WINGS SO SOFT

Dani Finn

DRAGONHEART PRESS

XII
III
VI
IX
Kriti

Content Warnings

This book is intended for **adult audiences** and contains depictions of wartime violence, drinking, drug use, and explicit, consensual sex scenes, including light bondage.

Author's Note

Wings so Soft is a standalone in the Time Before trio, and no prior knowledge of any other books is required to enjoy it.

Though it takes place chronologically after *The Delve*, they share no characters in common and there is almost no plot overlap. The last book in the trio, *Cloti's Song*, is coming early 2024, and a side romance called *Jagged Shard* will come some time this winter.

The Time Before books take place 2,000 years before my Maer Cycle and Weirdwater Confluence books, and the series can be read in any order.

There are several cameos and little Easter eggs in *Wings so Soft* for those who may have read the other books, but that's it.

1

Uffrin squeezed the fine pincers with his aching fingers, grasping one of the tiny teeth of the cog and wiggling it gently until he felt it come unstuck. He laid it on the tray and dialed in the scope to the macro level. He spotted the manufacturing imperfection of one of the teeth in the adjacent cog, a slight lip mostly likely caused by a miscalibrated stamp. He sighed, laying down the pincers and selecting a locking spanner, then set to work removing the offending cog and replacing it with a fresh one. He gave the works a faint misting of ultralight oil and gently pressed the hatch closed, straightening one of the silk feathers that had gotten pinched when he'd opened it. He wished he had time to re-do that bit of the design, but it would have taken several days to re-configure the feather pattern on the entire device. It wasn't likely the humans would get close enough to notice anyway if it even saw action.

He tapped his gauntlet three times. The owl's eyes blinked open, and it twisted its head toward him without a hitch this time.

He raised one finger and pointed toward the far end of the workshop. It spread its wings and powered up off the table, swooping gracefully through the series of irregular rings that hung from the ceiling before returning to land on its perch.

"Aren't you just a gorgeous little machine,?" he cooed. The owl blinked and let out a little mechanical hoot. Uffrin cocked his head, turning toward the perch and staring into its yellow glass eyes. "Yes...you...are," he murmured, taking a step with each word uttered until he stood next to the perch. The owl blinked and hooted again, then raised its wings as if in greeting.

"It's time for me to get some rest, and we need to power you down too." He moved his fingers to the pad on his gauntlet, and the owl lowered its head to butt his hand. He smiled, almost forgetting for a moment that he had programmed it to do so, along with a few other gestures of affection he'd copied from the cats that begged for food outside the workshop. He chucked it under the chin, and it clacked its beak several times in response. He went to tap the pad to power it down, but his finger stopped in mid-air as he looked down at the owl's unblinking yellow eyes, which fixed him with an unnerving stare. He ran through all the behavior patterns in his head, but he couldn't recall one that resembled the repeated clacking.

His mouth half-opened in wonder for a moment. Could it be he'd forgotten something from the owl patterns? Not likely; he could recall from memory every strand he'd written since university, and he'd entered these strands himself. It was probably just a quirk of the orbus that powered it. They were a weird mix of magic and mechanics, and little idiosyncrasies of the mage who'd enchanted them sometimes snuck in. He shook his head and tapped the pad three times. The gleaming yellow eyes turned dull, the lids snapped shut, and the machine went inert.

Uffrin locked up the workshop and waved to the guards outside, who gave him curt nods in response. He picked up his circlet at the gate house and slipped it on his head as soon as he passed through the sliding gates into the dark streets of Kuppham. His stream was plastered with notes, mostly yellow, which he swept to the side. He checked the handful of orange ones as he wove his way through the crowds toward the Falls pavilion, where his favorite soup stall sat nestled between a tea house and an antiquities shop. The notes were mostly shop-related, and none of them needed to be dealt with until the morning. He swept them to the side and pulled up a flight view captured from a lens atop an owl's head. He watched it soaring above the deep green spikes of the conifers, banking around the edge of the clearing along the river.

He paused the view to order his soup, which was goat and honeycomb fungus. It wasn't his favorite, but he did like the texture of the fungus and the way the little compartments held the broth so it squirted into his cheeks as he chewed. He ate leaning against a counter, replaying the owl's landing on a bare branch high up in the pines. He wished he could see from the outside, the way it slowed to a stop, how it angled its wings. He had a notion to reconfigure the shoulder joint to allow for quicker stops. It would take half a day at least, and he wasn't sure he'd have time for that on top of the other maintenance and upgrades he'd planned before his mission. Maybe he could get permission to visit the aerie and see the owls landing up close. It probably wouldn't make much difference, but it needled at him, and he knew he would lose sleep over it until he tried.

He watched the view a couple more times as he wandered through the now-familiar rows of the antiquities shop, his fingers brushing lightly over scroll cases, oxidized weapons, and faux-antique Soulshape pendants that fooled only the tourists. Not that there were any tourists these days. He never thought he'd miss their clueless meandering, their clogging every restaurant and shop from the Middle Falls to the Forge. Most of the Maer in the streets moved with purpose, either to or from work, home, or food, except one pair of lovers who stood leaning against each other next to the fence overlooking the Middle Falls.

Uffrin paused to watch them. They leaned in close, noses touching for a moment, then angled their faces for a kiss, which was brief but looked tender. He felt a stirring as he watched, and he turned away quickly, not wanting to feel like a voyeur.

It had been forever since he'd kissed anyone. Not since last fall when he'd gotten blind drunk at the Artificer's Ball and made out with Jonta, an assistant orbus technician in the Forge shop. Uffrin didn't remember much from that encounter except for the way Jonta's nose whistled slightly when he breathed through it and the delicate little swirls his fingers made on the back of Uffrin's neck. Before that, there hadn't been anyone since Jaisey, and she was going to be a hard act to follow. Sometimes Uffrin wondered if he was meant to be alone.

He made his way back to his hightop and trekked up the seven flights to his tiny apartment. A wax-sealed rectangle of Maoti's handmade paper jutted from his mailbox. He picked it up, fingering the seal for a moment. He shook his head, a wry smile warming his cheeks as he made his way inside. She could have just sent him a message on the Stream like a normal Maer, but then she wouldn't be Maoti. He dropped his bag on the table and fell onto the bed, tearing open the letter.

Come visit when you get back was all it said. Uffrin fingered the rough paper, tracing his mother's sweeping letters with his fingers.

She hadn't said it, but her subtext was clear, and she was right, of course. It had been too long. He'd meant to come by. Several times in fact. But there were drinks after work sometimes, and other days he was too tired to trudge all the way up to the Bluffs. And every now and then, he just needed to relax with his tarpipe and the Stream for a little while after work.

He tapped his circlet back on and continued the owl view he'd been watching, soaring with the bird as it flew low into a canyon where the moon glittered off the river. It was a nice effect, though he wasn't sure if it was enhanced or natural. At any rate, he'd seen it before, and he flicked it away with a blink.

A view popped up of one of the great automatons crossing a river with only its upper turrets remaining above the surface until it emerged on the other side, water cascading down its shiny bronze sides. Its wheels spun in the mud for a moment before finding purchase and propelling it through the scrub brush. He'd spent his childhood watching automaton parades every Solstice, shouting along with the crowd. His heart would race as their scattershots shredded row after row of wooden targets with their faces painted harsh pink to represent human skin. War was a fantasy, a bedtime story, a cautionary tale. Everyone knew the Maer's military was so powerful, the humans wouldn't risk open war.

That illusion had cracked when the humans retook Mount Cope in a surprise attack, breaking the Great Treaty that had kept the peace for his entire life. Never mind the whispers that Mount Cope had originally been a human mine before the Maer took it over a century before; it didn't matter at this point. After Mount Cope, a generation of simmering tension boiled over. Attacks and counterattacks began in the borderlands, and the humans had struck the brightstone mines deep in Maer territory. War had begun, and it wouldn't end until oceans of blood spilled across the Silver Hills.

The automaton view was followed by one of a group of human soldiers in chains being marched along the road by a group of heavily armed Maer. Close-ups of the humans showed their skin-covered faces marked with cuts and bruises, their eyes bloodshot and sullen as they tromped through the mud. Uffrin wondered what kind of propaganda the humans were being fed by their leaders to send them to attack an enemy a thousand miles away. Whether they believed it any more than he did, or whether they too were just hapless pawns in this bloody game.

A ping pulled Uffrin out of the view, and he stared at the red note folded up neatly like an official envelope, complete with the facsimile of the Chief Artificer's seal. He blinked it open, and the rest of his stream went dark as the message filled his mind.

We've had to accelerate the timeline, Uff. You leave in two days. Get your machine sorted and be ready to meet your scout at quarter-dark tomorrow. PS: The Stream is going down at quarter dark tonight and won't be back on until half-dawn.

"Fuck," Uffrin muttered. He checked his clock and saw he had only a few minutes left before the Stream went down. He popped over to the military stream to see if there was any news, and the stridency of the propaganda told him things were going downhill fast. The Council's latest memorandum claimed the humans had been turned back short of the Archive Valley, "routed in a fierce battle," which Uffrin assumed meant the Maer had suffered heavy casualties. He slipped out of the military stream and tried to pull up the owl view again, but his stream went dark.

He opened his eyes and removed his circlet, dropping it on the bed beside him. His owl clock hooted quarter-dark, and he hooted back at it in annoyance. The interruptions in the Stream were the worst part of the war, besides the death and destruction and the likely downfall of his entire civilization. If all of Maerdom was going to go up in flames, he should at least be able to relax for an hour or two after work.

He sat up with a sigh, glancing at the books on his shelf, but he didn't feel like reading. He put his circlet back on just in case, but the Stream was still down. He poured a glass of mushroom wine, lit his tarpipe, and took a few puffs. His eyes wandered to his shelf again, to the lacquered wooden box he'd received as his last Solstice present when he was twelve.

He absently cleared the papers and assorted bachelor's debris from his desk. He wet a cloth and wiped the crusted bits of food and tea from the bronze-inlaid grid, then dried it off until it shone in the light from his brightstone lamp. He picked up the box, which had always seemed much bigger, and set it down to the side.

When he undid the latch and opened the box, a pang of nostalgic excitement swept over him as he stared down at the gleaming bronze pieces that would form the mechanical owl's skeleton. He removed each tray and set them around the edges of the grid: the structural pieces, the gearbox, the delicate bronze feathers, and the tools, which were a little small for his adult hands. He'd spent hundreds of hours building and rebuilding the kit as a child, dreaming of making mechanical owls with wings so soft, no one could tell them from the real thing.

If only little Uffie could see him now.

The paper that held the instructions was worn and brittle, but he didn't need them anymore. He'd assembled the owl a hundred times, though it had been quite a few years since he'd last touched it. He gazed out his window, watching the space to the west for the owl that seemed to roost on one of the nearby hightops. It was hard to imagine a wild owl living in a city like Kuppham, but the park below the Middle Falls had a fair number of trees, and gods knew there were plenty of rats, mice, and small birds to eat.

The city was eerily quiet outside his window, with very little of the bustle and laughter that usually echoed up from the Forge pavilion. His head buzzed from the tar and the gleam of the tiny pieces. It would take several hours to assemble the device, and without the Stream to occupy his mind, sleep was as elusive as a gutter sparrow. He laid out the curved ribs along the grid in the orientation he knew from long memory, slid the tool tray closer, and set to work.

2

Mara stood on the rooftop, leaning against the rickety railing, watching for Cleo's shadow to come wheeling around the neighboring hightop. Cleo usually did a sweep through the park, then hunted along the river if she came up empty. If she caught something in the park, she'd come in over the Forge pavilion, but if she'd had to seek out prey along the river, she'd come in from behind the row of hightops. If Mara wasn't ready, Cleo would swoop in and land on the rail next to her. If Mara's arm was up, Cleo would land on her bracer, prey hanging limp from her beak. Mara enjoyed the little game, and she was pretty sure Cleo did too.

A flash of movement spun Mara's head around, and Cleo stood on the railing behind her, tucking her wings, with a bird's neck clamped in her beak.

"Ooh, a gutter sparrow! Someone's on top of their game tonight!"

Cleo raised her wings as if in victory, then dropped the inert lump on the railing. She cocked her head at Mara and let out a little *coo* as her wings settled down her back. Mara picked up the still-warm carcass and put it in her pocket, then folded her arms across her chest. Cleo double-hopped toward her and pecked at the pocket, then swiveled her head up to stare at Mara with wide, unblinking eyes.

"All right, clever girl, enjoy the spoils of your predation." Mara palmed the bird and placed it on the railing. Cleo gave her another soft *coo* and flapped up onto her roost, then quickly tore into the bird with her beak and talons.

Mara stared out over the city, an odd tinge of sadness creeping over her at how dark and quiet it was. Though she hated the brash noise and harsh lights that had marked Kuppham in normal times, the gloomy calm that reigned now was almost worse. She'd been avoiding the news lately, but she didn't need to follow the Stream to see how badly things were going with the war. It was etched on the faces of passersby, the slump in their silhouettes as they hurried through the streets, the grim determination of their steps.

She'd lived beneath the specter of looming war for so long, it was hard to believe it had finally begun. Every few years there was another border skirmish, and each time, the tensions were diffused. The cycle had repeated her whole life. But when the humans took Mount Cope two years ago, everything changed. Never mind the whispers that it had originally been a human mine before the Maer took it over a century before; it didn't matter at this point. War was upon them, and its thirst for blood was insatiable.

Now, instead of talking about the weather, Maer exchanged rumors about the war, little hopeful bits they'd cobbled together against the gloom. She'd overheard Maer talking about the victory at the Archive Valley, but the tone in their voices told her it had been a costly one. The humans were coming, and all the propaganda and automaton parades in the world weren't going to make a damned bit of difference. The Maer were about to be blasted back to the Time Before.

Once Cleo had finished her meal, Mara reached up and gave her a scritch on the back of the head, which Cleo accepted, though Mara knew she didn't really like it. Cleo ruffled her feathers afterward, then turned and hopped into the roost, a wooden box with a slanted roof and a round hole on one side. Cleo cooed, and Mara gave the side of the roost a gentle tap, then descended the three flights to her cramped room.

She hung her circlet on the hook on the back of the door and fumbled for a match to light a candle. Open flames were forbidden in the hightops after a fire had destroyed an entire row a few years back and killed several dozen Maer, but she hated the harsh light of brightstone. She used the still-burning match to hit her tarpipe a couple of times, then fell back on her bed and watched the shadows from the candle dance on the ceiling. She set some water on to boil, then opened the worn book of vintage erotica she'd bought at the River Market bookstall the weekend before. She flipped through the pages, stopping to study a few she hadn't spent enough time with.

One showed a Maer warrior with chunky muscles leaning against a table, her armor half off, being eaten out by her squire. The warrior had an almost bored look on her face, but the way she cupped her hand behind her squire's head was kind of hot. Mara flipped the page and saw a pair of male lovers crushed together amid a tangle of grapevines with oddly phallic-shaped clusters of grapes blocking the view of their privates. Their eyes were locked with a tender intensity as one hovered over the other, his arms braced on the muscled shoulders of his partner, whose hands gripped his rounded behind. Lowra, as the artist was known, was famous for the emotional depth of their pieces, and this was one of their finest.

The gleam of her circlet on the door caught her eye, and Mara knew she should have checked it before the Stream went dead. It was supposed to stay on until three-quarters dark, but it had been going down earlier and earlier. There was probably a meeting at half-dawn, which was rude for a group that worked with night birds, but the Shoza seemed to make it a point of pride to disrupt her sleep schedule whenever possible. She was on duty tomorrow night, so she'd have to catch a nap during the day or pay for it dearly on watch.

She was an uneasy combination of wired and exhausted, so she made a cup of darkroot tea, hit the tarpipe one more time, and settled in with a book of epic poetry, hoping it would lull her to sleep. Much to her surprise, the characters on the page took on fresh life in her mind, their declarations of love and revenge touching her deep inside. She almost shed a tear at the tale of King Egaborth, the lyrical passage where he sat in his golden tower surrounded by finery, staring out at the ocean, despairing at the meaninglessness of his life.

He stepped up onto the railing, feeling the chilled breeze across every hair on his body as he stood balanced between his life and the endless sea. Three beautiful wives and a dozen children filled his castle, but his heart was empty for he had nothing left to strive for, no challenge left to overcome.

He gazed out at the islands on the horizon, their undiscovered wonders blooming in his mind like fungal gardens in every shape and color of the soul's prism. His heart lurched for a moment as he glanced down at the dark waters below, crashing white and furious on the rocks. It would take a great leap, he knew, but the alternative was a slow, withering death, surrounded by stagnant comfort.

He spread his arms wide, crouched, and pushed off with his still-mighty legs. He flew through the air like a flaming arrow arcing down, down, ever down toward the cold embrace of the sea.

Mara snapped the book shut, tears surging from her eyes. Such a dusty old tale should not have moved her like this. King Egaborth's selfishness had always pissed her off, but her nerves were raw and exposed these days. The High Council had declared a state of emergency throughout all Maer lands, and she had lost the freedom to roam outside the city. She mourned the wild spaces, such as they were, around Kuppham. The city walls had never felt so much like a cage.

She wondered what this place must have been like in the Time Before, when only fire and sweat and song moved the hearts of Maer, when no one dreamed of gears or brightstone or the Stream. If the war with the humans went as badly as everyone seemed to think, perhaps Kuppham would be once again what it was. Owls would nest in the crumbling remains of their towers, swooping down to feast on cliff rats and marmots, and the sound of bells and shouting and machines would be replaced by the haunting calls of the birds carried on the winds whipping through the valley.

Mara woke to the sound of gutter sparrows squeaking outside her window. She wondered what they were called before there were gutters, where they lived, what they ate without the Maer's detritus to feed them. Would they die out once the Maer empire crumbled, or would they adapt? She wondered if the Maer themselves could adapt, scattered throughout the Silver Hills, once the humans destroyed their cities. Or would they be enslaved, forced to work the mines for the humans, a subjugated race clinging to the vestiges of their stories and culture? She glanced at the tar pipe, eager to wipe these dreary thoughts from her mind. She sighed and put on her circlet instead as she set the water for her tea to boil, bracing herself for the inevitable.

She had one red message and one green, which intrigued her, but she made herself read the red one first. It was a meeting, of course, which hardly merited red, but anything from the Shoza was automatically coded red, so ignoring them was not an option. She scanned the text, and her blood chilled when she read the words: *Hoverball sighting just south of Kuppham.* She had heard of the humans' spying devices, glass balls that floated through the air, so small as to go unnoticed by the owls without the full attention of their handlers. Some of them were even said to explode. That meant night watch would be extra intensive, and they would probably double the number of owls, which would stretch the birds and their handlers to their limits. She had to be at the aerie at three-quarters dawn, which hardly left her time to wash up and grab a quick breakfast from the pavilion.

She poured her tea, then blinked the green message open. It was a view from Sugli, a retired handler who still consulted with the Shoza from time to time. Sugli sat with a valley owl on his shoulder, squinting as his fingers partially obscured the view for a moment. Mara giggled; Sugli was even worse with technology than she was, and he always seemed to forget which lens to look at.

"Mara, I trust you are well despite..." He coughed, waving his arms in the air, and the little owl's head swiveled to follow his movements. "Yes, well, anyway, I received a request from the Assistant Chief Artificer, and I immediately thought of you. One of her artificers wants to do a consult—something about the wing orientation during high-speed landings. I thought maybe you and Cleo could help him out." He reached his hand absently to his shoulder and ruffled the neck feathers of his owl, which pecked at his fingers in irritation. "It has to be today, I'm afraid, and while I'm sure we could reach out to someone else, I hope you won't mind showing him whatever it is he needs to see? You are the best in the business, after all. Send me a message if you're up for it, and I'll put you in touch."

He gave a pained smile and shook his head. "With all that's been going on, the mechanicals are going to be taxed to the limit, and I wouldn't be surprised if some of you get called away from the city as well. Things are going badly, I'm afraid, much more so than has been reported. It will soon be all hands on deck. I'm not supposed to tell you that, but I doubt the Shoza have enough time on their hands to go pawing through my views, so there you have it." He coughed several times, looked down at his hands for a moment, then back up. "Stay safe, wherever you end up, and do come visit me some night when you're not on duty." His finger obscured the view again, then it went dark.

Mara took a gulp of her tea, hoping it would chase away the aftereffects of a poor night's sleep. Between the morning meeting and having to make Cleo perform tricks for some gearhead, she was barely going to have time for her nap.

3

The elevators were out of service, so Uffrin struggled up the stairs to the aerie, which sat high in the West Bluff. He stopped at a windowed landing to catch his breath, his lungs burning from the unaccustomed exertion. He tapped on his circlet out of habit, but the view from the landing distracted him, and he tapped it back off. The stacked and layered buildings of Kuppham spread out from the river and rose halfway up the bluffs, where the penthouses of the wealthy afforded views like this. The river ran white as it gushed into Forge Lake, which was icy green, then turned white again as it spilled down into the valley below. Uffrin took a few deep breaths, then continued his torturous climb. When at last he arrived at the roost, he was soaked in sweat and huffing for breath.

"You must be Uffrin." The voice belonged to a short, plump Maer with a thickly braided beard and hair swept back in a messy bun. She handed him a cup of water he hadn't asked for and seemed to study him as he drank.

"Yes, thank you for meeting with me. Mara, is it?" he gasped between gulps. She nodded, eyeing him from head to toe and raising her eyebrows.

"I hope the stairs weren't too much for you." Her voice had a friendly tease to it, which softened as she continued. "I've given up on them ever repairing the elevators at this point." His eyes followed her gesture toward the elevator cage behind her, and on the way back, Uffrin caught himself glancing down at the generous curve of her breasts. When he snapped his eyes back to meet hers, he was sure she had noticed.

"No, it's good for the, uh…it's good to move the muscles, you know." He laughed weakly, and she flashed an inscrutable smile as she took his empty cup and set it on a table. *Stupid, stupid,* he chided himself.

"Well, you've got a few more flights to go to get to the aerie. Follow me." She turned, her cloak whirling behind her as she moved with quick steps toward yet another set of stairs. He followed her up, struggling to keep pace with the steady clomp of her sandals and struggling even more not to stare at her round behind as she powered up the stairs.

They emerged into a room with a high ceiling and wide-open windows starting at waist height on two walls. Patches of mist drifted by, and between them, Uffrin saw the cliffs on the opposite side of the valley. The High Chancellor's palace occupied the upper levels of the cliff, adorned with shiny copper flags that flapped in the wind. He saw movement out of the corner of his eye, and he looked up to see a huge shadow bearing down on him. He ducked, and the shadow coalesced into an owl, which landed silently on the bracer on Mara's outstretched arm. She buried a giggle in her other hand, looking down at Uffrin, eyes sparkling with amusement.

"Uffrin, meet Cleo. Cleo, Uffrin. He's not used to the real thing, I can see." She held a finger out to the bird, which pecked it gently. It had small, tufted ears and wide cupped rings around its yellow eyes. Uffrin was pretty sure it was a crag owl, the kind his mechanicals were mostly based on. He stood up, touching his hair and beard out of instinct, and forced a little laugh.

"She's so quiet," he said, staring at the owl's silvery gray feathers, which almost seemed to glow in the shadows of the unlit aerie. He took a tentative step toward Mara, eyeing the thick talons and sturdy beak, which could no doubt rip out his eyes and shred his flesh before he could blink. The owl's head swiveled to follow him, and he stopped as it fixed him with what felt like a menacing stare.

Mara moved closer and swung her owl arm toward him. He gave a little start as her sharp elbow and soft hip touched him. Mara giggled but stayed close, too close, putting a hand on his shoulder as she moved the owl right in front of his face.

"Don't worry, I won't bite. But Cleo might if you touch her wrong."

Uffrin froze, staring at the curved golden dagger of the owl's beak, picturing what it could do to him. Part of his mind was also picturing Mara biting him, what that would feel like, what part of him she would bite. He shook off the thought, which was hard, as he could feel her heat radiating into him, but there was something comforting about the gentle touch of her hand on his shoulder, and his focus returned to the owl.

"She's beautiful," he said, studying the soft blanket of feathers covering the owl's chest and the seamless way its wings folded into its body. "She's a crag owl, right?" He turned to look at Mara, whose eyes watched him, bright with what looked like amusement. He wondered for a moment if the hair on her cheeks was as soft as the feathers on her owl's wings. He felt all at once ashamed and excited and very, very confused.

Mara nodded, releasing her hand from his shoulder and turning her arm so he could see the striated white, gray, and black feathers on its back. Its head rotated smoothly, its eyes staying locked on his.

"She's almost two years old, in the prime of her youth. I may be a little biased, but I think she's the best owl in the parliament."

"The what?"

"A group of owls is called a parliament," she said with a tone that might have been lightly mocking, but there was a kindness to it as well, an indulgent quality. "Don't you study owls before you, you know, make them?"

"Well, we do, yes, but not..." Uffrin stared at the owl's wings, the patterns of stripes and color that repeated perfectly across a thousand different feathers. How did the feathers know to take on those patterns? What mechanism, already present in the egg, programmed them to do so?

"You can touch them if you like." Mara's hand rested on his shoulder again, and she swung the bird closer. "She won't bite you as long as she's on my arm."

Uffrin felt her breath on the hairs of his cheek, and his chest tightened. It didn't mean anything, couldn't mean anything. Some Maer were just like that. Touchy. He wanted to shirk away from her touch or lean into it, but instead, he steeled his nerves and reached out his hand toward the gray and black striped wings.

"Gently," she said, her hand pressing into his shoulder. Sweat soaked his armpits as his fingers brushed the downy soft feathers layered so delicately over each other. The owl's golden eyes bored into his, but it did not move or flinch as his fingers slid down toward the wingtips. He ran them down the other wing, and Mara's fingers squeezed his shoulder just a little tighter.

"Gods, she's amazing," Uffrin whispered, turning up to look into Mara's eyes, which were a warm hazel-brown, with a glint of mischief.

"Best girl," Mara said, releasing his shoulder and rotating her arm so the owl faced the wide, open window overlooking the valley. "But I expect you came here to see her fly, right?"

"Well, yes. I've seen them before, when I was in study, and I've watched a lot of views, but it's the landing I'm most interested in right now. Especially how their wings move when they land at speed, the angle of force. Can you..." He glanced up at her head, which was unadorned with a circlet. He knew they used circlets for surveillance, but he wondered whether she could control the owl without one or if it was so well trained she didn't need it.

"I can show you whatever you want to see. You want to check out her wings first?" Mara fished her circlet out of her pocket and fitted it on her head, and the owl's wings slowly opened, more than an arm's length from tip to tip, and light gray on the inside, like on its chest. Mara rotated her arm, and Uffrin leaned in to study the angle at which the wings protruded from its back.

"Can you...make it flap a little?"

The owl's wings whooshed downward, then back up several times, then settled into its back so neatly it was hard to believe it even had wings.

"If you want to see a landing at speed, we'll have to let her out in the valley. Come." She put her hand on the small of his back and guided him toward the opening. A chill breeze wafted in as they approached, and the owl ruffled its feathers a little and moved from foot to foot.

"Somebody's ready to show off," she said, smiling indulgently at the bird. She removed her hand from Uffrin's back and gestured toward a pointed tower just below with a half-dozen wooden platforms arranged around the edges. "Watch." She held her arm out the window, and the owl raised its wings and powered off into the air, wobbling against the breeze for a moment, then turning to bank smoothly out over the valley. It flapped hard away from them and up, up, up, then whirled around tightly and shot down with a few strokes of its powerful wings, slicing through the air toward the tower. Uffrin was sure it was going to crash and bounce off into the valley below, but at the last second, its wings flared out and flapped several times, and it landed on the platform as lightly as a butterfly on a flower.

"Gods, that's incredible!" Uffrin wished he'd thought to bring his lens to capture the view. It had gone so fast, he hadn't had time to fully process it. "Can you make it circle and land again?"

"Only if you stop calling her 'it.'" Mara's tone was a little less glib but still friendly, he thought.

"Of course, Cleo. Best girl, as you say. Would you mind asking her to circle around and—"

"You don't need to repeat yourself, Uffrin. Just be polite and use her correct pronouns. She's not a thing." She bumped him with her hip, which was soft and substantial and gave Uffrin a little twinge of desire, amplified by the sideways smirk she flashed him. Gods, was she hitting on him? Surely not—it was unthinkable—no one hit on him, not ever. He was nerdy and scrawny, his chest was concave, and his body hair wasn't thick or lustrous like some. He was just being overexcited and stupid, as usual.

"She's going to take off now if you want to study that too." Mara's hand was on his forearm now, and Uffrin could hardly focus on the bird, but when it spread its wings—when *she* spread *her* wings and launched off the platform, something clicked. The angle of her wings changed in a way that showed greater rotation in the shoulder joint than he had realized. Cleo soared out into the valley, wheeled around, and dove again. When she pumped her wings to land, he saw it again, that flexible angle, as if the joint could not only rotate but also pop in and out a little. That would be hard to replicate with the automatons, but perhaps with the right springs, he could make it work.

Mara offered to show him again, and he agreed, though he'd seen what he needed to see and could already picture the little tweak that would allow the joint in his machine to flex in and out. After the landing, she ran Cleo through a few training routines, and Uffrin watched in awe, no longer bothered by Mara's near-constant touching, as the owl wove in and out of various rings and wooden tubes laid out below. It was a much more challenging course than the ones at the lab. He knew how much more agile flesh and blood owls were than mechanical ones, but seeing it up close like this really brought it home how much work remained to be done. He itched to get his fingers on his tools, to open up his machine and see what he could do.

Uffrin gave a start when Cleo finally swooped in and landed noiselessly on Mara's bracer, her bright yellow eyes intense and inscrutable.

"Would you like to hold her?" Mara asked, laughing as he shrank back, staring at the owl's powerful talons. "Not barehanded, obviously." She pointed with her eyes to a row of leather bracers hanging below one of the windows.

"I—maybe next time," Uffrin managed, glancing from the bird, whose eyes bored holes in his confidence, to Mara, who covered her mouth with her hand, but he could see her smile in the creases around her eyes.

"All right then, next time it is." She blinked, and the owl flew up into the darkness of the rafters. She unbuckled her bracer and hung it with the others, then returned to stand even closer than before, now that the owl was no longer on her arm. "You're welcome here whenever you like, though I keep weird hours since I'm on night duty half the time. Send me a message if you want—I'll just share my stream." She pressed the dot on the front of her circlet, and Uffrin tapped his into life and accepted the share. "It's mostly owls and other birds, plus some ancient poetry and the like, but you can message me any time." She touched him again on the arm as she said it, sending a dizzying tingle to his head. *Gods, what did that mean? Did that mean—*

"Right, of course, any time, I will, I—" He paused, closing his eyes before they could stray down to look at her breasts again. "I absolutely will when I get back from mission."

Her eyes fell, and she pulled her hand back and turned away a little. "That would be lovely. Well, be safe wherever you go. I know you can't talk about that stuff."

"Thank you. I'm sure it will be fine. The scouts are first-rate, and it's not like I'll be going toe to toe with the humans or anything."

They stood awkwardly for a moment, then she touched him on the shoulder again.

"It's been a real pleasure to meet you, Uffrin."

"Oh yes, so much. I mean, I'll hit you up in a month or so when I get back. And maybe I'll see if I can get permission to show you around my shop and see some of the mechanicals. I mean, you showed me yours..." Uffrin's face boiled with embarrassment, and Mara's cackling laughter did little to cool it off.

She took his hand in hers, still giggling. "I would love for you to show me yours any time it's convenient for you."

The Stream went out just as Uffrin returned from meeting his scout, a taciturn Maer named Erliss with dark eyes that looked like they'd seen too much. They seemed to know the territory well, and it was as Uffrin feared—he was heading to Burrows Valley, not far from the Archive Valley, where the humans had been repelled at great cost but were regrouping. Though the action report hadn't spelled it out, Uffrin had heard that they were preparing to bury the Archive and evacuate the valley.

He sighed, hit the tarpipe, and sat down at the desk where the gleaming toy owl sat fully assembled from the night before. He fingered the little tools, figuring he would take it apart since there were no views to watch and he didn't feel like reading. His mind drifted to his meeting with the owl handler, and a smile crept onto his face. He'd barely had a chance to check out her stream during the day since he'd been busy with the adjustments to his machine, but it had been pretty much as she'd said: owl views, many of which he recognized, some ancient poetry, and illustrations of antique erotica, the kind they carried in the bookstalls down at the River Market. He wished he had the Stream so he could look through them, but it wouldn't be back up until the morning, and by then, he'd be too busy to take full advantage. He loved the fact that she had these funky illustrations on her stream, and he was desperate to study them further.

He hit the pipe again, replaying his visit to the roost, trying to summon Mara's image in his mind. His loins stirred as he pictured the curve of her hips, her ample breasts, the mischievous sparkle in her eyes. He heard the sound of her laughter, felt the way she bumped him and touched him, and his heart twinged. Gods, he hadn't crushed on anyone so hard in the longest time, and the fact that she had actually shared her stream with him was an unthinkable piece of good fortune.

He'd all but written off any chance of romantic contact as news of the war got grimmer and the city's mood puddled like wastewater around the leaf-clogged sewer drains. He'd even wondered if he'd ever have sex with another Maer again. It could be weeks or months, but probably not years, before the city was under siege, and he was so bogged down at work that he hardly had the time or energy to go out. Not that there was much of a bar scene left these days, with most of the soldiers gone and everyone working frantically to get things made and stored away in the event the worst came to pass.

It figured that he would meet someone like this right when he was about to go off on mission for a month. By the time he got back, she might have forgotten him or moved on to someone else. A Maer like her would not lack for company if she wanted it. Gods, he had to at least send her a message tomorrow before he left. But what would he say? He could do a view, maybe with his owl on his shoulder. It was against protocol, but he doubted the Shoza had time to stalk people's messages these days. And Mara would love it. He pictured her watching it, her face lighting up with amusement, crinkling around her eyes as she laughed. He felt himself rising again, and he reached down to touch himself a little.

It wasn't just her shape, as pleasing as it was, that stoked his imagination. It was the way she seemed to take him in in his entirety, to see what he was and be amused, or maybe even a little more. He pictured the light brown of her eyes, splintered with yellow shards like exploding stars, and the spark of those explosions sent a jolt straight to his heart. He saw her tilting her head just a bit as she leaned in to kiss him, felt the hum of her stifled laugh buzzing into his lips, the wet warmth of her tongue caressing his, the heat of her body flowing over him.

She would push him down, moving with strength and determination, rubbing against him with a light pressure that would nearly push him over the edge before their clothes were even off. And then they would lay fur to fur and heart to heart, their bodies interlocking, moving in undulous union, straining together like vines climbing each other up toward the blinding sun. Time would slow as they crushed against each other, arms trembling, eyes locked together until the moment flooded away and she collapsed on his chest, rumbling a little laugh into his neck as her body slowed, then finally stopped.

4

Mara grumped her way up the thousand stairs to the roost as the sunset painted the covered sky a muted yellowish pink. The winds had calmed somewhat, so hopefully, down in the valley below the falls, the air would be nice and still. She and Cleo had trained with marbles hung from lengths of string. Cleo had had no trouble catching them, but spotting them was going to be almost a question of pure luck, as they didn't seem to trigger the owl's prey or self-protection responses. No one knew what the range of the hoverballs was, but someone somewhere was controlling it. She couldn't imagine it being much more than twenty miles, which was the supposed range of the latest orbus. She could reach thirty miles with Cleo on a good day.

When she reached the roost, she was tired and thirsty and in the mood for absolutely no one's bullshit. She quickly downed a cup of water, mumbled half-hearted greetings to her fellow handlers, and hurried out to the aerie. The falcon crew was still on duty, the agile birds weaving through the forest until the owls arrived to keep the night watch. Cleo flew down as soon as Mara had her bracer strapped on and blinked at her eagerly. Mara stuck out her nose, and Cleo gave her the customary double-peck. She stared into the bird's eyes, sensing the eagerness, the yearning to fly free. Although, in fairness, the lure of fresh meat might have had something to do with it.

Mara dangled a mouse by its tail. Cleo's head bobbed up and down, and she shifted her feet. Mara swung the mouse over, and Cleo eyed it, motionless, impassive, until it passed right in front of her beak. She snatched it with a suddenness that never failed to catch Mara off guard. Cleo snapped her beak a couple of times, then swallowed the morsel, her head swiveling out toward the window. She knew another mouse awaited her on her return, and she seemed eager to spread her wings. Mara put on her circlet and quickly found her bond with the bird. Cleo's eagerness was almost too much to bear, and Mara pushed out a calming vibe, though she sensed Cleo wouldn't calm down until she felt the wind beneath her wings. Mara pulled a glass marble from her pocket and held it between her thumb and index finger directly in front of Cleo's eyes.

"This motherfucker right here is the target," she said, and she heard one of the falcon crew laugh from behind her.

"We're hunting ghosts now," he chuckled, then slung his bag over his shoulder and flashed her two fingers as he descended the stairs.

"This motherfucker," Mara whispered, then pocketed the marble and held her bracer out the window. Cleo fixed Mara with her golden eyes, then swiveled her head to face the valley and powered off, disappearing almost instantly from view as her colors faded into the growing darkness.

Mara sat on one of the lumpy chairs, closed her eyes, and flipped her mind to owl's eye view. She saw the lake glimmering with reflected lights, and her view slanted downward as Cleo descended, cruising just over the falls. The bird dropped suddenly, diving, gaining speed, then evened out and slowed near the bottom. She cruised through the forested valley with measured flaps, scanning the area along the river for a single tiny glass ball.

Mara was a little out of sorts; she hadn't had much of a nap after her meeting with the artificer, and it had been a fitful one. Her mind had flitted between images of the hoverballs and persistent flashes of Uffrin, the intensity in his eyes when he studied Cleo, his awkward half-smile. Even now, she struggled to keep him out of her mind so she could focus on the elusive glimmers in the shadows. He'd been so easily flustered whenever she touched him, and it only made her want to touch his wiry little body more. He was so gentle, and his eyes had this soft gleam like one part of his mind was always dreaming. *Dammit, Mara, focus!* She chided herself and brought her attention back to the valley. She spotted a few other owls and a number of small rodents, which Cleo no longer needed reminders not to go after, but no little glass balls.

Cleo felt powerful, purposeful, as she scanned the valley, cruising as slowly as gravity and physics would allow. Mara was able to keep the owl's focus near Maer height, which the hoverballs apparently always traveled at. She cruised along the river as it meandered down the valley. According to superstition, the gods had broken the mountain in two to form the lines of steep cliffs on either side of the little forested strip along the river. There wasn't much room for a human to hide, but spotting a hoverball would be next to impossible.

When Cleo reached the place where the valley widened into a plain, she turned around, running closer to the eastern side of the valley, along the base of the cliffs. It was trickier flying, with more dodging between trees, but Cleo was made for this, and she was a marvel of creation. When Mara had first bonded with Cleo, it had taken a while to trust her to navigate the forest at speed, but now she had made her peace with Cleo's patterns, and it was a calming experience, better than anything on the Stream.

She focused as best she could on looking for the hoverballs. Her mind did wander on occasion, drawn inexorably to the little artificer, who had stammered so adorably when she'd caught him checking her out. She wondered what he'd do if she took ahold of him and laid a big kiss on his pouty little mouth. He'd probably forget his own name, but she could make him forget more than that, forget everything except her body on his. She would pin him down and—

Cleo's jolt of alarm snapped Mara back to the present, and she saw it for just an instant as they flew past it: a tiny glint among the trees, like a drop of water hovering where it had no business being. She soothed Cleo, who wanted to fly back and catch it, but that wasn't protocol. She urged Cleo to land in a nearby tree, facing the direction the hoverball would approach Kuppham.

She sent a message back to the command center and got an immediate response. They would send a team through the tunnel below the falls, but it might take some time for them to find it. She watched the forest through Cleo's eyes, focusing on the area between two pine trees, where she sensed it might pass. They sat for no more than a minute before the ball floated into view, moving at the pace of a Maer walking. At that speed, it might be in sight of the falls before the ground team found it.

She restrained Cleo, who wanted to go after it, and opened a voice stream to the command center.

"Tell me what you see," said the operator.

"A hoverball—I'm sure of it. A little glass ball floating about five feet off the ground headed up the valley on the east side of the river."

"A team has already been dispatched. They should arrive within minutes."

"It might not be fast enough. If it gets close enough to see the falls, who knows what information it might be sending back to its handler. To the humans."

"Are you seeking authorization to pursue and terminate?" His voice was so flat he might as well have been an automaton.

Mara paused, wishing she had an answer. Some hoverballs were said to be explosive, and if she lost Cleo, she wasn't sure if she'd ever recover.

"Yes. It just passed us. We'll keep close and wait for the order."

"Stand by."

Mara urged Cleo out of the tree, and she flew until they saw it again, moving eerily between the trees, silent, nearly invisible, and unhurried. Cleo landed again, and Mara's voice stream came back to life.

"Seize the device and bring it to the roost. We have a special container ready for it."

"Bring it to the roost? Do we really want to show them—"

"Seize the device and bring it to the roost," said the operator, with perhaps a hint of impatience. "Remember the protocols."

Mara shut off the stream and pushed Cleo out of the tree, perhaps a little forcefully, but Cleo didn't need much convincing to swoop in and snatch the marble out of the air. Mara clutched the armrests on her chair as she flew Cleo straight up into the canopy, dodging between branches the whole way back so whoever was watching the stream wouldn't have any landmarks. She hoped Cleo's talons would obscure most of the view anyway, but she followed the plan that had been laid out in the meeting she was suddenly glad to have paid attention to.

Cleo rose from the canopy into the mist from the falls, touching her talons to the water at the very top before flying at top speed straight toward the roost. The theory was that the water would obscure vision for long enough to disorient the viewer, though no one really knew how the devices worked. One of the handlers held out a large black box, and Cleo flew in the window, dropped the ball in the box, then flapped over to land on Mara's arm as she struggled to flip views without getting dizzy.

She heard the clunk of the box and the sound of latches being tightened. The box was hustled out of the aerie by two Shoza who had not been present before. Cleo's bright eyes stared into hers, and Mara smiled and raised a finger to her beak, receiving a gentle peck in response.

"Good girl," she cooed. "Good girl gets extra treats."

Mara slept fitfully but late after her shift, not waking until three-quarters noon. Though she did not remember her dreams, she woke with the taste of bile in her throat, which it took several scalding cups of darkroot tea and a stale cheese roll to exorcise. Her circlet glinted ominously on its hook on the door, and she groaned as she slumped over and put it on. To her surprise, the only messages were a yellow reminder that she was on shift the following night and a green message with an unusual insignia on it that looked like a clockwork cog and an owl had been spliced together. Her heart leapt as she realized who it must be from.

She sat down on her bed, straightening her hair absentmindedly, and opened it. It was a view, and the opening image was Uffrin staring down at the lens with an owl on his shoulder that had to be mechanical, but it was a surprising likeness of the real thing.

"Hi, Mara, this is Uffrin, which I guess you might have figured out from my insignia because who else would have that, right?" He blinked a couple of times, then half-turned his head toward the owl. "This is my machine, which *technically* I'm not supposed to put in a view, but you showed me yours, right?" He looked down and fiddled with something, and the owl's head rotated all the way around, then it emitted a fairly convincing *hoot*. "It was lovely meeting Cleo, and you, of course. Mostly you, but I like your bird too." He shook his head as if in embarrassment, and his finger tapped the lens, and the view went dark for a moment. When it flickered back on, he was laughing nervously. "I'm not very good at these, if you can't tell.

Bit of a babbler, really, but I digress. Anyway, it was so, so nice to meet you—and Cleo too. Hi, Cleo!" He waved, and Mara giggled; did he think she lived with her owl or something?

"I'd love for you to come down to the shop sometime, once I'm back from mission." He ducked his head and looked around with a guilty grin, putting his finger over his lips and winking. "I'd love to show you what this machine can do. Maybe you could give me some pointers!"

He held out his finger to the owl, which butted it with its head, more like a cat than a bird, but it was so cute, Mara couldn't stop the broad smile that grew on her face. He gave it a scritch on the head, which it seemed to lean into, then it straightened up and stared into the lens for a long moment. Its eyes must have been glass, but they were so perfect she was sure they were of magical construction. It hopped off his shoulder and peered into the lens, almost seeming to sniff it for a moment, then gave it a headbutt, just as it had Uffrin's hand.

Uffrin lifted the lens to his face, and his eyes were wide with amused surprise.

"I never told it to do that," he said, then leveled his eyes at the camera. "Anyway, I really appreciate your help, and I..." Uffrin paused, looking down for a moment, and when he looked back up, he was biting his lip and squinting a little. "It's just that I really enjoyed meeting you, which I know I said before, but I hope when I get back, we might...you might meet me at the Forge pavilion for some soup, and I can show you around the shop. If you want." He reached out and tapped the lens, which went dark. Mara waited for it to come back on, but the view was over.

"What an absolute dork," she said, smiling into her beard as she sat down at her desk to compose her response.

5

Uffrin sat staring at his stream over a cup of tea, the last time he would be able to enjoy this simple pleasure for a very long time. He was due at the north gate in an hour. Once he passed through, there would be no Stream, a casualty of the humans' exploding hoverballs, which had taken out two dozen signal towers in a single night.

The view he was half-watching, of a sparrow chasing a hawk through the sky, was interrupted by a flash of green. He quickly dropped the view and pulled up the message, which was text only, from Mara.

Thank you for showing me your wonderful machine. I didn't catch its name—does it even have a name? I loved the way it headbutted the camera. Anyway, it was really nice to meet you, and I absolutely love the soup stand at the Forge pavilion, if it's the one I'm thinking of, where the chef wears the little rings in his ear? I look forward to having a bowl with you and seeing your owl. And you, of course.

Be safe, and hit me up as soon as you're back!

--Mara

He reread it several times, picturing her saying the words, the little smile that could barely contain the universe of mirth inside her. Gods, why couldn't he have met her a week or two before? He had half a mind to ditch the mission and go running off to the roost, calling her name like one of the mad characters in the classic heartstory views making some grand foolish gesture. They'd only just met, but he couldn't keep her out of his mind:

her eyes, her curves, the mocking lilt of her laughter. This was going to be a long trip.

He met his scout Erliss at the north gate. As before, they were quiet and professional, acting more like a bodyguard than a traveling companion or a partner. They wore the usual nondescript gray cloak of the Shoza, with black leather armor spiderwebbed with bronze filaments that must have been magically hardened. They carried a bow over their shoulder and a wicked-looking blade, long and thin and made of a silvery metal that looked a lot like steel, though it was hard to imagine even the Shoza using such taboo weaponry. Erliss' countenance did not invite inquiries, and Uffrin was not disposed to pry.

"We have a week travel on foot to get to our position," Erliss said, looking Uffrin up and down. "Maybe a little longer. I've brought fortified sporecakes to last us that long, and we should be able to resupply from the relief station just south of the valley. And I hope to shoot something fresh along the way." They shrugged the shoulder with their bow over it.

"Well, that sounds lovely. I brought some dried figs, tea, and whiskey, so..." he trailed off as Erliss cocked one eyebrow.

"What kind of tea?" they asked in a surprisingly warm voice.

"Darkroot. It's all I drink. I just hope I brought enough. I doubt the relief station will be able to resupply us on that."

"You might be surprised. Shall we?" They gestured toward the gate, where four guards stood waiting to turn the big wheels that operated the mechanism. The clanks and groans of the massive gates swinging open vibrated Uffrin's bones, and his chest tightened as he walked out of Kuppham and into the gray mist shrouding Valleys Road. He tapped his circlet, but there was no trace of the Stream, only the dark beacon of the signal tower looming amid the ether. He pocketed the circlet and tried to take a deep breath, but it felt like he couldn't fill his lungs more than halfway. Which made it difficult to catch up with Erliss, who was marching steadily down the road, apparently unaware of his little moment.

Erliss maintained their silence throughout most of the day, shepherding Uffrin to the side of the road whenever a group of soldiers slumped by, bedraggled and limping. They passed the hulking carcass of an abandoned automaton whose wheels, tracks, and turret had been removed; presumably, it had broken down and been raided for parts. Uffrin had never understood the appeal of the great machines, given the resources and Maerpower required to build and maintain them. They broke down far too often and could only travel on clear surfaces, despite what the propaganda views showed. He was glad he'd chosen to work with the smaller machines, though as the straps of the heavy case carved grooves into his shoulders, he wondered if he could take this for another month. He'd only been on shorter missions before and nowhere near as close to the front lines as they were going to be. He hoped he had the strength to make it as far as Burrows Valley.

He opened the case when they set up camp, and while Erliss was off hunting, he flew the machine in a couple of wide circles in the sky, maintaining the link through his circlet and steering it with his gauntlet. Everything was working perfectly, and the views were clear, even at a distance, thanks to the next-generation convex lenses he'd installed. He saw a larger group of soldiers camped out a half-mile ahead, huddled around small fires, passing around what looked like a tarpipe. He wished he'd brought his with him. Something about traveling with a Shoza had given him pause, and he needed his wits about him in case any human hoverballs were lurking about.

He made a small fire, scrounging what little kindling he could from an area that had been used by too many soldiers to have any real firewood left. It was just enough to make his tea, and Erliss brought back a dry branch for the fire along with a scrawny marmot.

"Got any more of that darkroot?" Erliss asked out of the corner of their mouth while gutting and skinning the marmot with shocking efficiency. Uffrin shuddered to think what a Shoza with those skills could do to a living Maer, though it was a comfort to know Erliss was on his side. He poured the dregs of the tea into his cup and brewed a fresh pot, which was quicker now with the added branch to bulk up the fire. Erliss trussed the carcass on a metal skewer, rubbed some kind of spice mixture over it, and arranged it over the fire, then scrubbed their hands with sand and rinsed them in the trickle of a creek that ran alongside the road.

"Thank you," they said as they took the offered cup of tea. Their eyes looked softer in the growing dusk, less guarded perhaps, but they said nothing more as they squatted, staring at the fire and sipping their tea.

Uffrin was at a loss for what to do with no Stream, no tech, and no tarpipe, and he ran through a dozen things to say to start a conversation. Erliss' silence snuffed each of them out before they escaped through his lips. It was a surprise, then, when Erliss turned to him and spoke.

"You were born and raised in Kuppham," they said. It was not a question, and Uffrin's head buzzed with the thought that Erliss had been researching him, though it was hardly surprising. He had to do security checks every month or two, so nothing about his life was unknown to the Shoza.

"Yes, actually. My mothers and father still live there as well. A city boy through and through. How about yourself?"

Erliss rotated the marmot, which had begun to brown underneath, sending a stream of juices sizzling into the fire.

"I'm from the country," they said. "Not far from where we're headed, in fact." Uffrin waited for them to continue, but they just stared into the fire, draining the last of their tea. After a couple of minutes, Uffrin couldn't take the silence anymore.

"Is that where you learned your hunting skills?"

Erliss shot him a dead-eyed glance, then their face scrunched into a gentle smile. "My mother hunted frasti, in part to keep them away from the sheep, but also for the fur and the meat, of course." They glanced back down into the fire. "Not too many frasti left out there these days, though."

"I guess that's good," Uffrin said, though he sensed from Erliss' tone that maybe they didn't agree. "I mean, for the sheep."

Erliss nodded gently, turning their eyes from the fire to meet Uffrin's. "You ever tried it?"

"Once or twice, at Solstice dinners. My family eats mostly vegetarian, though, so we never had it at home." Frasti stew was considered a delicacy, one of the many peasant dishes popular with the city's wealthy. The meat was terribly expensive, so it was only served on the most special occasions.

"I'm vegetarian too when I'm not on mission." Erliss checked the marmot and turned it again. It had shrunk a bit and browned on several sides, and Uffrin's stomach was starting to growl at the smell. Marmot was far from his favorite, but out in the cool mountain air, with the intriguing aroma of the spice mix, it smelled heavenly.

"Gods, that does look good, though. Fresh killed, cooked over a fire—it's just like the Time Before."

Erliss let out a single chuckle.

"What?" Uffrin said, feeling suddenly self-conscious.

"Nothing. It's a very Kuppham thing to say, talking about the Time Before like it was some kind of paradise." They pulled out a square of sporecake, broke off a corner in their teeth, and passed it to Uffrin.

"Well, I'm sure it wasn't all good," Uffrin said, nibbling on the sporecake. It actually tasted kind of good, very salty, a little earthy, but it left a slight greasy coating on his tongue.

"Maer claimed their mates through violence," Erliss said. "They killed each other over the best hunting territory."

Uffrin washed down the last bite of sporecake with his now-cold tea. "Well, yeah, but so do we, don't we? With the humans?"

Erliss fixed him with an intense stare that made Uffrin want to crawl inside his fur.

"Do you see the humans as just Maer without hair, then?"

It was a trap. No one uttered these words, least of all to a member of the Shoza. No one except his mother and her followers, that is. Maoti had toned down her speeches once the war began, but she still walked a fine line between philosophy and sedition. No one working with the government could openly follow her, but Uffrin was sure many did in secret. Could Erliss be a practitioner? It was hard to imagine, but then again, so was the end of civilization, yet it felt like he was living it.

"You probably already know this, but Cloti is my mother."

Erliss' eyes grew wide, and something like awe fell across their face for a moment before it returned to its normal inscrutable expression.

"So, it's true," they murmured, then looked up, eyes sharpening a bit. "Scouts don't have access to that kind of information. The details of your private life are considered classified."

"Well, that's small comfort if I can believe you."

"I know why you think you can't, but you can. I'm just a cog in the machine, not the machine itself."

"But if the machine turns, every cog must do its part or be ground to dust." Uffrin felt a sudden spark of inspiration like he used to get in his university days, drinking tea and arguing over books at the riverside tea houses.

Erliss raised their hands, nodding their head gently. "I understand. I was just making conversation, and I got a little carried away. It's why I don't speak much, as a rule."

Uffrin smiled despite himself. "You can let yourself get carried away any time you want. It's boring out here with no one to talk to."

Erliss's mouth twisted into a grim smile. "You may be wishing for boredom once we get to our destination."

6

It was market day, so Mara stopped by the group house where her sister lived for their weekly trip. There wasn't as much reason to go to market these days; Maer had stocked up as best they could, and with the army getting first crack at any supplies, it was a crapshoot. But it was market day, and tradition was tradition. She didn't like the idea of Kaela going by herself, though it probably would have been fine. Kaela got herself to work and back, bought her groceries at the corner market, and seemed to be doing well enough. Maybe Kaela wasn't the one who really needed this weekly trip.

Kaela was standing outside, her serious eyes following Mara along the street as she approached.

"Kaela dear, how are you?" Mara pressed foreheads with her, then pulled her in for a hug, which Kaela squirmed out of, blinking apologetically. She smiled, nodding slightly, and gestured toward Mara.

"Oh gods, I'm fine, I guess, given..." Mara gestured around, and Kaela gave a pained wince. "But believe it or not, something happened this week that did not entirely suck." She held out her elbow, and Kaela slid her arm through and grasped her hand tightly, eyes wide with curiosity.

"I met a boy."

She babbled about Uffrin as they walked through the streets, which were much emptier than they had any right to be on market day. Kaela nodded, squeezing Mara's hands when she told her of his cute little smile and how he flinched when she touched him. Kaela's whole body convulsed when Mara told her of Uffrin's stammering after she caught him checking her out. Kaela bumped her with her shoulder and hip, and they made their way down to the market. Mara let a few thoughts dribble out—nothing substantial, just enough to keep the gloom away.

They managed to find fresh-grilled orbnuts, some passable carrots, and a pair of squabs, not bad by recent market standards. There had been some nice-looking thistle greens, but Kaela had always hated the texture. They sat on a low stone wall that ran around a papery-barked beech tree and ate orbnuts, prying open the shells and popping the little salty globes in their mouth, letting the castoffs pile up on the stone.

"So, tell me something good."

Kaela frowned, shaking her head slightly, then threw up her hands and let them slap down on her knees.

"I get it," Mara said. "It's hard not to think about all of that. Say, want to come up to the aerie with me? See Cleo and the other birds? Might be a nice change of pace."

Kaela half-smiled and shook her head. She was afraid of heights, and the only time she'd ever been up there, she'd clung to the wall and been too afraid to even approach the owls. Mara kept hoping if she tried it again, she might gain a little confidence, but she wasn't going to push it.

"Want to go down to the River Market and check out the book stalls?"

Kaela's face brightened, and she nodded rapidly. She loved books, especially illustrated ones, and Mara often bought her one on market day if she had time and money. At this point, money was the last thing on Mara's mind, and she needed the distraction. They finished their nuts and made their way down the curving cobbled street toward the River Market. The book stalls were busier than the food market; everyone seemed to be hoarding old books as well as food. Kaela picked out a worn manual on fishing, which was odd since she'd never fished, but Kaela wanted what Kaela wanted, and it was only a couple of fen. Mara impulse-bought another book of antique erotica, which Kaela eyed with a little grin.

"Go ahead, take a look," Mara said, handing it to her sister. Kaela had never shown any interest in anything sexual, but there was no reason why she wouldn't have the same thoughts as anyone else. Kaela's eyes widened and lit up with mirth as she flipped through the pages, covering her mouth as if stifling a laugh at an illustration of three female Maer climbing a giant's erect phallus, one of them hanging upside down with her legs wrapped around it and a wild grin on her face.

"You can have it if you want," Mara said, but Kaela closed the book with a smile and handed it back, hugging her fishing book to her chest. "Suit yourself, but if you ever change your mind, I have more than a few back at my apartment."

Spatters of chilly rain began falling as they walked along the river path back toward Kaela's group house, and Mara tucked both books in her bag to keep them from getting wet. The rain dampened their enthusiasm; Mara didn't talk much on the way back, and Kaela showed no signs of wanting to engage. She was too busy eyeing the passersby, her sharp eyes seeming to analyze each one before flitting to the next. Whatever was going on in Kaela's mind, no detail escaped her notice.

Mara gave her a longer-than-usual hug when she dropped her off, which was awkward because Kaela was clutching the book to her chest.

"Enjoy your book, and I'll see you next week, yeah?" Kaela nodded, staring down at her book. "And listen, hey." Mara put a hand under Kaela's chin, and Kaela looked back up, her eyes soft and open. "If you ever need me, have them send me a message. I'll come just as soon as I can."

Kaela blinked, pulling Mara's hand away, and turned into the group house, where the steward was holding the door open.

Mara played around on the Stream when she got home, watching views of baby owls hatching, their purplish-pink wrinkled skin streaked with a few wisps of wet feathers. It always cheered her up a bit, but she had seen pretty much all the owl-hatching views there were to see more than once, and she got bored. She pulled up Uffrin's view and watched it again, wondering what he was doing, what it was like out on mission. He hadn't said where he was going or what he was doing, but given his line of work, he was probably headed close to the front line to do aerial surveillance using his machine owl. The orbuses were said to have a range of up to twenty miles, so hopefully, he wouldn't have to get too close to the fighting, but she worried about him, soft little thing that he was. If something went wrong, if he got separated from his scout, how would he defend himself? She popped over to his stream, which she had promised herself she wouldn't stalk, but if it was going to rain all day and the Stream was going to be down all night, she had to do something.

He didn't post much—just a few short views of tools and mechanisms, but when she went far enough up his stream, she saw what looked like an old family portrait, and her jaw dropped. He stood, probably five or more years younger, between three adults, two females and a male. One of the females she immediately recognized as Cloti. How in the world had Cloti's son grown up to be an artificer? She searched through her memory, trying to picture anything in his demeanor that suggested Cloti's practice, but nothing came to mind.

Mara didn't practice regularly, but she had gotten into it when the fad swept the Stream. She'd been to a couple of Cloti's sessions in the park, in part just to see who would be there and what the scene would be like. She'd expected it to be more elaborate somehow, but it was literally just Cloti and an acolyte leading meditation cycles, with a couple of hundred Maer sitting in a big circle around them. It was silent meditation, without any direction other than Cloti's movements and the occasional tinkle of a little bell, which the acolyte would ring whenever it was time to change positions. Mara liked it better on the Stream because there were fewer distractions, and she enjoyed the soothing background noises Cloti used. She wasn't a big fan of Cloti's political philosophy—Cloti believed that humans and Maer were the same people—but those posts had been restricted since the war began anyway.

She hopped over to Cloti's stream, selected the beginner practice, and opened the view. Cloti sat in a flowing, colorful robe on a reed mat in a tranquil garden next to a fountain, whose burbling sound was amplified in the view. Cloti smiled beatifically, closed her eyes, and put her hands to her forehead, pressed together with the fingertips pointing up. Mara paused the view and sat down cross-legged on her mat, which she hadn't used in months, then started again from the beginning.

As she held her hands up, she concentrated on the pressure of her thumbs on her forehead, letting it build inside her. She'd always liked that part. Though her arms grew weary, the pressure of that single point of contact buoyed her until she lost awareness of her arms, then her legs, then the rest of her body. She floated in this space until the sound of a tiny bell brought her attention back. She followed Cloti's movements through one cycle and the next, bringing a quiet peace to her heart. The bell sounded to move her hands to her forehead for a third time, and no sooner had she reached the new position than the Stream cut off suddenly, and her mind went dark.

Mara opened her eyes and glanced out the window, but it couldn't have been past quarter-dark. The Stream had been cutting out at half or three-quarters dark, but this was a new low. She removed her circlet and examined it, but the tiny pinpoint of light still glowed from the dot on the front; there was nothing wrong with it. She stood up and looked out the window at the passersby in the streets, but no one acted as if anything was wrong. She gazed down at her mat again, thinking she could just continue the practice on her own, but she'd been pulled out of it so abruptly, she wasn't sure if she could just jump back in.

She sighed, set some water on for tea, and hit the tarpipe a couple of times. Cleo would soon be looking for her on the roof, and she smiled as she pictured the owl's little game. Whatever happened to Kuppham and the Maer, Cleo would be fine. Better than fine, most likely, though she was pretty sure Cleo enjoyed their bond. If the city fell, if the Maer were dispersed to the far corners of the Silver Hills, the owls would always have the cliffs, the woods, and the wind.

7

Uffrin studied Erliss as they traveled, as he was sure Erliss was studying him. Neither of them brought up Uffrin's parentage or the question of the humans and the Maer, but the dance they did around these topics was more awkward than the conversations themselves would have been. Once they passed Geivert, they saw quite a few more soldiers returning from the front, and their grim faces sank Uffrin's mood lower. Erliss insisted they not talk to anyone, given the sensitive nature of their mission. The few times they had been asked their business by a patrol, Erliss had a few quiet words with whoever was in charge and lifted a flap on their armor to show their badge, and they were allowed to pass without comment.

One evening as Uffrin was returning from relieving himself, he thought he saw Erliss' fingers curled into one of the hand moods Maoti was so fond of. Erliss had slid their hand into their pocket at his approach, but the flicker of their glance suggested guilt unless it was part of an elaborate ruse to draw him out somehow. The Shoza hadn't been bothering Maoti of late; since the war had started in earnest, they had bigger frasti to roast than a cult based on meditation and fantastical worlds. Maoti's published tracts had become less political and more mystical, which must have made Paodo happy since her opinions had gotten him into hot water at work more than once. Years ago, she'd written a treatise stating that humans and Maer were the same people, only with different amounts of hair. Paodo had nearly lost his appointment, only keeping it with Maoti's written promise not to speak on the topic again.

Uffrin blinked at Erliss, then opened his case and gazed at the silky feathers and golden glass eyes. The machine came to life the moment he tapped his gauntlet, headbutting and gently pecking his hand as he undid the straps that held it secure in the case.

The owl hopped up on its case, staring into the darkening sky, then rotated its head around so it stared directly at him. Uffrin cocked his head at the owl. It was an odd series of behaviors; though each one was part of its repertoire of movements, he had not instructed it to do anything. The headbutting and the pecking were automatic, though it might have been a little more enthusiastic than usual. But the way it looked at the sky, then back at him—it was hard to see anything in its built-in response patterns that would account for it. He was sure it was just a strange combination of circumstances that had triggered these responses, but a small part of his mind did wonder if the rumors about the orbus were true. Some said the newest orbuses sometimes did things they weren't supposed to, even developed rudimentary personalities. A glitch of the artificing process, or a mage losing control during enchantment.

Whatever the case, his machine's behavior was unusual, if not exactly concerning. It had done nothing wrong, had not failed to obey any commands, and had functioned in every way as expected. But as he met its eyes, his finger hovered over the pad on his gauntlet, and he wondered for a moment if it needed him to tell it what to do. He sighed and tapped the circle test pattern, and the machine powered off into the night sky.

In her message, Mara had asked him what its name was, and though he'd always hated the idea of treating his machine as a pet, he'd started to ruminate on what to call it. He could name it after Uncle Soamu, who'd helped inspire him to take up the study of artificing, but it didn't feel like the right fit. Soamu was too ebullient, too sarcastic. If the machine were truly developing a personality, which he still doubted, it seemed more introspective, warmer somehow. He'd have to think on it a while. The view from the machine's flight was clear, with nothing but a four-Maer patrol on the road, and it soon fluttered back down, landing on top of its case and poking its head down inside.

"In you go, friend," Uffrin said, gesturing toward the case without using his gauntlet, and the owl hopped down and backed into position, letting out a small mechanical hoot as its golden eyes blinked up at him. "Well, I'll be," he said, squatting down to eye level and sticking out his finger for a peck. The owl closed its beak gently around his finger, which it had never done before, then let go and headbutted his hand. He ran the back of his hand gently over the top of its head and down its back, enjoying the feel of the silk beneath his fingers. Though the silk feathers were marvelous in their way, they lacked the downy softness of Cleo's wings, which haunted him in spare moments. The owl emitted a sort of purr, and its eyes half-closed, just like the cats its affection patterns were based on. He shook his head and secured each of the straps, and the owl's head cocked down to watch his fingers. When he had finished, the owl fixed its gently glowing eyes on his once again, blinked, then its eyes went dark, and it powered down with a low whine. Uffrin hadn't laid a finger on his gauntlet.

As they got to within a couple of days of Burrows Valley, larger groups of soldiers marched past them. Erliss spoke with one of the commanders for several minutes. Uffrin noticed a figure with the group wearing a mage's gauntlet, and he wondered about the magical side of the conflict. The humans were said to have mages with destructive powers that far exceeded what the Maer's gauntlets were capable of. Though he didn't expect to get close enough to the fighting to be in danger from weapons, he was less sure he'd be out of harm's way if there were mages about. Erliss returned, waiting until the soldiers had passed by before speaking.

"She said the bulk of the human forces have pulled back, but they've sent exploding hoverballs to sabotage the automatons. More than half have been put out of commission, and the rest will be pulled back soon to defend the Giant's Pass, which is only a day away. The Archive has been buried, and the forces that remain are preparing to join them once the automatons have been moved." They shook their head. "It seems the automatons were not the great assets the High Council had hoped."

The next day, they joined a makeshift camp in a small pine valley cleft by a stream. They found a plot of mostly level ground with easy access to the stream, which had been dammed to make a bathing pool, and below that, there were latrines. Erliss spotted a falconer and scout and approached them, speaking for a few minutes. Uffrin made a small fire out of pine needles and a few small branches, though the area was picked clean of any real wood. He wished he could go talk to the falconer, but he trusted Erliss' instincts.

"They don't know much more than we do, but they've been training their bird to hunt hoverballs."

"But wouldn't they just explode and kill the bird?"

Erliss wobbled their hand in the air. "Most of them don't explode. They're just lenses, basically, for whoever is looking on the other side. And apparently, the exploding ones are pinkish purple and a little bigger, more like this." They held out two fingers a couple of inches apart. "The birds can sometimes crack them against a rock with their talons and break them before the mages trigger them."

"My machine could crush them with its beak," Uffrin said, feeling strangely defensive.

"Can it spot them at night?"

Uffrin shrugged. "In theory? We've only done test runs in the barn, so who knows what it will be like out in the field. It can see just as well as a real owl, though its hearing is not as sensitive. If I'm paying attention, I should be able to spot them, and if I do, my little friend can definitely catch and destroy them."

"I sure hope so. I don't know about you, but I'm going to catch some sleep while we're in relative safety." Erliss lay down on their bedroll and pulled their hood over their eyes.

Uffrin did the same, but sleep proved elusive. His mind flashed with visions of the Stream, of little glass balls floating in the air, of Mara, laughing, touching his arm, pulling him in for a kiss. He stirred at the thought of the teasing glint of her eyes, her soft body pressing into his, how she'd push him down and have her way with him. Though he still dared not touch himself with so many Maer about, he took comfort in knowing that when he returned, he might just stand a chance of making his daydream a reality.

8

Mara grew restless and irritable as the demands on her and Cleo increased. They were now on duty every other night, but she struggled to sleep during the day. Though she tried her best to avoid getting caught up in the news from the war, with Uffrin headed toward the front lines, it was hard to resist. It was even harder to parse the reality from the fictions spread by the propaganda machine, but she gathered that there had been something of a lull in the fighting near the Archive, and a number of automatons had been sabotaged by exploding hoverballs, or poppers, as everyone was calling them now. She assumed Uffrin was involved in night surveillance since that was the whole reason for the mechanical owls. Though the Maer had a large number of vultures and falcons, Mara was one of only two dozen owl handlers in the city, and she didn't think there were too many elsewhere either. It was hard to imagine a machine being able to do what Cleo could do, and she was desperate to see Uffrin's owl up close.

In the view he had sent, it had seemed rather affectionate, though she knew it was just a series of patterns. She wondered if he was as involved in the behavioral side as he was in the mechanical side. At school, she'd been delighted by the little turtle automaton one child's mother had brought in for show and tell. She'd sent it scurrying around the classroom, controlling its movements with a special gauntlet. Orbus technology had surely advanced quite a bit since then, so they were no doubt much more autonomous, but the mechanicals still needed a handler within twenty miles unless the range of the orbuses had increased significantly. Then again, with the secrecy surrounding everything from the magical tech industrial complex, anything was possible. She wondered if Uffrin could really get her access to his workshop; the artificing compounds were notoriously hermetic, like the orbuses themselves. But even if he couldn't get her in, they could still go for soup. Soup was a start.

One afternoon, as she was idly floating through the Stream instead of napping, she saw a view of one of Cloti's sessions in the park. It almost looked like a picture since Cloti and everyone else held their hands pressed together atop their heads for quite a while, but a bird flying by showed that it was a view. Soon the arms lowered together to their laps, and the stillness returned. Mara recalled that the sessions started at half-dark, and she wasn't on duty that night. What did she have to lose? Maybe it would help her sleep; she had to admit she was curious to see Cloti close up, especially now that she knew Cloti was Uffrin's mother. She had a bite, grabbed her mat, and headed out along the river path, feeling refreshed by the cool air blowing off the water. Fall had officially begun, but it had been warmer than usual, so the river breeze was a welcome lift to her spirits.

She went early, hoping to get a spot close enough to see Cloti. She arrived to find several dozen Maer already seated on their mats in a semicircle around an elaborate inscription in the stone. She had seen it before, on flyers at the market advertising Cloti's practice, but she hadn't paid it any attention. The figures flowed together and curled around each other like seaweed. She was pretty sure it was a message of some kind, though it didn't look like any alphabet she'd ever seen or heard of. The closest thing to it was the old alchemical mystography she'd seen in some of the books at the River Market stalls.

"Do you know what it means?" asked a quiet voice from a bright-eyed young Maer seated closest to the circle.

"I'm sorry, I don't," Mara replied.

"Would you like to know?" There was an openness in her voice that was reflected in her face, and she scooched her mat over to make room. The Maer on either side of her moved accordingly, and Mara nodded thanks and sat down on her mat next to her.

"Yes, please." Mara's curiosity was piqued by the Maer's gentle frankness and by the symbols themselves, which seemed to undulate as she stared at them.

"To find the Thousand Worlds, you must seek within, as without." The Maer's voice was stronger, steadier, as she spoke the words. Mara knew of the theory of the Thousand Worlds from her studies, but she had never believed in alternate realities or travel through time and space. She had to admit there was something appealing about the notion of connectedness in the old religions, the idea that all things were part of a greater whole. She felt that sometimes when she was flying with Cleo; they each existed in a separate version of reality, walled-off and inaccessible to each other, but through the circlets, she could break through those walls. Mara noticed none of those seated around her was wearing a circlet, which was quite unusual. She quickly removed hers and tucked it into its pocket, smiling apologetically.

"I can see you're new to practice. Welcome. I'm Juiya." She crossed her arms across her chest, and Mara repeated the gesture.

"Mara. Thank you for making room and for..." Mara's eyes fell on the inscription once again, and she began to follow one of the lines with her eyes, around innumerable loops and flourishes and long connecting curves, around and between like a vine on a trellis. She grew dizzy before she managed to follow it for more than a quarter of the inscription, but it seemed to be one continuous line that circled back in on itself.

"What is in me is open to you." Juiya bowed slightly, then covered her mouth, suddenly giggling. "Sorry, I know that sounds weird if you don't practice." She touched Mara's arm as she spoke, and her laughter was infectious. "It just means—"

"I don't think it sounds weird at all," Mara said, putting her hand on top of Juiya's and thinking of her connection with Cleo, how their minds were open to each other. "What is in me is open to you too."

Juiya's eyes half-blinked, and she put her hands together, then let her palms spread apart like a pointed egg. The group took in a collective breath as sandaled footsteps approached. Cloaks rustled as everyone put their hands together at their hearts at the same time, and a Maer approached, full-figured and dressed in flowing robes in shades of green and brown. She must have been in her fifties, and she scanned the crowd with gentle eyes and a smile that said she saw each and every one of them.

Mara's heart clutched when Cloti made eye contact with her as if, for that brief moment, they had shared more than just a glance. Cloti had seen her, really seen her, and it felt like she approved. Mara's chest warmed with the sensation, and when Cloti lowered herself to sit and held her palms out to the crowd, Mara stuck hers out energetically, hoping to recapture the feeling of being connected to this amazing person. She'd heard of Cloti's charm, but sitting ten feet away from her, it was almost palpable, a real physical thing that was just invisible to the usual means of perception. Her hands moved to her lap in time with Cloti's, and they sat, unmoving, breathing together, just her and Cloti.

Cloti's movements were slow and subtle and a lot more physically challenging than Mara expected. She raised her arms slowly toward the heavens, so slowly that Mara's arms ached as she mimicked the movement. Just when the burn got to be too much, Cloti's hands touched above her head, and she lowered them to her lap. In those periods of recovery, Mara's consciousness seemed to expand just a little bit outside herself. She felt as though the edges of her being were just out of reach of those around her, like a fingertip brushing over the fine hairs on the underside of a wrist. By the end of the practice, it felt like the space between herself and Juiya had closed even further. She could feel Juiya, almost physically, like iron pulled toward a lodestone, though they sat half a Maer's length apart.

When Cloti finished her final cycle of movement and stillness, she pushed up to standing without using her hands and spread her arms wide, seeming to embrace the crowd, which had swelled to more than a hundred practitioners. Juiya sat up straight, her eyes glued to Cloti, her face bright with anticipation, which seeped into Mara, though she had no idea what she was excited for.

"Thank you all for sharing the part of you that is in me and accepting the part of me that is in you. We each wear our isolated little lives like turtle shells, only poking our heads out to the wider world when we feel it is safe." Mara found herself nodding, less at the words than at the tone, which somehow communicated a layer of meaning beyond words. "But as we look at the world around us, it is anything but safe. War is upon us, disease, uncertainty, and loss." She paused, clutching her hands together, but the beatific smile never left her face. "Should we then remain enclosed, ever hesitant, hoping that our fragile shell will protect us when the hammer falls?" Mara shook her head, fully entranced by Cloti's words and moved by a warmth that welled up inside her. Cloti spoke of imminent doom, but hope moved beneath her words like an undertow.

"These are dark days for the Maer. No one can see the future, but everyone can read what is written on the walls. No wall stands forever. If, as some believe, the end is not far off, we must ask, the end of what?

Of this city, its gates and towers, its houses and markets, perhaps. Of the workshops and machines, the laws and regulations? Perhaps. Of the life of comfort and ease many of us enjoy? Perhaps. But even if the worst should come to pass, if everything we fear turns true, it will not herald the end of the Maer. We will endure, as we did in the Time Before; we will survive, we will change, and we will adapt. The Maer that emerge in the Time to Come may be better, stronger, and wiser than we are now."

"Carry this thought in your minds as you return to your lives amid the turmoil and stress of the days we are living. Think not of the darkness of tomorrow, of the destruction wrought by the divisions we have sown amongst ourselves. Look to the future, when the Maer will be reborn through the forge of history, by common struggle and unity of purpose. Cleave to each other, and prepare yourselves, not for the end, but for the beginning."

Everyone stood as she finished, and their silence was louder than any applause. Cloti put her hands to her heart, bowed, and everyone suddenly relaxed. Juiya turned to Mara, her eyes wet with joy, and threw her arms around her. Mara wrapped her bony body tight, both of them rocking gently side to side, until Mara felt Juiya's grip loosen, and they released. Cloti had drifted over toward them, and Mara's heart leapt when Cloti reached out and touched her shoulder.

"I'm glad you could make it," Cloti said, squeezing gently as if speaking to an old friend.

"Gods, of course, I wouldn't...that is, I've been watching a little on the Stream, and I thought..."

"I'm glad to know those views do some good. I'm never on myself, but my wife helps me put them out there. I'm Cloti since we haven't formally met." She reached out her hand, not so much for a handshake, but to take

Mara's hand in hers and hold it. Her hand was warm and soft, her grip gentle but stable.

"I'm honored," Mara managed. "Also, I'm Mara."

"You have some experience with sharing minds," Cloti said, her kind eyes falling on Mara's.

"Only with birds," Mara said, looking down in embarrassment.

"How delightful!" Cloti took Mara's arm in hers and steered her toward a path leading into a lightly wooded area of the park. Mara glanced back at Juiya, who watched with an amused expression on her face. Maybe Cloti did this kind of thing all the time. Cloti sat on a bench and gestured for Mara to join her.

"Any kind of birds in particular?"

"Owls, mostly. Though I have trained with other raptors, as well as crows."

"And your owls... They keep the city safe?" Cloti's voice had an odd timbre to it, as if she didn't quite believe it.

"They are our eyes and ears in the night."

"Well, I shall sleep better knowing we are in good hands." Cloti let go of Mara's hand and gazed off into the forest. Mara looked in the same direction but saw nothing other than trees and a few practitioners making their way back home through the park. It was hard to fathom someone as important as Cloti spending this much time with a random Maer she had just met, but she sensed no impatience, no hurry to do anything but sit on this bench and look into the trees.

Cloti shifted in her seat, fishing something out of a pocket of her robe. "Take these." She laid two thin copper discs with an engraving of an eye filling the circle in Mara's hand. "When you have time, look into the eye and see what you can see."

"Thank you, I will. They're...beautiful." Mara turned the discs over and over in her fingers. They were shiny-smooth on the other side, so she could see her blurred, coppery reflection in them. She looked into the eye, which was engraved with remarkable detail, down to the thousand striations of the iris and even a few squiggly veins in what would have been the whites.

"Do three slow circles around the outside with your mind, then three around the iris, as slowly as you can go. Push through the center until you lose your vision in the emptiness and see where that takes you."

"I will. Thanks again." Mara looked down at the coins, puzzled. Why did she need two?

"One is for you, and the other is to pass on to someone else who might appreciate it."

Mara pocketed one of the coins and kept the other in the palm of her hand.

"I think I might have someone in mind."

9

As they made their way along the edge of the stream, Uffrin could not stop staring at the masses of automatons arrayed at the cleft where two valleys met. He counted eighteen of them, each the size of a small cabin, gleaming bronze mottled with spots of oxidized green, fitted with fixed-mount arbalests and scattershot catapults. The scattershots were the Maer's deadliest weapon, able to shred armor and flesh from a distance, cutting down whole rows of enemies with a single burst. Hundreds of soldiers, artificers, falconers, scouts, and other assorted Maer milled about. Some were busy with the machines, while others trained, napped, or played dice.

"I can see why they call it giant's pass," Uffrin said, gazing along the two valleys, each of which had a wide road leading through it.

"It's a natural choke point," Erliss commented. "Anyone headed toward Kuppham has to go through here unless they want to go hundreds of miles around."

"I can see that, but aren't they kind of sitting ducks out in the open like this?"

"Why do you think we're here?"

Uffrin's heart sank. It all made sense now. "We're here to protect the automatons from hoverballs."

"Glad you worked that out on your own. Let me check in with my superiors and get our assignment. You stay here."

Uffrin wanted to object, as he'd been dying to get a close-up look at the automatons, but he didn't relish the idea of wading through that swarming mass of unknown Maer to do so. Maybe he could get a private tour later. When Erliss left, he set down his case and opened it to make sure his machine hadn't shifted during their travels. He tapped his gauntlet, and the owl's eyes flickered into life. It strained against the straps in an apparent effort to headbutt his hand.

"Easy now, friend," he said, holding the back of his hand out and letting the owl touch it with its forehead. "You're going to see some real action tonight. Better save your strength."

The owl emitted a low hoot that was little more than a purr, then its lights went out. Once again, without his having touched his gauntlet.

There was no way the machine had understood what he'd said; though it had sensitive hearing, there was nothing in the patterns for speech recognition, though a prototype of a new orbus was said to be voice-activated. Uffrin would believe that when he saw it. But there was no denying that the machine had correctly interpreted his actions and powered back down of its own accord. The orbus' power supply would last for up to a month of continuous operation. It had only been used for a total of a few days at most, but there was no sense in using it when not strictly necessary. It did have an automatic shut-off built in, but it shouldn't have powered down so quickly.

Movement among the automatons caught his eye, and he watched as several of them began moving to the side to make room for a new arrival, whose top was blackened and its armaments shattered. It lurched behind the front line, and the other two automatons moved back into position. A crew immediately swarmed the new arrival as soon as it stopped, swinging themselves up onto it with tools to pry the remnants of the catapult and arbalests off. Though the scattershot catapults were quite deadly, he wondered about the overall efficacy of the automatons. They took a crew of 2 to operate, not to mention the support personnel required to move and maintain them. And they turned out to be vulnerable to the humans' most potent and annoying weapons, the hoverballs.

Erliss returned, carrying steaming bowls that set Uffrin's mouth watering even before he knew what they contained. When he smelled goat, his spirits soared, and he held the bowl up under his face for a few seconds before he even picked up the spoon. It was thin and light on meat, with only a few chunks of turnip to bulk it up, but it was salty and hot, which he craved more than anything after a week of eating sporecakes and barely seasoned marmot.

"We've been assigned to Burrows Valley, the one to the east." Erliss gestured with their spoon in between bites. "It's full of little caves, so we'll hole up in one of those near where it opens up to the Geurla Forest. The bulk of the human forces are thought to be past the Archive Valley, but the vultures can't see through the forest canopy, so you'll be sending your friend there in." They eyed Uffrin's case while spooning a chunk of turnip into their mouth. "Should be another day's hike, and we'll have to be on the lookout. A hoverball was caught and destroyed in the valley just last night. They think the humans controlling it are in the forest, but they could be in one of those caves in the valley."

Uffrin chewed a piece of gristle, picking out a shard of bone and flicking it to the ground. He'd hoped to stay behind the safety of the automatons, and Erliss' description of the valley did not inspire confidence.

Erliss seemed to sense his discomfort. "Not exactly what you were expecting, I take it?"

"No," Uffrin admitted. "I mean, I'm an artificer! I spend my days in a workshop with bright lights and tiny tools. I never fully realized what I was signing up for."

"Every Maer in the Silver Hills is signed up, whether they wanted it or not."

Uffrin's breath grew shallow as he pictured the humans sweeping over the land, the silver flash of their swords, the black smoke churning from razed villages, the red fury in their eyes. Erliss' hand touched his arm, and he sighed a shaky smile.

"We should get moving if we're going to find some good cover by nightfall. I studied a map of the valley, so I have an idea where to look for some caves that will serve us well." They squeezed Uffrin's bicep, then tilted their bowl to slurp the remaining broth. Uffrin choked down the rest of his stew, though he had lost his appetite. He doubted they'd be eating anything hot in the next few days.

The entrance to Burrows Valley was guarded by a half-dozen automatons and a contingent of soldiers, who nodded at them as they passed. The valley stretched before them, with a stream flowing down the center, dotted with boulders amid the little pools and rapids. The road ran along the north side of the stream, but they walked a narrow path near the rise to the south, where stretches of grasses and occasional clumps of pine trees would provide some cover. Erliss stopped occasionally to scan the valley and the hillside, then gestured him forward. They never said if they saw anything, and the landscape looked empty of all life except for birds and the occasional lizard. Shadow fell over the valley as the sun dipped below the mountains. Uffrin pulled up his collar, though the sun's warmth still radiated from the rocks all around.

Erliss motioned for him to stop, then summoned him with a subtle gesture.

"See that little ridge up ahead?" they said in a low voice. Uffrin nodded. "The map showed a few caves not too far up. Once we get to the base of it, I'm going to scout them out, and I'll let you know when it's safe."

Uffrin glanced around the cave, which was big enough for a half-dozen Maer and looked to have been slept in before. Several piles of rushes were spaced around the remains of a fire, though none of it looked especially fresh to his untrained eyes. Erliss crouched in the entrance, studying the valley through a field scope. Uffrin set down his case, opened it, and checked to make sure everything was secure. The machine looked sad somehow, though its features were still in the shadowy half-light of the cave.

"You'll get to have some fun tonight, Friend." Uffrin closed the case softly so the snap was almost inaudible. Erliss stood up, turning to him and holding out the scope.

"We're not alone in the valley." Uffrin's heart lurched into his throat at the words, but Erliss' unworried tone took the edge off. "Free Maer," Erliss said, pointing with their chin.

Uffrin raised the scope, at first fixing it on a pair of vultures circling overhead, which he suspected were controlled by Maer like Mara. Erliss' arm touched his to lower it, and he followed a stream of smoke down to a series of holes in the rock.

"Looks like maybe a couple dozen," Erliss said. "Four or five families in that group of caves just below the little cliff there."

"Yes, yes, I see them!" Uffrin whispered, not that Maer over a mile away could have heard him. "What are they doing there?"

"Living." Erliss did not continue, and Uffrin let the silence stretch on as he scanned the dwellings, which had worked stone around the cave entrances, with stairs cut into the cliffs with rope guards and metal handrails. The Maer milled about, working, playing, talking, as if a wave of destruction weren't looming over them, building to an inevitable crash. Uffrin lowered the scope and handed it back to Erliss.

"Yes, well, do they pose a threat?" Uffrin asked delicately, sensing Erliss' empathy toward the Free Maer.

"Not to us, but if I were a human scouting party, I might want to watch my step. You can bet they see everything that goes on in this valley."

"Meaning they already know we're here?"

"They already know we're here." Erliss gripped Uffrin's shoulder. "That's a good thing. They're on our side."

"So does that mean we can make a fire, and maybe if you happen to shoot some small animal or bird, we might, you know..." Uffrin placed his hand over Erliss', and they shared a smile.

"I doubt there's much game to be had between the Free Maer and the hunters from the camp. And besides, the Free Maer may know we're here, but hopefully, the humans don't."

"So, no fire?"

"No fire." Erliss pulled a bag of jerky from their pack and offered Uffrin a stick. It was as tough as a sandal strap and twice as salty, but it had a kind of sweet heat to it once he got it worked a little softer. They chewed in silence for a while, staring out at the darkening valley.

"Should I bring out my friend now?"

Erliss blinked their assent, and Uffrin opened the case. The owl's eyes were already lit, and it purred and pecked at him as he undid the straps. It hopped atop the case, its head swiveling around and stopping as it faced the opening. It stared for a moment, turning slowly to scan the valley, then rotated back to fix Uffrin with its bright yellow eyes.

"Somebody's ready for action. Yes, you are." Uffrin put on his circlet, which felt heavy since he hadn't worn it much on this trip.

"Do a high scan along the valley, then enter the forest canopy a mile or so in and fly low on your way back." Erliss pointed here and there in the valley as they spoke. "I'll keep watch while you work."

"Sounds good." Uffrin sat on his folded bedroll, leaning against his pack. He shifted around to get comfortable, and the machine clacked its beak several times. "All right, all right. You want to fly? Let's fly."

He found the pad on his gauntlet by touch, and the machine's wings fluttered into action. It sped out of the cave entrance, climbing up into the sky at a swipe of his fingers. He saw purple-tinted clouds through the view as the machine rose up, then leveled off, showing the valley in sharp detail. He zoomed in on a few areas of scrub or tall grasses, flying the owl as slowly as gravity and the winds would allow. Nothing larger than a bat moved in the valley, and other than one standing guard, the Free Maer had withdrawn inside their cliff houses, the low glow of hearth fires betraying their presence within. He combed the valley, taking time with each area of cover, scanning one before moving to the next. After several miles, the valley opened out into a rocky meadow with a few conifers growing along the creek, becoming denser until they spread into a wall of forest a mile or so beyond the valley edge. He flew the machine over the forest for a few minutes, then sent it gliding down, slowing to pass through a hole in the canopy and flutter onto a convenient branch.

He swiveled the owl's head slowly in all directions, but nothing moved in the forest. He sent the owl flying in a zigzag pattern back and forth through the forest to cover as much territory as possible. The conifers' branches interlocked to make an almost impenetrable ceiling in places, which did make Uffrin nervous, but Friend seemed to anticipate his movements and flew cleanly through. He saw no sign of anything in the forest, and he sent the owl up to survey the area, following the line of trees along the stream.

Just as it began to thin out nearer the valley, a dark shape caught his eye, almost indistinguishable from the tree it leaned against. Only the faint flutter of its cloak in the breeze gave it away. The owl started descending, but Uffrin nudged it back up, wondering if that had been a pattern response or if the damned thing was somehow making decisions on its own? He flew it to the end of the trees, then wheeled and circled around, a little lower this time to get another look.

The hooded figure stared down at something that glinted in their cupped hands. It was impossible to get a bead on it without hovering directly above, which Uffrin feared might draw their attention. His best guess was that it was a scrying lens, most likely connected to a hoverball. He circled around again and saw a pair of figures creeping across the valley toward the treeline with what might have been javelins in quivers across their backs. They entered the line of trees at the valley end, difficult to follow as they ducked from tree to tree, but they were clearly heading in the direction of the hooded figure. Uffrin had the owl continue circling high above, catching occasional glimpses of the two figures, who split up as they neared their target. The hooded figure remained immobile, staring down at what Uffrin could now see was definitely some kind of lens. The lens disappeared, and the cloaked figure whirled around just as one of their pursuers closed in, jabbing the figure with a knife. A cry of pain reached the machine's auditory sensors, and the sound of repeated blows, juicy, squirting sounds. The cloaked figure slumped to the ground.

The owl pulled downward, and Uffrin restrained it, but as he watched the two figures rummage through the fallen mage's cloak, he sent the machine diving down, swooping in to land about ten feet away. He flared the wings, and the owl sent out a muted trill. The Maer pulled javelins from their quivers and stood poised to throw. The owl lowered its wings and hunched its body, softening its trill further. The Maer spoke, still tensed, and though he could hear the words, Uffrin could not understand their speech. He sent the owl forward one hop, and it blinked its eyes and clicked its beak together. The Maer lowered their weapons, and one of them advanced cautiously, speaking directly to the owl. Uffrin heard a word that sounded like "human," and then the Maer pointed to the dead mage, whose hood had fallen back to reveal a face covered in skin except for a trim mustache and goatee. It was as revolting as it was fascinating, but Uffrin snapped his focus back to the Free Maer facing his machine.

The owl hopped forward again, cooing at the Maer, who smiled a little and said something to their partner. Uffrin distinctly heard the word "Shoza," and the owl chirped at the word. The Maer slid the javelin back into its quiver, crouched, and held out a shiny object that looked like a pocket watch or a foldable mirror on a chain long enough to be worn as a necklace. They held the object out, dangling from its chain, and the owl hopped forward and gently grasped it in its beak, then secured the chain in its talons.

The Maer smiled with wonderment, and the owl sent a purring trill toward them and headbutted their hand. The Maer cooed at it as one might to a cat or a baby and held out their hand for further headbutting. The owl rotated its head to blink at the other Maer, who had approached and crouched down as well, and the owl headbutted them, then hopped backward, raising its wings. The Maer stood, backing up a little, and Uffrin sent the wings fluttering with a quick swipe of his finger. The owl raced off into the sky, prize clutched in its claws. Uffrin let the owl fly back on its own, following the homing pattern, and he removed his circlet as soon as it flew into the cave and dropped the device at his feet.

"Well done, Friend," Uffrin said, still a little groggy as the contours of the cave came back into focus. The owl raised its wings and let out a series of quiet trills, then hunched down again and hopped forward to peck gently at his fingers.

"You did so good!" Uffrin chucked it under the chin, then raised the device on its chain to study it in the faint light filtering in from outside. It was made of cold metal, steel, most likely, and the case was engraved with symbols he couldn't make out in the darkness. He fumbled around with his fingers until he found a nub, which he pressed. It popped open, revealing a mirrored surface. He stared into the mirror but saw very little in the shadowy cave, and after a moment he grew dizzy, and snapped the case shut.

10

Mara scanned the valley through Cleo's eyes with increased confidence now that she knew they could spot and capture a hoverball. After a long shift, they found nothing, and she struggled through her torpor to stand up to retrieve a mouse for the bird, who stood on a perch clacking her beak.

"Here you go, girl," Mara said, dangling the dead mouse by its tail so Cleo could snatch it out of her hand, then turn her head up and swallow it down in three quick snaps. "Are you ready to go home?"

A soft hand touched her arm.

"Before you go…"

Mara turned to see Leasse, a tall, soft-spoken handler she was friendly with but didn't see enough of.

"I was wondering…that is, me and a couple of the other handlers were hoping you could do a little demonstration? Of how you caught the hoverball?" Leasse raised an eyebrow hopefully, biting her lip. Mara noticed several of the other handlers listening in. Looking at her. As if she was some kind of authority just because her owl caught a marble. She shook off her doubt and pushed out a smile.

"Sure. Why not. How about we come in an hour early tonight, and I'll rig something up."

The smiles of the other handlers lifted Mara's heart, and she leaned in close to get eye-to-eye with Cleo.

"Are you ready to teach everyone your tricks?"

Cleo cocked her head, searching Mara with her inscrutable golden eyes. She swiveled her head toward the window and ruffled her wings a bit.

"*Fly away, fly away,*" Mara sang the old nursery rhyme under her breath as Cleo flapped off into the darkness. "*With eyes so sharp they pierce the night and wings so soft in silent flight, fly away...*"

Cleo was already on the railing when Mara emerged onto the roof of her hightop, weary from the climb. It always seemed harder than the stairs to the aerie, despite being one-twentieth as high. She laid the chicken liver she'd gotten at the market on the railing, and Cleo inspected it for a few moments before snatching it up and swallowing it in one gulp. The first light of dawn etched pink outlines of the mountains, and Cleo's feathers glowed in the reflected light. She turned her head toward Mara, her iridescent eyes blazing fiery gold as the first rays of morning sun hit them just right.

"Such a pretty girl," Mara cooed, holding out her hand to Cleo, who hopped closer and gave her a gentle peck. She wondered what was going on in Cleo's mind, whether she saw Mara as an owl or a Maer or if she even thought of the world in such a way. When Mara wore her circlet, she could connect with Cleo and see through her eyes, but she never quite felt like an owl, never got into Cleo's headspace in that way.

She thought back to the day in the park when she'd felt Cloti's energy pouring into her, the hint of a deeper connection she didn't yet have the training to achieve. She wondered if she could find a similar bond with Cleo. Her magical training had been entirely focused on using the circlets; without them, she couldn't do much. There were mages who eschewed magical tech, relying on the power of their minds, boosted with various philters and herbs and the like. The training schools in Kuppham did not teach such "primitive" methods, which were said to be common among the Free Maer.

Brightstone chips were getting harder and harder to come by; if the humans took Kuppham, there would be none whatsoever. The circlets could supposedly be used without the chips, but it took a great deal more mental and physical energy—and a different skillset, which Mara hadn't trained for. Would it be possible to gain that skill, to figure out how to use the rings to communicate in some way without the brightstone? The rings themselves were magical, and the brightstone chips boosted their power, but there must be a way to use them without it. She wondered if Uffrin would know more about the tech, given his line of work.

Her heart squirmed as she thought of him out in some distant valley, flying his little nameless mechanical owl, with humans and their hoverballs lurking all about. He was such a tender little thing, afraid of his own shadow; how would he cope with the terrors of war? She wished she could wrap herself around him and keep him safe. When he came back from the front, she was going to take him to bed and make him feel so safe his shouts would wake the neighbors. She hummed in her throat as she thought of the little sounds he'd make as she kissed him, how he'd stiffen at the lightest touch. The end of the world wasn't going to stop her from ravishing that Maer's body—

Mara gripped the rail and tried to relax, breathing heavily. Cleo ruffled her feathers, then turned and flapped up to her roost and ducked inside.

Mara held up her hand to block the sun, which had suddenly risen above the mountains and peeked between the hightops at her. Somewhere out there, that same light shone on Uffrin's face, casting a warm glow on the coppery hair on his cheek. Did he think of her as he blinked into the morning sun? As he hiked for miles through mountain passes? As he lay awake touching himself, was it her face he saw? She closed her eyes and smiled, picturing the shy glances he'd stolen when he thought she wasn't looking. He was into her. And she was into him. It was just a matter of time before they got to put their fantasies to the test.

Mara did a morning routine using a new view from Cloti's stream showing a water lily slowly opening until its petals lay flat against the glassy surface of a pond, which reflected the pink and lavender clouds of dawn. A dragonfly flew up and landed on the flower, its wings mosaics of iridescent cells striated with the colors of the sky reflecting up from the water. A second dragonfly landed just in front of the first, raised its tail, and touched it to the back of the other one's head. The first dragonfly curled its tail beneath it until it touched the abdomen of the first one, and they stayed in this heart-shaped form, swaying in a gentle breeze, for several minutes. They detached from their contorted position and flew off in separate directions, then the flower slowly closed again, and the cycle repeated itself.

Mara moved her arms along with the opening and closing of the flower and contorted her fingers to try to imitate the connection between the dragonflies, like the hand moods she'd seen in some of the other views. With each cycle, she breathed more easily, and her fingers found the moods less awkwardly until, at last, she let her hands fall into her lap and pulled out of the view. She pulled off the circlet and stood up, feeling light and airy.

She made some clove tea, her backup because of the darkroot shortage. She'd need to get to the market early to try to re-up her supply before they ran out. She stood by the window with her tea, watching the gutter sparrows flit in and out of the eaves like crossbow bolts. She tried to imagine what their little lives were like in the chinks and hollows of the city's buildings. Cleo had brought her gutter sparrows from her hunts on many occasions, despite their speed and agility, and she wondered what life was like for those that remained when their mother or father or partner or child never returned. She supposed death was part of their life, but that didn't mean they didn't feel sorrow or loss.

There was a line at the tea vendor, but she managed to procure a small bag at double the usual cost, enough to last her a week, perhaps, unless she cut it with something else. Rumor had it that the bulk of the tea was going to the military. She didn't begrudge them their morning lift, given how dreadful their circumstances were. News on the Stream had told of a lull in the fighting, which probably meant the humans were preparing for another big push. She hoped Uffrin was safe, wherever he was, and she hoped he would contact her as soon as he got back. She knew the army had a few mobile communication posts, and soldiers could occasionally send brief messages to their loved ones. She didn't expect Uffrin to reach out, but she still checked her stream several times an hour, just in case. She checked as soon as she got home from the market, and her heart sank when she saw nothing but yellow and orange messages she had already ignored more than once.

Mara sighed as she removed her circlet and hung it on the door. She needed at least four hours sleep plus a shorter nap before duty tonight. Since she'd drunk only clove tea this morning, she was feeling sleepy already, but her brain wouldn't settle down. She sat on the bed and flipped through her new erotica book, which was heavy on natural settings. It showed Maer intertwined beneath waterfalls, atop high cliffs, and beneath flower-covered trellises, with leaves, clouds, and splashes of water covering most of their naughty bits. When she opened a page near the middle of the book, her breath caught at the image.

A female Maer with extravagant hips and breasts was riding a wiry Maer with his hands tied behind his head. Her hands gripped around his neck as she stared down at him with an almost malicious grin, and the look of tender joy on his face stretched Mara's smile wide. She touched herself, imagining her as the Maer on top with Uffrin beneath her, hands tied, muscles taut against the restraints. When Uffrin got back from the front, she would ride his tight little body like a rail. She worked herself up quickly, picturing Uffrin's soft eyes, his tender lips, his utter submission to her will. She bit her hand to stifle her moan as she came, then fell back into her pillow, eyes closed, and let the patter of rain in the gutters lull her into sleep.

Leasse stood staring out the wide window into the valley as Mara entered the aerie. Her hands were clutched in front of her, and she jumped up and gave a little yelp of delight. She held out her bracer, and her owl Seeli swooped in, landing awkwardly and spreading her wings. A string dangled from one of her talons, which clutched a marble, explaining the awkward landing.

"You're the smartest and bestest owl in the parliament," Leasse said, holding a mouse just out of reach until Seeli closed her wings.

"Don't let Cleo hear you say that."

The owl snatched the mouse while Leasse spun toward Mara, a joyful smile plastered to her face.

"Did you see that?"

Mara gazed out the window as she pulled on her bracer. She noticed a little sparkle beneath one of the platforms, then another in the middle of one of the rings, then several more.

"You set up a whole obstacle course!" She gripped Leasse's free arm and got a timid smile in return.

"I hope it's—"

"Leasse, it's fantastic! Much better than the training we got at the meeting."

"Which is why we're glad you elected to lead the training this evening."

Sergeant Kay had a way of sidling up out of the ether after having listened in on conversations long enough to join them as if she'd been there all along. Which made sense for the Shoza director of avian surveillance.

"Sorry, Sergeant, I hope we didn't—"

"Just...Kay, please." She held out a gloved finger toward the platforms. "Show me what Cleo can do before the others get here."

Mara ran Cleo through the course, picking up the marbles one at a time and bringing them back to put in the box Kay held out. The other owl handlers straggled in as dusk neared, and the aerie apprentices climbed out and re-set the marbles on their long strings. When the course had been laid, Mara turned around and noticed everyone staring at her. She glanced toward Kay, who had vanished, leaving her in charge, apparently. As she looked from face to face, she saw glimpses of hope that had been absent from the aerie of late. She didn't really believe a little training with marbles was going to make much difference with the human armies supposedly marching toward Kuppham on two fronts. But seeing this light in eyes that had been dull and hopeless for so long buoyed Mara's heart.

It's fine, she thought. *I've got this.*

She pulled a marble from her pocket and held it up.

"Call your birds down," she said, and the half-dozen owls that weren't already on the handlers' arms fluttered down in silent concert. The handlers formed a semicircle around her, and she stepped forward, holding the marble up high.

"This motherfucker right here," she said to a chorus of chuckles, but every Maer and owl's eyes were fixed on the marble. "There are twelve of them hanging from the platforms and hoops, one for each owl, thanks to Leasse's hard work." She gestured toward Leasse, who did a little curtsey at the quiet applause. "The real ones are like lenses, and we think the humans can see anything visible through the glass. The trick is to make sure the birds clutch it completely in their talons to obscure the field of vision." She dangled the marble in front of Cleo, who picked it gently out of the air and closed her talons around it. Everyone nodded, and she passed the bag of marbles around, watching as the handlers practiced with their owls.

"Now, who wants to go first?"

11

Uffrin sat outside the tent of the Master Artificer, waiting for the promised audience. The mirror Friend had captured was stored in a lead-lined bag in his pocket. A grumpy-looking mechanic stormed out through the tent flaps, and a high voice summoned him from within.

"Come in, come in," said a Maer about the age of Maoti as Uffrin slipped in through the opening, still wearing his case on his back. She was wiry and upright, with an almost military bearing, though her leather apron, toolbelt, and lens cap left little doubt about who she was. Voliare was a legend, having designed the first truly autonomous Guardian, which had presumably been buried along with the Archive it was designed to guard. She had been instrumental in improving the mobility and versatility of the automatons, though some felt her passion for the devices had swayed the military to invest in technology that cost more money and Maerpower than it was worth.

"You work with the owls, third generation orbus, correct?" She eyed his case, which he unshouldered and set on the wooden planks that made up the floor.

"Yes, we got the new orbuses a couple of months ago, and I finished modifications to the machine just before we left."

"Let's have a look, shall we?" She opened his case without asking and had Friend unstrapped and set on the table before he had time to object. Uffrin went to unstrap his gauntlet to hand it to her, but she tapped on her own gauntlet, and the owl's eyes popped open before he had the first strap undone.

"How did your gauntlet bypass my imprint lock?"

"Child, I invented the orbus." Her fingers slid across the pad on her gauntlet, and the owl spread its wings, then tucked them. "I see you implemented the wing modification you requested permission for." Friend's wings flapped several times, then folded again. "You increased the range of motion by maybe 15%, but that could come at a cost in durability." Uffrin swallowed, watching as the hard glint in Voliare's eyes softened in appreciation. "Let's see how it performs."

Friend fluttered upward, then zipped around the tent, hovering in each corner before flying back and hovering again. He landed neatly on the table and emitted three high trills. Voliare's eyebrows furrowed, and she leaned in close to the owl, which gave her nose a gentle peck, then headbutted the hand she held out.

"You used cat behavior patterns?" she asked, still staring at the owl.

"Just a couple, for the close-up interactions. I thought it might be useful to make it seem less threatening. It actually came in handy with the Free Maer, I think."

Voliare shook her head, turning halfway toward him. "We've told them they need to clear out. When the humans come, we can't protect them."

"Well, without their help, we wouldn't have this." Uffrin lifted the bag from his robe and set it on the table. Friend hopped over toward it and pecked at it, then swiveled its head toward Voliare and trilled.

"We'll get to that in a minute. But what are you saying, little one?" She leaned her face in close to Friend, who cooed and headbutted her nose, then reached out with one claw and slid the bag closer to her.

Voliare shot Uffrin a surprised look, which might have been tinged with a hint of pride.

"I don't suppose you put that pattern in it, did you?"

Uffrin shook his head, picking at a tangle of his beard. "It has developed a few quirks."

Voliare ran the back of her hand down the owl's chest, its fine silk feathers ruffling with the movement. Friend reached up with one claw and gently moved her hand back, then let out a bright trill.

"Incredible," Voliare whispered. "The magic of the third-gen orbus is adaptive, so I expected some behavioral evolution, but nothing like this." She tapped her bracer, and Friend's eyes snapped shut, and it powered down with a faint whine.

"The machine still performs up to spec. Better, even." Uffrin tried to quell the desperation creeping into his voice.

"Yes, I should say. I'm not sure a real owl could have done as well. You can put it away now. I'm going to have a look at the little treasure you've brought me."

As Uffrin secured Friend in the case and snapped it shut, she sat down at a table, set the bag under a brightstone lamp, and flipped her lenses down. They were the finest Uffrin had ever seen, with dozens of adjustment rings up and down their length. She pulled on a pair of black suede gloves, then opened the bag and pulled out the case.

"We've only captured one of these lenses, and it was cracked. I could guess how it worked from the construction, but I never got to try it out." She opened the bag and pulled out the case, whose designs were intricate and quite beautiful. She inspected the outside for some time, especially the hinge and the nub, then finally opened it. She studied the glass closely, then flipped up her lenses and stared intently into it. Her eyes narrowed, and her jaw clenched with concentration, then she smiled.

"I tried to look into it, but it just made me dizzy," Uffrin said, gesturing toward the device.

"You're not trained as a mage, are you?"

Uffrin shook his head. He'd long suspected he had a touch of the gift, but he'd always been more drawn to the mechanical aspect of artificing. He didn't have the patience for the kind of meditation magic his mother was into.

"It's a fine line to do both, I can tell you. The thing is—" she paused, finger in mid-air, at the sound of boots scuffing the ground outside the tent. "Come in!"

A grease-smudged mechanic slipped through the flap, bowing briefly to both of them.

"Sorry to intrude, Master, I just—"

"No intrusion, Gert. Uffrin here was just leaving." She flashed Uffrin a quick smile. "You're on for another week and a half, I think? See if you can catch us another." She clapped him on the shoulder. "Go ahead, Gert." She shifted her gaze to the newcomer, and Uffrin shouldered his pack.

"Rear lift piston on one of the mediums is fucked."

"Well, unfuck it, son! What the hell do we pay you for?"

Uffrin slipped out, glad he hadn't chosen to work with the great automatons, which were neither particularly great nor strictly speaking automatons, but neither of those things was public knowledge. He made his way through the busy camp and found Erliss by the valley water station.

"All good?" they asked.

"Good enough." Uffrin wished he could have stuck around and asked Voliare a hundred questions, but instead, he filled his waterskin and followed Erliss down the now-familiar path into the valley. Ten more days, he thought. If he could survive that, he'd be on his way back to Kuppham, the Stream, and his date with Mara.

They intercepted one more hoverball a few days later, but the human mage had spotted Friend flying overhead, so Uffrin had kept it at a distance. Having seen what their exploding hoverballs had done to the automatons, he was not keen to see what other destructive magics they might be able to hurl at his machine. The mage had returned to the woods and headed north. Uffrin had shadowed them through Friend for the rest of the night, then flown it back close to dawn. The mage had not returned, and the only thing distinguishing one day from the next was the specific cave they holed up in and the game Erliss had been wily enough to catch to supplement their sporecakes. They managed to bring back something more days than not, and they ate snakes, marmot, lizards, chunky millipedes, frogs, and small birds of some kind. They cooked them during the day when the humans were less likely to be about. Uffrin was not normally an adventurous eater, but a steady diet of sporecakes made each fresh-killed meal a delicacy. He even enjoyed the nutty crunch of the millipedes, though they cleaned him out something awful and he was hardly able to eat anything the next night.

Uffrin looked forward to Erliss' morning hunts when they were sure to be gone for at least an hour, leaving him time to tinker with Friend's machinery or catch a quick wank. He was normally quite omnivorous in his fantasies, but his thoughts kept coming back to Mara: the twinkle in her eyes, the way she touched him, her generous curves. He pictured them in a dozen different scenarios, most of them starting with her pushing him against a wall in the aerie, her soft breasts pressing into his chest, her mouth devouring his as her hands roamed over his body. He would run his fingers over her hips, then slide them around to squeeze her large, round buttocks, kneading and holding on as she worked him over. She would push him roughly to the ground or lay him gently down, her eyes hot with lust but still twinkling with bemusement.

Sometimes she toyed with him, stroking him gently with one hand while kneading his chest with the other, pressing him against her wetness but not letting him in until he could take it no longer and spilled all over himself. Other times she would shove him in straightaway and ride him remorselessly, the wicked grin on her face morphing to a rictus of concentration, followed by a groan of surprised pleasure as she ground against him and drained him into her. A couple of times, she gripped his hair in her hands and pressed herself into his face, sliding back and forth and moaning as he pleasured her with his tongue. Her indomitable desire moved him like a gauntlet controlling an automaton built for the sole purpose of giving her whatever she wanted.

The way back was cold, wet, and muddy. The fall rains had hit with a vengeance, and the creek that ran alongside the road had swollen to a river that left little room to walk. Uffrin shuddered to think of the automatons trying to move around in the mud. The soldiers they saw trudging toward the front lines bore it with grim stoicism, rain dripping from soaked hoods onto the wet-matted hair on their faces. Uffrin dried his boots by the fire on one of the rare nights without rain, and the stench would have chased him away from the fire had his feet not so desperately needed the warmth. There was almost no game to be found, so they subsisted on increasingly stale and damp sporecakes, and Uffrin went to bed every night hungry and sick to his stomach. Erliss was even more laconic in the rain than in normal weather, but as they neared Kuppham, their spirits seemed to lift a bit, and their tongue loosened up.

"What will you do with your time off?"

Uffrin opened his mouth to answer, then frowned. Was that what he was going home to? Time off before a return to the front lines? Was that to be his future now, until the war was over? Given the way things were going, it didn't look like a future he wanted anything to do with. He thought of Mara and the future he'd imagined with her, one with considerably more snuggling and less peril and misery.

"I've got a date, actually." His heart lifted as he pictured himself sitting across a table from Mara, sipping hot soup, her eyes smiling at him over the rim of her bowl. "At least I think I do." His chest tightened as doubt suddenly seized him. Was it really a date? Could she possibly be interested in him? And could someone like Mara really last a whole month in the city during such stressful times without being swept away by someone taller, stronger, and more handsome, not to mention physically present?

"Would that be the person you were thinking about every morning when I went off to hunt?" Erliss' words carried no malice or mockery, though their tone was not without a hint of amusement.

Uffrin felt his cheeks flush and his ears burn, but he laughed in spite of himself. "Was it that obvious?"

"I'm Shoza. We're trained to notice everything. And besides, it's what I would have done. Not a lot of privacy out there."

"All right, fair enough. And yeah, yes, gods, this Maer has really gotten under my fur. We only met the once; she handles owls, real ones, and does surveillance around the city, I think. But we exchanged messages, and we're supposed to get together when I get back."

"I hope it's everything you imagined," Erliss said drily.

"What about you, nosy-pants? You got anyone waiting for you?"

"I'm sure I do; I just haven't met them yet."

"Well, I hope you meet them and they exceed your expectations."

They walked in contented silence for the rest of the day. The sun came out, giving Uffrin's heart a much-needed lift until it ducked behind the hills. As they approached the gate, Erliss stopped him with a hand on his forearm.

"It's been a pleasure traveling with you, Uffrin. I hope to be assigned to work with you again sometime."

"Oh, absolutely! You've been amazing." He wanted to share his stream with Erliss, but he figured they already had access to it if they wanted, and he wasn't sure if Shoza were even allowed to use the Stream in their private lives.

They were separated going through security, and Uffrin didn't see Erliss when he emerged on the other side into the city streets, which were much quieter than they had any reason to be. He sat down on a bench, placed his circlet on his head, and let the Stream wash over him, flooding him with a barrage of sensation so intense he had to restrict the flow for a little while as he readjusted. He shunted all the messages to the side and let himself be carried away in views of mechanicals, owls, and the last part of an old dungeon adventure view he'd started right before he left. When the view was over, he stood up and pocketed his circlet. He usually kept it on as he walked through the streets, but he'd grown accustomed to the quiet, and he let his mind wander as he headed for the Clockwork Baths. He needed to get cleaned up and clear his thoughts so he could decide how to word his message to Mara.

12

Mara slumped home through the misty gray streets, having finished a second night on duty in a row. She hardly had the energy to pick up a cheese twist at the River Market, but her stomach was angry from fatigue and the long night's surveillance, so she waited in line with a half-dozen Maer who looked just as tired and grumpy as she. Some, she guessed, from having been up all night, others from getting up early to go to work. The cheese twist was a meager thing, with less than half the cheese they had before the shortages began, but she wolfed it down on her way back to her hightop, wiping her greasy fingers on the lower inside hem of her robe.

"Fuck," she muttered as she trudged up the stairs and remembered she'd forgotten to pick up a treat for Cleo. She stopped in her apartment for a shred of jerky and brought it to the roof. Cleo was waiting for her, hopping along the rail and pecking hopefully at her pocket. Mara set the jerky down on the rail, and Cleo glanced at it, then turned her bright yellow eyes up to Mara hopefully.

"Sorry, girl, it's all I've got." Cleo reached out a claw for her pocket and leaned over to peek inside, then settled down to peck at the jerky once she'd seen there was nothing else to be had. Mara reached out and stroked the top of Cleo's head with two fingers. Cleo slunk below her touch, picked up the jerky in her talons, and flew up to her roost.

Back in her room, Mara downed a cup of water and fell back onto her bed. She was off duty for one night, then back on for two more. A third of the handlers had been sent off on surveillance out of the city, some to the north, others to the east. Rumors were swirling about an imminent human offensive on multiple fronts, and there hadn't been any activity in the valley since the Maer had sent a battalion to the old Three Cliffs Fort. The Maer's relations with the South had become strained in recent years, and some thought the Southern kingdoms might allow the humans from the North safe passage through the East Pass and along the Plains Road. It would be a long way to go, but Kuppham was the southernmost Maer city, so it made a kind of sense. Mara's head spun with the dreadful possibilities, and she hit the tarpipe and let herself drift into a fitful nap.

When she awoke in mid-morning, she made a cup of half-strength darkroot tea cut with ground cloves since the darkroot shortage had only gotten worse. She was fidgety and irritable, her weary mind buzzing in a dozen directions at once. She pulled out her mat and her circlet, hoping a few cycles would take the edge off. She'd been trying out some of Juiya's views when she wanted something a little lighter. She found one of a little waterfall no more than a foot high that must have been in the river by the park. The view showed the water pouring over the rocks in an endless glittering sheet. A pair of hands moved through a set of moods, starting with the simplest shapes and progressing into complicated finger-twisting forms that challenged Mara's spatial abilities. The final mood in the progression was a heart shape with interlocking fingers pressing against each other to maintain the perfect tension. The cycle continued backward, in decreasing order of complexity, until the last mood was the same as the first, palms pressed together, fingers pointing toward the sky.

She exited the view feeling calm and refreshed, and she was about to remove the circlet when a flash of green drew her attention to her message box. Her heart leapt when she saw Uffrin's little mechanical owl logo.

Dear Mara,

I've made it back to Kuppham alive and well! I hope you're still up for a bowl of soup, and I got clearance to bring you into the workshop if you want. I know gears and silk feathers probably aren't your thing, but I'd like you to meet Friend. Let me know if you're free sometime. I'm in town for a few weeks, and my schedule's pretty much wide open.

Uffrin

Mara read it, reread it, read it once more just to make sure, then took off her circlet and clasped her arms across her chest. A bowl of soup and a mechanical owl. What could be more romantic?

She fretted about her response, what to say, when to say it, and whether to send it via text or view. He'd sent her a view before, and she'd responded with a text, so maybe she should send him a view? But she'd just gotten up, and she badly needed a bath. Not that he'd be able to tell through the view. But maybe it would seem too forward to respond to a text with a view?

She really wasn't very good at this.

It was easy enough to talk to Maer face to face when she could hear the subtle tones in their voices and read their body language. But communicating through the Stream had always felt awkward, which was why she didn't do it as much as most of her peers. And now most of her Stream time was spent meditating, but she wondered if that didn't sort of defeat the purpose?

Focus, Mara.

She decided to send a simple text, though she spent several minutes pondering and writing it down in a notebook before she finally composed it and sent it.

Hey Uffrin! Glad to hear you're back, and I would absolutely love to have soup with you and meet Friend! I'm off tonight if you get the message before then. I could meet you at quarter dark if that suits you? Looking forward to it!

--Mara

The moment she sent it, she felt a pang, wondering if she'd sounded too enthused or not enough. She fretted the paper she'd written it on for a while, then tore it out, balled it up, and bounced it off the wall neatly into the wastebasket. She pulled the circlet from her head and pocketed it, then pulled it out to check her messages again a minute later. There were none, of course, except for the yellow and orange ones she was not going to read. If they needed her badly enough, they could send a runner. Otherwise, this was her life to live, and she was going to live it. There was no telling how much time she had left before her way of life changed beyond recognition.

She took a few minutes with her new vintage erotica book, eager for a distraction. She found an image of two lovers draped around a pillar that kept their bodies apart but left their arms and faces free. One of his hands rested on her hip, the other brushing against her chin, and her hands grasped his head with splayed fingers. They were locked in a rather strenuous-looking kiss, lips smooshed together, cheeks contoured with movement. There was an ineffable tension in their stance, the way they wrapped around the pillar, eternally bound but kept apart. Another page showed one female Maer pushing another against a wall, hands pinning her biceps against the stone, one thigh pressing between her legs as her lips quirked a spicy sneer.

She made up her mind to buy another book by the artist, whose name was not listed, but each drawing had a vague scribble that looked like a signature beginning in S. Her bookseller would know. Tomorrow was market day, and she'd bring Kaela down, maybe buy her a book too. What the hell else did she have to spend her money on? She pushed to the side the thought that all Maer currency might soon become obsolete, worth nothing more than the bronze it was made of. If humans even used bronze.

She read some poetry for a while, checked her messages, then read some more. She made tea, contemplated the tarpipe but decided against it, checked her messages again, then stood up suddenly, hands clenched at her sides. She had to get out of this apartment, out into the air, cold and damp though it was. She stuffed her lens case and waterskin in her bag, donned her rainskin and boots, and trudged out into a fine mist floating down almost like snow, though it wasn't quite cold enough for that yet. It was going to make catching a view more complicated, but hopefully, the trees would block the mist if she could get set up under the right one. The streets were oddly quiet as she made her way along the river to the park.

Some of the trees had lost their leaves, but others had not, and she scoped leafy trees with a clear view of conifers, where her quarry would be easier to spot. This time of year, the pine-pickers were getting ready to migrate south. They were busy feeding up before the big trip, so they were easy to spot flitting from tree to tree, picking at spots of sap. She found a nice spot beneath a lowland oak whose canopy was browning but intact, right next to a cluster of featherpines. She saw movement as the birds flitted into the upper levels of the pines at her approach, but by the time she had set up her lens and dialed in the right magnification, the birds had resumed their activities, having no doubt correctly judged her not to be a threat. She watched for a while, capturing some decent views and a couple of stills of the birds feeding. She would definitely post the one of the bird with a nugget of dried golden sap in its beak and smaller specks dotting its rich brown chest feathers that so perfectly matched the color of the bark.

The mist became a drizzle, and the tree started leaking onto her lens, so she had to dry it off and pack it up. Just as she snapped the case shut, a dark shape plunged from the upper branches of the featherpine and snatched a startled pine-picker off the tree, sending shreds of bark and brown feathers flying. The wood hawk flapped back up onto its branch to tear apart and devour its prey in a matter of seconds. Mara half considered pulling her lens back out to try to get a still of the scene, but she figured bird viscera was the last thing Maer wanted in their streams right now. And besides, did a thing somehow not exist if it was not recorded and shared with others? Could things not simply be in their moment, then gone forever, their beauty only enhanced by their ephemeral nature?

She wandered back through the park, her rainskin and boots keeping her comfortable despite the chilly drizzle. She bought a flatbread and some bean dip at the River Market and had a melancholy little picnic at her desk with some clove tea, watching her rainskin on the door drip a puddle onto the floor. She knew she should get a towel to soak it up, but she couldn't bring herself to care. She devoured the bean dip, which was garlicky and spicy, though the flatbread was a bit limp due to the weather. She tossed the waxed paper into the bin, wiped her hands, downed the dregs of her tea, and put her circlet back on, hoping that maybe this would be her lucky time.

Her heart raced at the sight of the green message, which she opened almost without noticing Uffrin's logo.

Meet me at the soup stand at the Falls Pavilion at quarter dark. The spicy silver stew is to die for! Friend and I are looking forward to seeing you!

Uffrin

Mara's heart quivered, and a warmth spread throughout her chest and up to her head. It had been a very long time since she'd been this excited about anything.

13

Uffrin looked in the mirror at his hair (tousled) and the braids in his beard (uneven), then swished a cup of water and swallowed it. He stared at his comb but decided it wasn't worth it. He could never get his hair to do what he wanted, and he was awful with braids. Mara didn't seem like the kind of Maer who would mind. Maybe he would even come off as cool in a don't-care-about-appearances way. It was his only shot. He checked his messages one more time just in case Mara thought better of it and canceled, but there was nothing but a handful of yellow and orange messages, so he stuffed the circlet in his pocket, along with a few extra coins from his reserves. He wanted to pay for Mara's soup, but he didn't want to be patronizing, so he'd play it by ear.

The Falls Pavilion was busier than he expected; vendors got first crack at whatever supplies hadn't been commandeered by the military, and the market had been pretty bare, so a lot of folks weren't able to cook even if they wanted to. There was a bit of a line at the soup stall, and he hovered near the side to make sure there would be enough since they often sold out. Two pots of red broth simmered on low burners, with chunks of vegetables and fish floating amid the bubbles, setting Uffrin's mouth watering. He worried that fish might not be the best choice in case there was going to be any kissing—was there going to be kissing?

He flushed at the thought of Mara's plump lips, her tongue slipping in to brush against his, and he had to adjust his stance as he felt his loins rise. He walked around near the back of the line, checking the big water clock, which read quarter-dark exactly. He scanned the crowds for Mara's rounded figure, to no avail. He pulled out his circlet and checked it again, but the Stream was already dark. It had been going down earlier and earlier, with even some midday outages, and he tried to imagine what life would be like if it went dark forever.

Though it had been a struggle at first, he'd ended up enjoying his Stream-free time on his mission. And what the hell did he really do on the Stream, anyway? Watch views of Maer displaying their tools, aerial dynamics breakdowns, the occasional sex stream, and of course, the messages. He could definitely do without those. He put his circlet back on, forgetting the Stream was down, then slipped it back into his pocket. A warm hand landed on his arm, and he spun around to see Mara smiling at him, radiant in a flowing orange robe reminiscent of the Solstice season.

"Uffrin!" she said, her eyes dancing in the reflected light from the lamps on the ceiling.

"Mara, I'm so glad you came!"

She clasped both of his forearms and leaned her forehead in to touch his. The comforting smells of muskwood and cinnamon reached his nose as he pressed his forehead into hers, feeling the warmth of her body, her full breasts brushing against his arms. He was almost dizzy when they pulled back, and he let out an awkward giggle.

"You look good," she said, still holding onto one arm, looking him up and down. "I hope it wasn't too rough out there."

"Oh, it wasn't too bad," he said, hyper-aware of her hand on his arm. "Shall we get in line?"

Mara guided him over, never letting go, her soft hip bumping against his as they stopped behind an older couple who stood silent, holding hands.

"Did you see any action?" she asked, gripping his arm a little tighter, her eyes ablaze with excitement.

Uffrin paused, thinking of the human mage being stabbed to death by the Free Maer, the way their lifeless body slumped against the tree.

"Nothing too dangerous," was all he said.

"I know you can't talk about it, but...was it as bad as they say?"

"I didn't see much, to be honest. Certainly, no armies of humans bearing down, if that's what you're imagining. Mostly just a lot of waiting and watching."

"Sounds all too familiar." Mara released his arm to scratch her face, then placed it against the small of his back, so casually, like it was the most normal thing in the world. Uffrin's heart felt like it would hammer right out of his chest. "Surveillance here has been pretty quiet too. I think Cleo's getting bored."

"I expect boring's going to be looking pretty good before long." Uffrin shuffled forward at the pressure from Mara's hand as the line moved.

"That soup smells amazing. I haven't been here in forever!" Mara slid her hand around Uffrin's waist, leaning into him and standing on tiptoes to try to see over the couple in front of them, pressing her soft flesh into his side. Gods, was she doing this on purpose? Uffrin let his hand touch her back just for an instant, then removed it when she lowered back down.

"It's the best soup in the city, as you can tell by the line. I come here after work way too often."

"So, is your lab nearby?"

"Yes, just a few minutes' walk, in the Artificer's Compound. I told my boss you're a consultant helping me perfect my machine's flight mechanics."

"Ooh, a consultant!" She squeezed his arm and pressed into him for a moment. "Do I get a special badge?"

"No, but I'll let you wear mine if you want when we get there." He fished the gear-shaped bronze badge out of his pocket to show her, and Mara snatched it from him before he knew what was happening.

"Let's see, *Junior Mechanical Technician.*" She held the badge up to inspect it, and Uffrin pulled her arm down. "What do you have to do to be a senior technician?"

"It usually takes another five or so years, though..." He stopped the thought, pulling at the badge. Mara held onto it for a moment, smiling up at him, then let it go with a pout. "Sorry, we're not supposed to show these around. Thieves and such."

They moved to the front of the line, and Mara stepped forward and said, "Two bowls, please, and two copper ales."

The vendor nodded, slapped the counter, and said "Two soup, two copper" over their shoulder to a short, tawny Maer working the prep station. She paid before Uffrin knew what was happening. "I hope you like copper ale," she said, touching him on the arm again.

"Yes, of course. Who doesn't?" He wasn't supposed to drink before going into the workshop, but he doubted the guard would notice or care. Security had gotten pretty lax since a lot of the guards had been sent off to fight, and the replacements weren't always the best trained.

They stood at a counter since all the tables with chairs were taken. Mara raised her cup to clonk with his, then drained half of it in one long swig. Uffrin took a smaller sip and set down his cup. It was a little past its prime, but Mara didn't seem to care, and before he knew it, she was digging into her steaming soup with the wooden fork and spoon, sucking the dangling noodles into her lips with a little smacking sound.

"Gods, this is so good," she murmured as she chewed, closing her eyes for a moment. "But, like, so spicy!"

"It's not too spicy, I hope?" Uffrin took a tentative bite with his spoon, careful not to slurp or drip it into his beard. He coughed as the spice penetrated his nose and throat, and Mara giggled, covering her mouth with her hand.

"There's no such thing as too spicy for me." She took a spoonful of the broth, and the smile that bloomed on her face set Uffrin's heart fluttering. "Mmm! Uffrin, you might be right. This really is the best soup I've had in, like, ever!"

They chatted a bit about the soup, about the weather, about everything and nothing. The soup was light on noodles and vegetables, which was hardly surprising, given the shortages, but it had a decent amount of fresh silver with that silky texture he could never find anywhere else. Mara finished before he did, and he grew increasingly self-conscious as she watched him slurp up the last of his noodles and drink the remaining broth. She fetched a bowl of water and a towel from the cleaning station, and they rinsed their fingers and faces, then returned their crockery.

"Thank you for the soup," Mara said, hooking her arm into his as they exited the pavilion, though she was the one who had paid. "I feel all warm inside." Warmth spread throughout Uffrin's body as Mara pressed against him.

The streets were dark, as half of the brightstone streetlights had been stripped of their stones for the war effort, but Mara's arm in his and the pleasant patter of their conversation gave the mist-slicked cobbles a buttery glow. He couldn't possibly be living this moment, feeling her fingers slide up his wrist and trace across his palm on their way to interlocking with his. She spoke, he responded—anything at all, pure nonsense; he had no idea what he was saying. She laughed and kept touching him, and before he knew it, they had arrived at the compound gate. A slightly nervous-looking guard eyed Uffrin's badge, then gave Mara a thorough checking-out before waving them through. Uffrin didn't care for this guard at all, not in the slightest.

Inside, the compound was empty, with only a couple of lights on, none of them near his shop. He touched his badge to the lock, but it didn't click open as it should have. He tried it again at different orientations and angles, but the lock did not respond. He felt around in his pockets for the keys, which he seldom used, but thank gods he had them on him. He opened the door and tapped on the lamp over his worktable. Mara hovered close enough that he could feel her body heat, and he had to sidle out of the way to turn around without brushing into her.

She laughed and touched his arms. "Don't worry, Uffrin. I won't bite."

Uffrin's throat caught at the devilish look in her eyes, the glossy sheen of her lips. She wasn't... Was she going to kiss him? Was he supposed to kiss her?

"No, of course, why would you—" He stopped cold as she pulled herself up to kiss him, gripping both his arms and leaning her body against his. Her lips were even softer and warmer than they looked, and he gasped a little when she pulled away so quickly. Her hands trailed down his wrists to his hands and, finally, his fingers, which she held onto for a moment before letting go and turning to gaze around the shop. She turned back to him, her eyes equal parts excited and serious.

"So, where's Friend?"

14

Uffrin unlocked a drawer with a tap of his badge, the kind of magical tech Mara associated with the Shoza. He turned to her before he opened it, a lock of hair flopping down over his eyes as he spoke.

"Now, I'm absolutely not supposed to show you this, but I'm caring less and less about what I'm supposed to do these days. You know what I mean?"

"You speak my language."

He opened the drawer and retrieved what looked like a heavy-duty channeling gauntlet with a circular bronze pad affixed to the back of the palm. He slid his hand into the gauntlet, which tightened on its own.

"It's a control gauntlet?" she asked, reaching out tentatively toward it.

"Exactly. It's okay; you can touch it. It's not on."

Her fingers found the smooth bronze of the pad, and as she slid them across it, the pad dipped a little in whatever direction she pushed as if it were on tiny springs, but its movement was so smooth it almost felt organic. She made sure to lean her breast against his arm as she played with the pad, then ran her fingers along the web of copper threads running the length of the gauntlet.

"It's incredible," she breathed. "Did you design that?"

"I wish," he said, shaking his head. "I just do modifications to the machine and some pattern imprint stuff. I don't really design anything."

"Pattern imprints?" Mara had heard that automatons could be programmed with almost any behavioral patterns the creator wanted, but she had no idea what that even meant or how it was accomplished.

"Think of it as a set of yes or no decisions, layered in patterns in a sort of grid. We add in threads with triggers and scenarios and plug in what we want it to do. It's tedious, but it's really cool when it all comes together." He tapped the pad on the gauntlet three times, and a golden indicator light flashed for a moment. Mara heard a faint mechanical whine from a corner of the room, and a pair of iridescent yellow eyes met hers when she turned to face it.

"Meet Friend."

He tapped a button on the desk, and the room lit up, revealing the mechanical owl he'd had on his shoulder in the view he sent. Its body was covered in feathers just like a regular owl, though the patterns were unusual. Uffrin's fingers moved on his gauntlet's pad, and the owl's wings fluttered into action. Mara's breath caught in her throat as it rose straight up, wings beating more like a hummingbird than an owl, then flapped toward them, silent except for a faint mechanical whine. It landed on a tray on the desk and spread its wings wide, then slowly folded them down on its back. Though no one would mistake it for a real owl, it was a remarkable likeness, down to the golden color of its beak and talons and the little tufts on its head.

"Gods, Uffrin, it's incredible!" she whispered, stepping closer to the desk. The owl let out a little tinny hoot, then hopped off the tray toward her.

"Hold out your hand," he said, touching her lightly on the back. "Don't worry, it won't bite."

She held out the backs of her knuckles, and the owl hopped toward her, fixing her with eyes that must have been glass, though they moved and blinked just like a real owl's. She moved her hand closer, and the owl head-butted her gently, angling its head sideways, almost like a cat looking to be petted. She let her fingers slide along its head, feeling its silk feathers, which looked almost real even close up. The owl blinked once, then hopped over to Uffrin, headbutting his hand and making a heart-melting sound like a high-pitched purr.

"Friend," Mara murmured. The owl's head swiveled back toward her, and it let out a little trill. She gasped, turning to Uffrin, whose mouth spread into a wide grin. "Does it know its name?"

"Apparently?" His head gave a little shake, and he said, "Friend!" The owl's head swiveled back to him, and he giggled. "That's a new one."

"A new behavior?" Mara lowered her face toward the table, and Friend hopped back over to her and pecked her nose gently, not unlike what Cleo did when she wanted a treat. "Did you add a new pattern then?"

"No, I haven't made any changes," Uffrin said, leaning his face in close. Friend turned to look at Uffrin, then pecked Mara's nose again and trilled. "I think it likes you."

Mara's heart lifted as the owl headbutted her nose and trilled again. How could a machine *like* someone? She wasn't even sure if Cleo liked her, though she suspected as much.

"I like it too." She ran her fingers over its chest feathers, which were not quite as soft as a real owl's, but they moved under the pressure of her fingers in almost the same way. "Uffrin, this is incredible. I never imagined..."

Friend hopped across the table to a little pedestal set in the corner and trilled at Uffrin.

"You want to see what it can do?"

Mara moved closer to Uffrin, letting her body press lightly against his, and put a hand on his back.

"Show me," she said into his ear.

Uffrin's fingers slid across the pad on his gauntlet, and Friend fluttered into the air and flapped to the far end of the workshop, where a set of rings hung from wires suspended from the ceiling at various heights. Friend hovered in mid-air for a moment, something a real owl could not do as well, then flapped through the rings, changing direction fluidly as it rose and dove, twisted and turned, then zipped back across the workshop and landed gracefully back on the pedestal.

"I'm still working on a few things; the landing is better since I made the adjustments after watching Cleo, but I'm not quite satisfied. I think with a little more work—"

"Uffrin, it's the most amazing thing I've ever seen." She gripped him by the shoulders, and his eyes grew wide, then fluttered closed as she kissed him. His lips froze for a moment, then moved with hers as she pressed into the kiss, pulling his body close, feeling his timid restraint melting, his hand sliding up to rest softly on the back of her neck. They kissed for a little while, softly, slowly, hands roaming with a light touch, then just as her fingers found his narrow ass and gave a good squeeze, she felt a peck on her arm and heard an excited trill. They broke from the kiss, arms still wrapped around each other, and looked down to see Friend blinking up at them, headbutting each of them in turn.

"I think it's jealous," Mara said, holding out a finger for Friend to headbutt.

"It just wants in on the action, I guess, don't you, Friend?" Uffrin held out an arm, and Friend hopped up onto his gauntlet with a flutter, sending Mara back a half-step.

"I don't suppose you gave it that pattern either." Mara studied the owl, who swiveled its head toward her and clacked its beak several times.

"No, I..." Uffrin's voice was soft, his eyebrows furrowed in concentration. He glanced around the room as if looking for lurking spies. "It's been...evolving, I guess you could say, in recent weeks. Making connections on its own. I'd heard it was possible, but until recently, I'd never seen it."

"Is it something about..." Mara paused, wondering if it was okay to ask about the orbus. They were the most widely known, closely guarded secret in all Maerdom, some kind of mechanical magical hybrid technology. No one quite knew what they were, but they were said to power all the automatons, big and small. "Something about the orbus?"

Uffrin lifted his arm to stare into Friend's eyes. "That's where all the patterns are laid, so it has to be. The newest generation orbus has an elementary autodidactic function, but even I don't know how it works. All I know is that Friend has been acting less like a machine and more like...I don't even know what."

Friend headbutted his nose and made that little purring sound, and Mara's heart purred along with it.

"I wonder what it would do if it met a real owl?" she mused out loud. "Would it even know what an owl was?"

"I did input a variety of owl-specific patterns to help it avoid conflict in case it came across a real one. Submissiveness, making itself smaller, retreating, things like that."

Mara's mind spun with the possibilities. Would Uffrin be able to get permission to bring Friend to the aerie? Probably not, given the secrecy surrounding everything related to the automatons. Maybe she could get Cleo to fly here one night when she wasn't working. She would love to see them interact, but she wasn't sure Cleo wouldn't rip Friend wing from wing.

"I'm going to put Friend away now, so we don't use up the power source in its orbus. I'm due to have it replaced, but things have been pretty tight of late, so I'd better play it safe. Say goodnight to Mara." He held out his arm and pointed at her.

Friend leaned in with his head, and she gave it a little scritch, the silk feathers soft under her fingertips.

"Good night, Friend."

Friend trilled softly in response, then flitted over to his perch and shut down with a low mechanical whine. Uffrin removed the gauntlet and put it back in the drawer, then looked up with an awkward smile.

"So, can I walk you home?"

"Maybe in a bit," she said, stepping closer to him, letting her hands touch his, then slide up his arms and onto his chest. She bunched his robe in her hands and pulled him in, kissing him gently until his lips started moving with hers. She gave him several more little kisses until the tiniest groan sounded from Uffrin's throat, then she pressed into the kiss, licking and biting softly. She let go of his robe and kneaded his chest with her fingers, leaning into him and pushing him against the desk. His hands moved up and down her back, over her shoulders, and finally down to her backside, cupping her cheeks with infuriating gentleness. She moved her hands around to grasp the back of his head as she pressed into him, feeling his stiffness beneath his robe, smiling into their kiss at the little whines he made. Part of her wanted to rip off his robes, mount him, and ride him on the desk until he cried for mercy, but his kisses were so tender, his hands so timid, that she wanted to bottle this moment and live in it forever.

Another trill sounded from the corner, and Mara pulled back from the kiss, turning to look over at Friend, whose yellow eyes were wide and un-blinking, staring right at them. She gripped Uffrin's robe again and pulled him back up to standing, kissed him one more time, then straightened his robe and patted his chest. They were both breathing heavily, and Uffrin was standing in that awkward way Maer did when they're trying to hide an erection.

"I suppose you could walk me halfway home," she said, sliding her fingers into his.

Uffrin looked at her with eyes so wide and full of joy, she almost rethought her decision not to lay him out on the table and have her way with him.

"It would be my pleasure," he said, raising her hand to his and kissing it.

15

The new orbuses were delayed, so Uffrin didn't have much to do in the shop apart from routine maintenance on Friend, who had weathered his travels without a hitch. Uffrin had been confirmed for two weeks off, minus the day and a half he'd already been home and would be on-call at the end of that time. From what he gathered, on-call almost certainly meant being sent back out the moment his leave was up. That gave him twelve days to see what this thing with Mara was. He didn't want to waste even one of those days, but he didn't want to come on too strong either. When he stepped out the gate and put his circlet back on, he had a green message, a view from Mara. He walked across the street and leaned against the wall of a warehouse to watch.

Mara was walking in the park, using a hand-held lens, so the view was a little shaky. She smiled at the lens, then closed her eyes and blew a kiss.

"Hi, Uffrin! I had such a great time last night! The soup was amazing, and Friend is incredible, and you..."

The view cut off, and when it restarted, she was sitting on a rock with the Middle Falls behind her. He knew exactly where in the park she was; it was a beautiful spot.

"Sorry, I can't walk and talk." She looked to her left and her right, then leaned in close to the lens so her face took up nearly the whole view. "Like I was saying, it was great to see you last night. I really like the soup, and Friend, and you." She paused, glancing to the side, a stray bit of hair blowing over her face. She tucked the hair behind her ear as she turned back to the lens. "I really like you, Uffrin. And I want to see you again. As soon as possible." She licked her lips, glancing away again for a moment, then back. "I work tonight and tomorrow night, but I'd be free during the day if you want to. I mean, if you're free. I like walking in the park. It's nice here." She moved her head and held up the lens to show the falls in the background, then moved her face back into the view. "Maybe you could come walk with me?" She pressed her fingers to her lips, then touched the lens, and the view went black.

Uffrin's head fell back and hit the wall of the warehouse, which hurt, but he didn't care. This was happening. It was really happening. He'd never been so instantly drawn to anyone, and to have her like him back just as fast? It felt like a mushroom dream. He wondered where she was now, if she was still in the park. The view had been sent about an hour ago, so most likely, she wasn't still there, and even if she was, he was due at his parents' house by half-dark. He pulled out his pocket lens, then thought better of it as he saw the guard tower on the compound. Using a lens within sight of the place was strictly forbidden, and that was not a risk worth taking. He moved around the corner, set up against a plain wood-shingled wall, and recorded a quick view.

"Hey, Mara, I had such an awesome time too! I'm wide open tomorrow, so maybe we could meet up for lunch or something and then a stroll in the park? I could do morning if that's better, or later, I just—" He paused the view, trying to think of what to say, how to not look like a dork, but his head was swimming. It was just a stupid view, after all. It didn't have to be perfect. He tapped the lens and stared into it. "I just want to say that I like you too, and I really want to see you again." He thought about blowing a kiss or doing the finger-lens kiss thing as she'd done, but in the end, he just did a little wave and smiled awkwardly, then tapped the lens off.

He sucked at views, and she was sure to think it was stupid, that he was stupid, and she would no doubt reconsider the temporary insanity of her attraction to him and not respond to this or any of his other messages henceforth. He sent the view anyway, then walked briskly in the direction of the park to blow off some steam.

The rains of the previous days had passed, leaving a clear, blustery day in their place. It took him until Skundir's Bridge to warm up enough that he could take his hands out of his pockets. He reached Middle Falls before long and stared at the rock where Mara had taken the view. Of course, she was nowhere in sight. Not that he'd been expecting her to just be hanging around almost two hours later, but he'd felt compelled to come here, to see the spot, as if somehow that would confirm that it had been real, that she had truly said she liked him and wanted to see him again. He checked his messages, but she had not responded. She was probably napping, he guessed, if she was going to be on duty all night. It had taken him some time to adjust to the unusual sleep schedule out on his mission, and he imagined it must be tricky to have two nights on and one night off.

He pictured her asleep on her bed in some small room in a hightop just like his, with a wool blanket covering her curvy form, her face holding that knowing smile even in sleep. He imagined what it would be like to wake up next to her, to snuggle into her warmth, feel her breath on his cheek, hear her little purrs of contentment as she wiggled her body in closer to interlock with his.

Gods, he thought, I've got it bad.

Paodo answered the door, standing tall and smiling as always, though his eyes betrayed a weariness beyond what lack of sleep brought. They pressed foreheads together, then Paodo clapped him on the back and ushered him in.

"You're early! Maofin and Maoti are just finishing up, I expect. They should be down in a moment." Uffrin rolled his eyes; it never stopped being awkward knowing his mothers were upstairs having sex while he was downstairs talking to his father. "Care for a dram of hotstone?"

"I'm going to need it." Uffrin sighed, shrugging out of Paodo's arm, which he'd draped all over Uffrin like when he was a kid. He slunk over to the couch and laid himself out. It was still big enough to sleep with arms outstretched, and he'd used it on more than one occasion when visiting.

"You seem to have come through the mission unscathed," Paodo called over his shoulder as he poured their drinks.

"I was never in any danger. And Erliss was the best scout. They made me feel safe."

Paodo laid the tray on the ottoman, picked up his drink, and clinked with Uffrin. The hotstone was smoky and full-bodied but soft on the back end, masking its potency with a touch of sweetness. His parents always had the good stuff. Paodo winced and pushed out a sharp breath as he set his glass down and leaned back in the armchair. His smile was genuine but also inscrutable, his mask against the darkness of the world, and it had the weight of an entire personality in and of itself. His eyes were the real tell, though. Dark, always dark, like he was looking too hard, seeing through things, into things that weren't meant to be seen. But always with that smile, no matter the circumstance.

"Hope it wasn't too grisly out there." Paodo stared out the window into the garden. "War is a horrid, evil thing, and you know I don't use that word lightly. It is the ruin of civilization, the death of what makes us truly

Maer." He looked down into his cup, picked it up, and drained it. "But," he said, wagging a finger in the air, "I retain hope that a peace treaty can be achieved, one that will allow both sides to avoid considerable losses and make reasonable concessions."

"Ever the optimist, Ludo." Maofin leaned in and kissed his cheek, then her eyes turned to Uffrin.

"Uffrin, it is so good to see you." She rushed over and took him by the shoulders, then pressed her forehead into his for a few seconds before wrapping him in a firm hug. He marveled at her strength, given her age; he supposed it must be one of the benefits of Maoti's practice, though he'd never seen the appeal. "And I must say you're looking well—fit, or fit enough, and a little harder around the eyes, which, honestly, I've always thought you could do with a bit more gravitas. It suits you. But then there's this thing all around you." She gestured around his head, and he felt his neck and ears flush as he realized what she was sensing. She walked in a slow circle around him, staring with that oddly distant look she got.

"Maofin, you can just ask instead of invading my private aura or whatever."

Maofin sighed, brushing his arm up and down. "You're right, dear, and I'm sorry. It's just that..." She paused, breathing through her nose, and her face brightened. "Is there anything good going on in your life, Uffrin?"

He suddenly wished she'd just read his aura, as it would have been considerably less awkward than whatever he was going to say next.

"It's nothing, really. I just..." He put his hand on Maofin's arm, rubbing her soft hair like he used to do when he was little. He looked her in the eyes and took a deep breath. "I met someone. She's...amazing, and I...I guess I'm really excited about it, but I don't even really know if it's a thing, so..." He looked down at his hands, and Maofin lifted his chin gently, raising his eyes back to hers.

"I like her already."

"Like whom?" Maoti's deep voice echoed across the room as she entered, clad in an embroidered green silk robe with a pink sash tying it together at the waist.

"Uffrin has a—" Maofin began.

"Let him tell it," Paodo interrupted.

"Tell me what?" Maoti took Uffrin's hands and leaned in with her forehead. When they touched, he felt the expected spark of warmth, exactly as she would give him before bed when he was a kid. His heart shivered with childlike joy at the sensation.

"I've just started seeing someone," he said before she could suss it out of him. He could never hide anything from Maoti. No one could.

"That's lovely, dear. How did you meet?"

"Through work."

"Another artificer? I thought you'd sworn off dating them."

"No, she's...an owl handler, actually. Her name is Mara."

Maoti's head flung back as she let out a single cackle. "About yea high, sharp eyes, curves for days?"

"Maoti!" Uffrin shook out of her touch. "Have you been stalking me?"

She raised her hands in self-defense, her eyes dancing with merriment. "Uffrin, I swear on all the hotstone in the world, it's nothing more than the most delicious coincidence. She came to one of my sessions in the park, and we got to talking afterward."

Uffrin's head felt ready to explode. "You talked to Mara?"

"Yes, I just said it. She's an absolute catch, by the way. She's got talent, that one, and she's cute as a button and nice to boot. Have you slept together?"

Uffrin smacked his forehead and closed his eyes in disbelief.

"Cloti, come on," Paodo said, tugging on her robe and pulling her to sit in his lap, where she settled with a sigh. "Not everyone wants to put out a news bulletin about the details of their private lives."

"It's fine, Paodo," Uffrin said, forcing a laugh, which he almost felt. "It's not like she's never grilled me about someone I'm seeing before."

"I wasn't grilling. Just asking, but I'm sorry for being too nosy. Have you had dinner with her, at least?"

"Yes. Last night, in fact." Uffrin suddenly smiled as he recalled Mara lifting her bowl to her lips to drain the last of the broth, her eyes locked on his over the rim of the bowl. "We went to the soup stand at the Falls Pavilion."

"Oh gods, did they have the spicy silver stew?" Maofin interjected, sitting down on the couch next to Uffrin. "That's to die for."

"You make a pretty good replica yourself," Paodo said, stretching out his toe to touch hers.

"They did, actually," Uffrin said. "It was so good! A little light on the veggies, if I'm being honest. Not surprising, given the shortages."

"Fresh vegetables are worth their weight in copper these days. If the humans don't kill us, the constipation will."

Between the three of them, they plied him with hotstone and needled him with questions until he spilled it all, though he was vague on the details of the kissing part. Paodo disappeared to check on dinner, and Maoti gave Maofin a surreptitious look. They both leaned in closer, their faces growing serious.

"Your father is under a tremendous amount of stress right now, though he tries his best not to show it." Maoti shook her head, and Maofin put a hand on her shoulder. "I think things are going worse than he lets on."

"There weren't many humans near the front, though. I only saw one, and he was killed."

Maoti closed her eyes, remaining still for a long moment, no doubt saying a little prayer for the human. She did that if she saw a rat get run over by a chariot or a dead roach on the sidewalk, not to mention every time they ate any kind of meat.

"Your father is an excellent interpreter," Maofin said, leaning into Uffrin's shoulder. "I'm sure he'll help the Chief Ambassador find the right words to stop the worst from happening."

"I don't know," Maoti said, her eyes going spacey, as they often did. "Some decisions cannot be undone. The world changes, and we either change with it, or it swallows us."

"Gods, Cloti, enough with the gloom and doom." Maofin kicked her foot playfully. "I want to hear how you met Uffrin's girlfriend."

"Like I said, she came to one of the sessions in the park, and we talked after."

"And you didn't have any inkling about her? Why she'd come?"

Maoti smiled behind her glass of hotstone. "I might have gotten a vibe from her, and sure, maybe I put two and two together. But I didn't want to say anything because I respect boundaries." Uffrin sighed audibly, and she shouldered him gently. "I try, anyway. Sometimes. But they just keep getting in my way. Honestly, why do we even bother having them?"

"Maoti, I've stopped trying with you. But since you've already had access to my girlfriend's innermost thoughts and feelings, tell me what you really think."

Maoti pulled back a little and gave Uffrin a deep, searching look. "I think she's got strength and curiosity in equal measure, and I'm pretty sure she's crazy about you."

Uffrin bit his lip to stop his smile, but it did little good. "I mean, if she stalked my stream to figure out who my mother was, then stalked you at a meditation session in the park, I guess she's not disinterested."

"And I expect you were 'not disinterested' yourself? She really is quite the hottie."

"Ooh, now I want to meet her too." Maofin tented her fingers, teasing Uffrin with her eyes.

By the time Paodo summoned them for dinner, a dishtowel slung over his shoulder and a slightly drunken smile on his face, Uffrin had gone through several cycles of embarrassment, annoyance, and acceptance. He'd known when he came over for dinner that there was no hiding anything from his mothers. As the hotstone gave way to ice wine and the fish and beans were laid out on a platter in the center of the table, he cared less and less. He let himself be swept up in the comfortable family banter until the last bit of sauce from the platter had been wiped clean with spongy flatbreads and chased down with even more wine. He wondered how much alcohol they'd squirreled away against the growing shortages.

When at last Paodo cleared the dishes and returned with his favorite mushroom brandy, Uffrin was drunk and happy and ready to crash on the couch.

Paodo raised his glass and held it out over the table to clink with theirs. "Here's to loves, old and new."

They all sipped the slightly bitter, earthy liqueur, and Uffrin sank back in his chair, feeling a bit maudlin in his drunken state.

"I really miss you guys, despite your absolute lack of boundaries." He raised his glass to Maoti, then the others, and took another sip.

"Our couch has no boundaries either if you feel like crashing for the night." Maoti winked at him, and he smiled at her, at Maofin, and at Paodo.

"It'll be just like old times."

When he awoke, his head was full of lead and splintered glass. He shuffled to the bathroom, then into the kitchen, where Maoti was sitting with a cup of steaming tea, staring into a candle on the table. It took her a few seconds to notice his entrance, and as her eyes drifted slowly from the candle to his, a faint smile grew on her face.

"I made you some tea." She stood up and drifted to the stove, then poured him a steaming cup.

Uffrin cradled the mug under his nose, savoring the pure darkroot, which he hadn't been able to get since his return. He stirred in some honey and milk and sat down at the table across from Maoti, who suddenly looked older than she had the night before and more tired, but her smile still warmed his heart.

"I hope I didn't tease you too harshly last night," she said, blowing on her tea and glancing up at him over the rim of the cup.

"It's fine, Maoti. It wouldn't be home without a little ribbing."

"I miss that, you know? Aefin is impossible to tease, and I hardly see Ludo these days since he's always working, even when he's at home. Do you know, he's up in his office right now translating part of that damned treaty? This is supposed to be his day off. I have half a mind to go up there and—" she stopped herself, smiling coyly. "He needs a distraction. Maybe you can get him to take you fishing or something."

Uffrin almost spit out his tea. "Paodo is the worst fisherman in the whole city. Besides, I expect the silvers have all been fished out, with the shortages at the market and all."

"Well, maybe you can catch some whiskers. We could make whisker-cakes."

"I'm hoping to meet Mara today. I need to check my messages—"

"Later," Maoti said. She hated when he got his circlet out around her. He'd have to check when he went to the bathroom. "Tell me about your mission. Not the classified stuff, obviously, but...you said you had a good scout?"

Uffrin told her all about Erliss, about the weird things they'd eaten, the caves they'd hidden out in. Her ears perked up when he mentioned having seen Erliss doing hand moods.

"Really? I've never heard of a Shoza practicing before." She stroked her beard, staring thoughtfully into her tea. "They could get in trouble for that."

"I guess that's why they hid it. Is it really so bad now? I thought things had quieted down a bit."

Maoti sighed, turning her mug in a circle on the table. "I've quieted down a bit at Paodo's request. It's too late for my words to make any difference anyway. They pushed ahead with the war despite the protests, and they're going to push ahead with their treaty, too, for all the good it's going to do. But the Shoza still follow me whenever I leave the house, and they're always lurking near my sessions in the park. I wouldn't put it past them to have a plant among the practitioners."

Uffrin's heart lurched at the thought. Did the Shoza really see Maoti as so dangerous she needed to be watched at all times? It seemed her past statements that humans and Maer were the same people had not been forgotten.

"Don't worry, I'm not in any danger," she said, and Uffrin scowled at the intrusion. "It's written all over your face, dear, and I understand your concern. I'm no fan of it either; makes it damned hard to find my center, knowing they're watching my every move and listening in on everything I say. I even cornered Doctor Nuidi at a party a few weeks ago and asked her point-blank. She said it was for my protection, that they feared a threat to my person, which is ridiculous, of course."

"Maoti, please do be careful." Uffrin slid his fingers across the table and locked them with hers. "I've only got two mothers, and you're one of my favorites."

"You know as well as I do that being careful isn't in my nature. The Shoza aren't going to do anything to me, not with my connections. They just want to keep tabs on me. And who knows? Maybe this Erliss is one of the ones they sent to spy on me. Maybe I converted them."

A door creaked open upstairs, and Maoti leaned in close, her face growing serious.

"Paodo will be down in a moment, but there's something I need to tell you."

"What is it, Maoti?" Uffrin asked, the hairs on his neck bristling at her urgent tone.

"You remember Eagle Lake, where we used to go camping years ago?"

"Sure, at the bottom of that interminable path with all the roots that kept tripping me."

"Do you know how to get there?"

Paodo's footsteps sounded on the stairs, and Uffrin searched his mind, then nodded. It was a week's journey, a little east of Gulham.

"Yes, but why—"

"If things should go the way we hope they do not, that's where I want you to go. We would meet you there."

"Maoti, what are you talking about? What do you think is going to—"

"Good morning, sunshine!" Paodo's voice boomed from behind him, reminding Uffrin of his lingering headache, which the darkroot tea had not entirely erased. Paodo touched Uffrin's shoulders and kissed the top of his head, then leaned down and kissed Maoti on the lips. "I hope your hangover is on the wane. Mine took a good few cups of tea to cure, and it wasn't much help with my translations."

"I'm feeling okay," Uffrin said, his stomach suddenly growling. Maoti stood up and moved to the counter, where a bowl was laid out, covered with a towel.

"I've got the dough all ready for the spiced nutbread if you're hungry?"

Uffrin's fingers found his circlet in his pocket, and he calculated how long it would take to make the nutbread. Mara would probably be asleep if she'd been on night duty, so there was really no pressing need to check his messages, but it niggled at him.

"Sounds amazing, Maoti. Let me just go get cleaned up while it bakes."

"Go ahead and check your messages. I know how it is to be young and in love."

"Except we didn't have the Stream back then," Paodo said, sliding his hands over Maoti's shoulders. She leaned her head back to look up at him, and he bent down to kiss her, rather more fervently than Uffrin needed to see.

"Towels are under the sink," Maoti called as he breezed out of the room and slipped his circlet onto his head.

His steps slowed as he saw the green message from Mara. It was a view, and he stopped in the hallway to watch it. She was standing on one of the landings of the stairs leading up to the Aerie, with the mist-shrouded falls behind her. She looked tired, but her eyes were happy, and Uffrin's heart pattered when she spoke.

"Hi, Uffie. I got your message. I'm going to go home and crash, but I'd love to meet you for a late lunch, maybe around half-noon? I'll ping you when I get up. There's this place that has these smoked boar sausages that are to die for and a bunch of little dips and stuff. I was thinking, I know it's kind of cold, but we could bundle up and have a little picnic in the park. Talk to you soon."

She pressed her fingers to her lips and pressed them into the lens, which then went dark.

"You heard back from Mara?" Maofin stood watching him from down the hallway, a sly smile on her face.

"Sorry," Uffrin said, slipping the circlet back into his pocket.

"No need to be sorry. Cloti hates the circlets, not me. Who do you think posts all her views for her?"

"Of course, I know, it's just..." He shook his head, unable to contain the smile growing on his face. "Maofin, I really like her, and I think I'm only going to be in town for a couple of weeks before I get sent back out."

"Well, then, I guess you better get moving if she's as hot as Cloti says."

Uffrin pushed down his annoyance and cracked a smile. "I'm going to go wash up. I'll catch you in a few. Maoti's making spiced nutbread."

She stopped to press foreheads with him briefly, then sauntered down the hallway toward the kitchen.

16

Mara napped fitfully, tormented by visions of an army of crouching humans slinking through the foggy valley toward the dam. She knew it was unlikely they'd be able to come through that way without advance warning, but she couldn't shake their sinister shape, the predatory way they moved, how their wicked steel blades glistened in the shadows. She tapped the tin to get the last few shreds of darkroot tea into the strainer and added some powdered cloves, which she was running low on, as the darkroot shortage had created a cascade effect on other teas as well. She slipped on her circlet and smiled when she saw the green message with Uffrin's logo. She had been meaning to make one for herself but had never gotten around to it. It was a simple text:

A picnic in the park with you sounds like my idea of heaven. I will await your message with my coat and boots on.

By the way, my mother says hi.

--Uffrin

Even the weak tea could not suppress Mara's smile or the fuzzy warmth that spread throughout her chest. She hoped Uffrin wasn't too mad about her not telling him about meeting Cloti. She'd totally meant to, had planned out how she would bring it up without looking like a stalker, but the soup had been so good, and Uffrin had been so excited to show her Friend, and then they had started kissing...She closed her eyes and relived the kiss, the timid way he'd touched her, the little groans he'd made as she teased him. He was going to take some prodding, and they had less than two weeks before he was sent off again. She might be sent on mission too, for all she knew, given how things were going. She wanted to take her time with him, to bask in the delicious early moments of this relationship, but time was not on their side. She wouldn't sleep with him today, she didn't think, but she couldn't just luxuriate in flirtation and courtship for months on end either. Uffrin was going to need a little push, and she knew just the thing.

Mara picked up lunch on the way to the park and found Uffrin waiting by the Middle Falls, sitting on the rock where she'd sent her view the other day, his shoulders jutting up around his ears against the cold. He leapt off the rock when he saw her, then stood awkwardly playing with his hands and smiling as she approached. His smile quavered as she set down the basket, gripped his coat, and kissed him, lingering just long enough for a little heat to grow, then pulled back, biting her lip.

Uffrin's eyes were wide, his smile incredulous, which only made Mara bite her lip even harder to avoid laughing or leaning in for another kiss.

"I brought lunch. Are you hungry?"

"Starving. And I swiped a bottle of wine from my parents." He pulled out a bottle from his bag. It looked like the good stuff, though Mara didn't have much experience with wine. "I believe you know my mother, Cloti?" His tone was light on the surface but a little crusty underneath.

"Uffrin, I was going to tell you—"

"Tell me that you stalked my stream, then stalked my mother, then didn't say a word about it?"

Mara cast her eyes down, pulling at a button on Uffrin's coat. She could tell he was a little mad, but there was a softness in his voice as well. He touched her arm, and she looked up.

"I should have told you." She picked up his hand and clasped it in hers. "It's just that...we were having such a nice time with the soup and then Friend, who is so amazing, by the way—I can't stop thinking about him!" She worried his fingers in hers, then looked up again. "And then we were kissing, and it was such a perfect evening. I didn't want to ruin it by bringing your mother into it."

Uffrin's face was still for a moment, then the hint of a smile crept over it.

"Since you brought lunch, I forgive you." He squeezed her hands, then raised them to his lips and laid a gentle kiss on them. Mara sighed in relief, giggling a little. She wanted to kiss him again, see that bewildered look in his eyes, but she didn't want to press her luck.

"Speaking of lunch, why don't you open that bottle while I get things ready. Have you tried the smoked boar sausage from the Fisher's Market? There's a butcher there who works miracles, and because most folks don't think of the Fisher's Market as a place to get meat, she actually still had some left!"

"That sounds so amazing!" Uffrin pried the cork off and produced two crystal goblets with copper-lined rims from his bag, where they had been wrapped in a silk scarf. "Swiped these from my parents as well, though I'll be returning them."

"Look at you, bringing a little class to our picnic." Mara straightened the tablecloth she'd set on the rock and laid out the sausage, flatbreads, and the tin of dip, as well as the wooden plates and her knife. She'd never realized Uffrin was rich—or his parents were anyway.

"I wouldn't have bothered, but if we're going to be drinking twenty-year-old wine, we should do it right." He poured them each a glass, and he raised his and said, "To Cleo and Friend."

They clinked and drank the wine, which was rich and smooth but with more bite than she expected. Mara picked up her knife and began slicing the sausage onto their plates. Uffrin tore off a piece of flatbread and tucked into the dip without waiting for her to finish.

"Mmm, so good!" He closed his eyes for a moment, his face contorted in delight. "Are these field beans?"

"Yes, with plenty of garlic and huppa seeds." She pushed a piece of sausage from her knife into her mouth. "Gods, you've got to try this sausage. It's to die for."

They ate and drank and made the smallest of talk, and Mara's heart warmed with Uffrin's every word, every gesture. He babbled with such pure foodie joy about the flatbread, how he loved the thicker style, and about the spices in the sausage. Even the way he chewed was cute, like he was searching some vast culinary archive to analyze every ingredient and technique. When they had finished, he poured them another glass of wine, and they clinked without words and drank, staring out at the falls. Mara shivered at the cold rock under her behind, and she moved the remains of their picnic out of the way and scooched closer to Uffrin, locking her arm in his and pressing against his side.

"So, what did you think of my mother? I have two, by the way, but Aefin's not famous."

"Honestly? She's amazing. I've kind of been dabbling with her practice, watching some views and stuff, so when I saw her on your stream—"

"When you stream-stalked me, you mean."

Mara squeezed his arm and scooched even closer so their legs were pressed against each other. "Yes. When I stalked you, I saw an old picture of your family and recognized her right away. I couldn't believe it!"

"Sometimes I can't believe it either. She's just Maoti to me."

"She's more than just famous, Uffrin. She's important. Like, her views are some of the most watched on the Stream. Have you ever practiced with her?"

"A little, when I was younger, but not since. Too close to home, I guess. Plus, my mind's always going in a thousand directions at once. I could never block out all the noise."

"Chicken and egg, maybe, but I get it. I'm not the best at it either, but with all that's going on, it helps me avoid drowning in the dark stuff." She almost asked him if he'd consider trying it with her sometime, but she decided not to press just yet.

"What about your family?" he asked.

Mara sighed, slipping her fingers between his. "My mom left when I was just a kid. Never knew where she went. My father lives in Gulham. I haven't talked to him since the Stream got restricted, but even before, we didn't correspond much. It's just me and my sister Kaela, who lives in a group house here." Uffrin squeezed her fingers, and she didn't want it to be weird, but it always was. "She's mentally disabled. Doesn't speak, though she understands most of what's said around her. At least I think she does. It's hard to tell sometimes. I see her on market day mostly; we go down and get a bite, sometimes browse the bookstalls."

"Is she a big reader?"

"She likes books, and she has the weirdest taste. The last two I bought her were an old fishing manual and a really technical book about farming. Not sure why she wanted those, but when she gets her mind set on something, there's no stopping her. And hey, who am I to judge what anyone reads?

I mostly read ancient poetry." She smiled, thinking of the book hidden in the bottom of her picnic basket, wrapped in an old tea sack.

"She sounds cool. You think I could join you this market day? I'd like to meet her. Since you've already met my mother, it only seems right."

Mara pressed closer against him. "I'm sure she'd like that. I may have told her a thing or two about you."

"What did you tell her?" Uffrin shifted to face her but kept his fingers locked in hers. His eyes were so soft, his half-smile so disarming she had no choice but to lean over and kiss him. His lips froze for a moment as if in surprise, but she pressed her case, and his mouth softened, inviting her in. She slipped him a little tongue, then kissed him once more and let her forehead fall against his.

"I told her how sweet you were, how you were cute and smart, how you built amazing machines. How much I like you." She rubbed noses with him, then angled sideways for another kiss. He opened up to her, caressing her tongue with his as she explored him. Her desire rose, and she slipped her fingers from between his and ran them up and down his thigh as they kissed. Her fingertips found his protruding erection, and she teased him with the lightest touch. He made that little sound again, that whiny moan in his throat, and she rubbed him with a little more pressure.

His fingers ran up her arm to knead her shoulder, and his kisses stuttered as she plied him, circling and squeezing, working his mouth with her tongue until his breath came in short huffs. She removed her hand and moved it up to cup his cheek, lightening her kisses until, at last, she stopped, letting their noses touch again as her own breath settled.

"I like you too," Uffrin said, followed by a shaky laugh. "I don't want to come off as a dork or anything, but I haven't liked anyone this much in a long time." His hands found hers, caressing her palms with the tender pads of his fingers, and her longing pulsed anew. She'd promised herself she'd wait another day. She was on duty again tonight, but the part of her that wanted to pin Uffrin to her bed and make him cry out in desperation was sending shockwaves through her body.

She pressed a hand to his chest and leaned in slowly, watching his eyes flit from her eyes to her lips, then close as she kissed him, softly this time, keeping her tongue at bay. She let her hand rise up and clasp the back of his neck, and his hands found her shoulders, then traced down across her breasts, moving in slow circles. She couldn't feel much beneath her coat, but it was about time he made a move, small though it was. His tongue brushed against her lips, and she let him in just a little as he kneaded her breasts gently, then slid his hands down along her waist to rest on her hips. If she hadn't been wearing a coat, he probably would have kept going, and she might not have stopped him, but she slowed down her kisses. He took the hint and found her hand, which was resting on his knee.

"Fuck, Uffrin, I wish I didn't have to work tonight." She kissed him again, giving it some heat, then pulled back. Uffrin's eyes were deep, almost hurt-looking, which only made her want to kiss him more, but she needed to be strong for now. If she didn't get a couple of hours more sleep before her shift, she would be useless.

"I understand," he said, squeezing her hands. "There's always tomorrow, right?"

"Yes. Yes! I want you to come to my apartment tomorrow night." She released his hands and moved her fingers halfway up his thighs. "Only if you want to."

Uffrin bit his lip, nodding, his eyes bright and wet, almost as if he was going to cry.

"Can I just say that I've never wanted anything more?"

"You can." She kissed him one more time, as lightly as she possibly could, humming in her throat at the flood of pleasure rushing through her body.

"I hate to say it, but I need to start heading back." She reached for the picnic basket, opened it, and pulled out the cloth-wrapped book. "But first, I brought you a little something from the bookstalls at the River Market."

Uffrin's eyes lit up in delighted surprise, and his smile grew as she handed it over. "For me?"

She nodded, and he turned it over in his hands, still wrapped. He toyed with the string but did not untie it. "This might seem funny, but do you mind if I wait until I get home to unwrap it? I haven't gotten a present in quite a while, and it will give me something to look forward to once you're gone."

Mara covered her smile with her hands, and Uffrin's face grew curious. "What?"

"Nothing. I hope it's a nice surprise."

"There's nothing better than curling up with a mystery book and a mug of tea on a cold, windy night. Damn, I wish I weren't all out of darkroot. I should have stolen some from my parents."

"Ugh, isn't that the worst? I'm even almost out of clove powder."

"Me too! Next thing, you know we'll be drinking mint tea day and night."

"Well, I hope you enjoy your surprise reading. I don't know if you'll like it—"

"Mara, if it's from you, I'm sure I'll love it."

She grinned wickedly. "I have no doubt. It's a favorite of mine, which I've read many times. I want you to do something for me."

"Literally anything."

"I want you to read it, think of me, and guess what my favorite part is."

"I will stay up until dawn to finish if need be."

Mara pictured Uffrin's face when he unwrapped the cloth and opened the cover, the confusion, the shock, the growing delight, and heat rose within her again. She ran her fingers through his beard, gripping it near the base, and pulled him in for a slow, deep kiss. His eyes stayed closed, his lips slightly parted, as she pulled away and slid off the rock to stand, her legs wobbly from sitting for so long on the cold, hard rock.

He carried the basket as they walked in silence, hands tightly wound together, through the largely empty park, then found their way through the streets to her hightop. He looked up at the building, which rose seven stories high, then back down at Mara.

"Fifth floor. Ring this bell here at, say, half dark?" She pointed to her button, marked 5-7, and Uffrin nodded, setting down the basket and wrapping his arms around her. He kissed her first this time, with more heat than before, and his hands found their way under the back of her coat and gripped her behind, pulling her to him, loosening the strings of her desire. All she had to do was open the door and invite him up, but after they had kissed for a minute, she pushed against his chest, forcing a bit of space in between them. She took a deep breath to steady herself, stooped to pick up the basket, and gripped his fingers in hers, then let them slip as she backed toward the door.

"Tomorrow night, then," he said, his hand hanging in the air where she'd released it.

"Tomorrow night."

17

Uffrin hit the tarpipe a couple of times while waiting for the water to boil for his tea, staring down at the cloth-wrapped book on his table. Something in the way Mara had reacted when he'd told her he was going to wait to open it had his curiosity fired up, and he needed a distraction. He was going to have to wait an entire day before seeing her again, and he was pretty sure they were going to sleep together tomorrow night. He thought of her soft lips and softer curves, the swell of her breasts beneath her coat, the supple heft of her behind. He knew he needed to rub one out before the night was over if he was going to have any chance of lasting when they finally got together tomorrow, but he didn't want to rush it. He didn't want to rush anything when it came to Mara, just as she didn't rush her kisses, keeping him on the edge at all times. Gods, was this really happening?

When his tea was steeped, he sat down at his desk, clicked on the lamp, and untied the string. The cloth was from a tea sack, the burlap rough and worn from many re-uses. A whiff of muskwood and cinnamon hit him as he unfolded the cloth, the scent she wore, and he wondered if she'd dabbed it on the cloth or if it just emanated from everything she touched. He slid the cloth out from under the book, which was old and worn, with a cover that must have once been black but was now a mottled gray. He flipped it over, picking up the tarpipe and raising it to his lips. He set the pipe down without hitting it when he saw the words on the cover in faded copper lettering:

Fantasies from the Time Before

Mara had said she was into ancient poetry, but this didn't look like any poetry book he'd ever seen. The must of old paper rose up as he opened the cover and saw an illustration of one Maer straddling another, her back arched and her hands gripping his thighs, pert breasts jutting toward the sky. Her partner held her round hips, his eyes greedily studying her svelte body. Uffrin's pants suddenly grew tight, and his mouth went dry. He took a sip of his tea, still staring at the drawing, and almost spit it out, it was so hot. He set the cup far away from the book and turned the page, one hand falling into his lap to press against his growing hardness.

The next illustration showed two Maer standing facing each other, their unrealistically large erections touching at the head. They leaned in to hold each other by the shoulders, lips just touching, eyes closed. The expressions on their faces were almost chaste in their sweetness. Uffrin studied the muscled dimples of their buttocks, the way their hands gripped each other's shoulders with strength and delicacy, and he loosened the strings of his pants and slid his hand inside, holding himself firm without moving.

He continued flipping the pages, and each drawing was more exquisite than the last, with Maer of all shapes, sizes, and genders engaged in an inventive variety of poses that spoke of the passion and genius of the artist. He loosened his grip when he felt himself growing close, then tightened it a bit each time he found a new illustration that was especially exciting. He laughed at an image of three female Maer hanging from a giant's phallus, legs wrapped around it like acrobats at the circus. He stopped at each picture, wondering which one was Mara's favorite, what her fantasy was, whether they could re-enact it together. His breath caught as he turned the page about halfway through the book. He knew without a doubt that this had to be the one.

The illustration showed a rather thin Maer with his hands tied behind his head, staring with longing and delight up at an exceptionally curvy Maer with enormous breasts who was riding him with her hands wrapped around his throat and a devilish glee in her eyes. The artist was obviously very fond of submission and dominance since there had been a number of similar drawings in the book, as well as eye contact, which was central to almost every illustration. They also had a knack for creating a mood just based on the expression on the figures' faces, their emotions and desires laid bare with a few deft strokes of the pen. Uffrin's heart pounded, and he pressed his hand down against his stiffness as he studied the drawing, the generous curve of her hips, the way her nipples just grazed his chest, and especially the knowing gleam in her eye, which reminded him of Mara.

She had given him this book and asked him to guess which one was her favorite. Did that mean this was what she wanted to do to him? He hoped to the gods that was the case; he'd never been restrained before, but it had long been one of his fantasies. He removed his hand from his lap, hit the tarpipe, and flipped through the rest of the pages, scanning for any other ones that reminded him of her. Though they were all interesting in their own way, and some quite arousing, nothing else fit the bill. He returned to the page, studied it for a long time, then closed his eyes and imagined the scene.

Mara's apartment would be a lot like his own, perhaps a bit messier and more organic, with feathers and books in place of tools and mechanical toys. She would kiss him, long and slow, working his body over with the lightest touch until he couldn't take it anymore, then undo his belt, roughly pull down his pants and yank his shirt over his head. Or perhaps she would sit back and watch as he removed his clothes at her command, twirling the rope in her hands with a devilish grin on her face. When he was standing naked, fully exposed, she would slip out of her robes so suddenly it would take his breath away to see her standing in the full glory of her curves, her knowing eyes watching his as he scanned her from head to toe.

She would expertly bind his wrists, then grip his beard in one hand and his behind with the other and lower him onto the bed, her heavy breasts pressing against him. She would pin his arms above his head while wriggling and sliding over him, crushing his mouth with ferocious kisses, devastating him with her tongue until he was gasping for breath, on the edge of explosion. She would rise up on her knees, grip him firmly, and guide him just inside. She would hover at that point for a moment, a wicked grin on her face, then sink down onto him with a breathy groan.

She leaned forward, smushing him beneath the softness of her breasts, and slid her fingers gently around his neck as she began moving, slowly at first, grinding hard against him with sure and powerful strokes. He tried to hold it inside, tried to keep his cool, but the fire in her eyes, the strength of her body, and the increasing urgency of her huffing breaths soon made resistance futile. Her eyes narrowed, and her grip on his neck tightened just enough as she moved faster and faster, pounding him into the mattress with each thrust of her goddess hips. She froze, exhaling in a shaky groan, clenching him inside her with such trembling power that he lost control and spilled in a seemingly endless series of spurts. She fell onto him, kissing him gently as the last tremors subsided.

"I love you, Uffrin."

Uffrin checked his messages in the morning and saw a red one from work, saying his new hotiron core had arrived, and they needed him to swap out the half-spent one today. They were getting tight with the hotiron lately, which was no surprise, given the movement of the great automatons, which were energy hogs. He still had a few half-spent cores in a special case in his locked drawer for emergencies; before the buildup to war, they didn't keep such close track of it. It would be good to have a fresh core in Friend, though he did worry a little about how it might affect its new patterns. The orbus had enough magical energy stored in it to function without hotiron for a time, but since he hadn't input the new patterns himself, he couldn't be sure what would happen.

The compound was bustling with activity, and Uffrin found out why when he picked up the new core. He was given a mission slip informing him of his next deployment starting the day after his current leave ended. He'd hoped for a little more time, but he wasn't surprised. The Stream had been abuzz with rumors of new movements by human troops, a big push before winter hit. If the Maer could hold them off until the snows came, the theory went, the humans would have to retreat back north of the Silver Hills until the spring, given their supposed susceptibility to the cold. Uffrin didn't put much stock in that line of thinking, as there were humans living in some places in the mountains already, but his opinion carried the weight of a single tuft of owl down.

Friend's eyes popped open as soon as Uffrin entered the workshop, and its head swiveled toward him.

"Good to see you too, Friend." Uffrin set the case with the new core on the table and retrieved his gauntlet from the locked drawer. Friend fluttered over at the barest touch of his hand on the pad, just a half-breath faster than usual, as if it had anticipated his movement and wanted him to think he had controlled it.

"Are you ready for some fresh juice?"

Friend headbutted his hand, then hopped over to inspect the case. It leaned in close, then hopped back over to the work tray. It turned away from Uffrin and tucked its wings down to expose the access panel.

"Let's power you down," Uffrin said, triple-tapping the pad on his gauntlet. The owl gave a low whine and went still. He unscrewed the panel, wondering if Friend was really powered off, but the machine gave no sign of movement. He removed the gauntlet and donned his visor, lead-lined gloves, and protective vest. He hated changing out the core because the gloves made it hard to hold his tools properly, but he'd done it dozens of times. He proceeded with utmost caution, removing the shielding and opening the interior panel to reveal the plum-sized orbus with its maze of copper filaments beneath a lacquered exterior. He held the orbus over the padded tray and carefully inserted the key. It popped open, searing his eyes with bright blue light from the hotiron, which his visor only dimmed a little. He picked up the fine clamp, his hands sweating inside his gloves, and maneuvered it inside the orbus to pull out the tiny ball of hotiron, which was no bigger than a marble. He held the clamp firm with one hand as he entered the code to unlock the hotiron case, getting it wrong the first time because of the clumsy gloves. He set it down in the 'used' indentation in the case, picked up the new one with the clamp, and steeled his jaw as he lowered it into the orbus, which flashed three times to show it had connected. He let out a long sigh of relief, then closed the orbus and put all the pieces back into place.

He shucked his gloves, removed his visor and vest, and took a long pull from his water bottle. Friend stood immobile on the table, and Uffrin picked it up and turned it to face him. He studied it for any signs of life, but Friend's eyes did not pop open. This should have been a good thing; the machine was not supposed to turn itself off and on, but the fact that it had done so when he'd entered the shop but not now was a little worrisome. He donned his gauntlet, took a deep breath, and tapped it to power the machine on.

Friend's eyes popped open, and it spun its head around and whipped its wings wide, then tucked them and emitted a soft trill. Uffrin held out his hand, and Friend leaned down and headbutted it. Uffrin's heart fluttered with relief. The head-spinning and wing-spreading were new but hardly surprising, given the development in Friend's personality of late. It felt weird to think of the machine that way, but how else could he describe behaviors that had not been part of any pattern imprint and that were unique to this machine?

"Are you feeling good, Friend? Do you want to spread your wings a little?"

Uffrin moved his fingers toward the pad, watching the owl's eyes watch his hand. Just before he touched the pad, Friend turned and fluttered into the air, hovering just above Uffrin's face, sending a faint breeze through his hair. Friend zipped off on a fast loop around the shop without any direction from Uffrin. It hovered again when it returned, then did another loop, flying in and out of each of the suspended hoops several times before returning to land on the desk in front of him.

"Friend, I'm very impressed by your initiative, but it's very important for you not to do that during inspection. You do understand that, right?"

Friend gave a soft hoot and hopped forward to headbutt his hand several times, angling into Uffrin's fingers like a cat trying to get petted behind the ears. Uffrin obliged gently so as not to dislodge the delicate silk feathers. They were in short supply and almost as difficult to replace as the hotiron. He sat back, and Friend stood straight up again, watching him. There was no way Friend could understand what he'd said unless the orbus had hidden patterns he wasn't aware of.

He worried about what would happen at inspection. The machine had to perform to the exacting specifications of the master artificers to be allowed out of the shop, and those that didn't were sent to another workshop for further examination. There was no telling what they would do to it, but he feared Friend's patterns would be reset, his memory wiped clean. The thought brought a lump to his throat. He leaned in close to Friend's face and pecked the owl's beak with his lips, eliciting another soft trill.

"Only with me," he said, pointing to himself. "Only here." He gestured around the workshop. "Not in the inspection lab." He pointed at the door, crossed his arms, then chuckled at his own ridiculousness. There was no way Friend could understand what he was trying to communicate.

Friend let out a firm trill, then hopped forward, touched Uffrin's nose with its beak, and swung its wings forward to wrap around Uffrin's ears in a little mechanical hug.

Uffrin went to the Clockwork Baths since he could use them for free, then stopped by the salon. A stylist sat reading in the empty shop, looking up in surprise as he entered. It seemed personal grooming had taken a hit with all that was going on.

"Just here for a trim?" the stylist asked, slipping a bookmark into the book and laying it aside.

Uffrin hesitated. It felt foolish to go to extra lengths for his evening with Mara; she wasn't the type who would care about such things. But it had been a while since he'd had sex, and it had been much, much longer since it had meant anything. He wanted it to be special. And besides, what else was he going to spend his money on? What would money even mean if the humans made it past the defensive forces and came for Kuppham?

"I'm going to need a full Maerscape," he said, pulling a ten-fen coin from his wallet.

The attendant popped out of his chair and slung a towel over his shoulder. "Glad to see there are still a few Maer left who care about personal grooming. Come on back." He gestured Uffrin toward a curtained-off area with an angled chair beneath an array of lamps hanging from the ceiling. "Just let me know when you're ready." He pulled the curtain closed, and Uffrin removed his boots and clothes and hung them on a rack on the wall. He rinsed his privates in the wash basin, though he'd just been to the baths; it was expected. He'd always loved the minty lavender scent of the soap they had here. It left him feeling fresh and fully presentable in any circumstance.

He summoned the stylist, who came in with his basket of scissors, clippers, and brushes and framed Uffrin's face with his hands.

"Going for a new look up top or just maintenance?"

"Just trim and neaten my hair and beard and go medium on the pubes. I'm not trying to look like a human or anything."

The stylist laughed rather too loudly and slapped him across the shoulder with his towel.

"I've done a few of those, and let me tell you, it's not pretty. Medium it is, then, and maintenance up top. I'll touch up your hands and around your nipples, too, if you like."

"Sounds good."

Uffrin relaxed as the stylist went to work on his hair and beard, humming a little bit to himself as he worked with deft snips and gentle flicks of his pick.

"Starting to smell like winter out there," the stylist said as he evened out Uffrin's beard, snipping a little here and there.

"Picnic season is just about over," Uffrin agreed.

"Might see some snow here in the next week or two if you believe the weather streams."

"They haven't been as accurate as usual since..." Uffrin didn't have the heart to finish his sentence.

"Well, if the snow comes early and hits hard, maybe it'll freeze the skinfuckers' balls off, and they'll go scurrying off back north for a while."

"Your lips to the gods' ears."

The stylist trimmed around his nipples, then went to work around his privates with a pair of scissors. His hands were quick but sure, and Uffrin stayed relaxed and unflinching as he worked.

"Special occasion?" the stylist asked, not looking up from his work. "Not that it's any of my business," he added a moment later.

"No, you're fine, and yeah, I've got a date if you can believe it."

"I kinda figured. Not much call for a Maerscape these days. Maer seem to be hunkered down a bit, which is a shame if you ask me. What better time to live your best life than when you don't know what tomorrow will bring?"

"You'll get no argument from me."

Uffrin closed his eyes and smiled as the stylist put on the finishing touches, then brought over a tray of perfumes.

"Anything special you'd like me to put on you today? I really like this rosewater, or you could try something in a muskwood, or maybe a lemon tea?"

"Rosewater sounds good. Just a spritz."

"You got it." He set down the tray, ran the brush through one more time, and sprayed once in the air above Uffrin's privates. Uffrin felt the tiny droplets hit him, and the air filled with the delicate perfume of the rosewater.

He tipped double, and the stylist put his hand to his forehead in thanks. "Good luck out there tonight."

When Uffrin got back to his apartment, he remembered to put on his circlet, which he'd completely neglected on the way home, walking through the cold streets with thoughts of Mara in his head. A smile grew on his face as he saw the message from Mara, then faded as he read the words.

I'm so sorry, Uffrin, but I've been called in to work tonight. Two of our handlers got sent on mission unannounced, and I've got to cover. It's the worst thing that's ever happened to me—I'm so looking forward to seeing you again, and they promised me the next three nights off, so I hope you don't mind postponing our date until tomorrow.

I can't wait to see you, Uffie! I want to hold you in my arms and ply you with kisses while you flip through the book and show me the page you think is my favorite. If you guess right, maybe we can do a little re-enactment of the scene.

Until tomorrow.

Uffrin removed his circlet and gently set it on the table, then fell back onto his bed with a long, whistling sigh. His wide eyes stared at the cracked ceiling in disbelief. How was he supposed to wait another day, especially when he only had nine more sleeps left before he was sent off to gods knew where? How many times would he see her before he left? How many kisses would she plant on his lips? And how many had been stolen by this cruel twist of fate? She'd said in her message that two of the other owl handlers had been sent away on mission unexpectedly. That meant Mara was at risk of being sent away, too—as was he. They had to make the most of every day, every moment, but Uffrin was alone at night while Mara was off flying with the owls.

He picked up Mara's book and his tarpipe from his desk and propped up some pillows on his bed. He made himself flip from the back this time since he'd only hastily inspected those pages, and he wanted to make sure he'd given each image sufficient consideration before he met with Mara tomorrow night. He had to make his guess count. He touched himself idly as he leafed through the pages, stopping to study the positions and facial expressions, the soft and hard looks in the couples' eyes. He found one particularly intriguing image of two Maer fellating one another, one upright and the other inverted, standing on his hands and leaning against a wall, and he gave that one a long look. Another showed a Maer with her legs spread wide, grinning with glee at a muscled Maer who crawled across the bed toward her, his massive erection looking like a fifth limb. Uffrin's excitement grew as he sensed he was nearing the picture he'd spent time with the night before, the one he hoped to re-enact with Mara the next time they met.

His pants grew tight, and his breath along with them as he turned the page and saw it as if for the first time: her gloriously exaggerated backside, the plump crease of her hips, her fingers around his throat, the fiery sweet glance they exchanged. Uffrin freed himself from his pants and lost himself in the picture and the mental image of all the things they'd do together. Once he'd finished and cleaned up, he closed his eyes and lay awake a long time, listening to the coos of the night doves, thinking of the gleam in Mara's eyes.

18

Mara exchanged a grim greeting with the aerie watcher as she arrived for her shift. Cleo had beat her here, and she flew down as soon as Mara had her glove on, clawing the pocket where she knew Mara kept her treats.

"Here's a nice little mouthful for you, night angel." She dangled the dead mouse by the tail, and Cleo snatched it in her beak and swallowed it with several quick convulsions of her neck. A boot scuffed behind her, and she turned to see Sergeant Kay standing with her arms behind her back.

"We got a raven today saying humans had been spotted below the valley, so be extra vigilant tonight."

Mara nodded. "Any more poppers?"

Kay shook her head. They'd lost an owl to an exploding hoverball a few days before, the first one they'd seen this close to the city. The concern was that they'd use them to blow up the dam, though it seemed like they'd need quite a few to pull that off, or maybe the lower gate. If the humans were really trying to attack from both sides, this was the only other way into the city, so whatever they tried, it would have to be here.

"If they send it, we'll catch it, won't we, Cleo?" Cleo stared impassively at her, then swiveled her head toward the darkening valley outside the open wall.

"Mind your bird."

"Always."

Mara slipped her circlet on and took a few moments to connect with Cleo, who was eager to take to the skies, as always. Mara summoned a view of an exploding hoverball the handlers had been sent on their private stream and shared it with Cleo, though she never knew if Cleo really saw views the same way she did. It showed a marble slightly larger than the regular hoverballs, with a faint pink glow, floating toward one of the great automatons. The view grew shaky as whoever was recording shouted, "Popper!" and backed up. A Maer leapt from the turret, yelping with pain as they hit the ground and started crawling away. Another one's head emerged from the turret just as the ball touched the automaton. A hot pink explosion filled the view as a boom roared all around. Cleo raised her wings and let out a little screech as she gripped Mara's glove, but she stayed put. The view grew jagged, spinning, then showed only the dusky sky, lit up on one side by what must have been the flames from the burning automaton. An agonizing scream ripped through the air, stopping suddenly as the view went black.

Mara pushed a calming vibe into Cleo, and the owl's wings settled down her back, though she still gripped Mara's hands a little too tight through the leather.

"We're going to stop that from happening," she whispered, trying to send a burst of courage to Cleo, whose mind seemed to sharpen a bit. The bird swiveled her head toward the open windows again. Mara stepped to the opening, held out her arm, and Cleo flapped off into the purple-gray night.

Mara guided Cleo low through the valley, keeping the image of the pink hoverball in her mind's eye. She flew straight along the creek, stopping to land in a tree here and there to scan the surroundings, but all was dark and quiet. Mara hoped the slight glow would make the hoverball easier to spot, but it was still a tiny object in a valley full of cover. She made a pass through the valley along one side, then flew Cleo back down along the other. Mara was tired and cranky since it was her third night on in a row, and her mind kept drifting to what she should have been doing tonight. She smiled as she imagined Uffrin leafing through the book she'd given him, touching himself, trying to pick which illustration would be her favorite. She wondered if he focused only on the ones with a male and a female in them, looking for figures that would recall him and her. Maybe he was more into the ones with two females or perhaps two males. Mara was pretty omnivorous when it came to erotica, and she figured Uffrin probably was as well, but there was no way to know. She hoped that once he'd seen the picture of the curvy Maer dominating her skinny tied-up partner, he would immediately see the resemblance and stroke himself slowly, thinking of them re-enacting it together.

Her mind snapped back into focus as Cleo's danger sense shot through her. She saw a feeble pink glow floating low to the ground among the scrub bushes along the northern side of the valley. It was about a half-mile from the dam and moving slowly enough it would take it a few good minutes to get there. She perched Cleo on a tree and opened a channel to the command center.

"We've got a popper, north side, about a half-mile away. It's moving low, which might be why we missed it the first few passes."

"I'll send out a detonation unit," the watcher said. "Keep an eye out for any more, and give me updates as it approaches."

Mara shifted back into Cleo's mind, watching the hoverball as it floated toward the city. She turned Cleo around and scanned the area again. She was about to swivel back to give chase when another glowing pink dot caught her eye, floating just above the river's surface. She opened the voice channel back up, growing dizzy for a moment.

"We've got another one right on the river," she said, struggling to keep her focus on Cleo.

"Skundir's balls," muttered the watcher, whose voice echoed in as if through a long tube. "You might need to snatch up the first one and try to let it explode in the air. I'll send for another unit, but it might take a minute."

"On it," Mara said, wincing at the spike of pain that shot through her skull at shifting back and forth so quickly. She urged Cleo forward, flitting through the forest, and they caught up with the ball a quarter-mile away from the dam, moving steadily at the pace of a fast walk. She scanned the area around the lower gate and saw three Maer emerge, wearing suits of thick padding and carrying what looked like large, heavy blankets. If she could eliminate the first ball, it would give them a better chance to stop the second. They might be able to stop both, but it wasn't a risk she could afford to take.

Time to be a hero, she sent to Cleo, then gave her a slight push, and the owl took it from there. She flapped a bit higher, then swooped low to the ground, catching the ball on the upswing and bursting up through the tree canopy and into the open air. Cleo flashed pain in her claw, and Mara's foot cramped as the feeling bled into her. The owl swooped back away from the dam, and the pain grew to a searing heat. Mara signaled release, and Cleo let go, then powered upwards, boosted by the force of the blast below, which flooded her sensors with a brilliant pink flash. Cleo tumbled about in the air, and she registered feather loss and some pain, but she was flying strong. Mara let her circle, trying to get a bead on the other hoverball, but the trees blocked her view. She made out the bomb squad, heading in the right direction, thank the gods.

She swooped in through a hole in the canopy, landing on the nearest branch to scan the forest. She saw it immediately, just fifty yards ahead, with the dark shapes of the bomb squad emerging from the underbrush. One of them threw their blanket over it, and it disappeared from sight as it fell to the ground. The other two blankets were quickly thrown over it, and the three Maer turned and sprinted back the way they'd come. Seconds later, the blankets exploded with a blinding burst of pink light, which Cleo's eyelids blocked just in time, but she saw spots when she blinked them back open. Flames roared from the spot of the explosion, a crater more than a Maer's length wide and nearly as deep.

"What's your status, Mara?" The watcher's voice rang in her ear like an off-pitch bell rung way too close.

"Cleo's okay," she said, taking a deep breath and blowing it out in a thin stream to keep the dizziness at bay. "Cleo got one, and the bomb squad got the other."

"I'm going to link with Kay and let her know what's happened. Go back and make sure there are no more out there."

Mara nodded, clenching her jaw at the pain twisting sideways through her head. She was dimly aware of footsteps and urgent conversations in the aerie. She urged Cleo out of the tree, and they did a zigzag pattern back down the valley, flitting from tree to tree and scanning the forest. They made it down to where the forest thinned, then rose up to scan the area but saw nothing. She wheeled Cleo around and dove back down among the trees, repeating the pattern on the way back. About halfway to the dam, she saw Seeli, Leasse's owl. She must have gotten pulled from half-duty and dragged out of bed straight to the aerie. Mara felt a hand on her shoulder, and Kay's voice echoed in.

"Bring her home, Mara. Let's make sure your hero bird is okay."

Mara wanted to hug Cleo when she flew in through the windows and landed on her glove. Cleo's claws were a little sore, and she'd lost a few tail feathers from the blast, but she carried herself with what seemed like pride, a hunter who'd caught important prey. Mara fed her a mouse, which she gulped down without hesitation, and Kay brought her another, tossing it so Cleo could snatch it without moving from her spot on Mara's bracer.

"You saved our bacon, girl," Kay said, walking around to examine the bird. Cleo clacked her beak, standing up tall and shaking her body to help the extra food go down. "Looks like you lost a few tail feathers, and there's a little singeing here and there, but you sure flew back here all right."

"Her claws are a bit tender, too, from holding onto the hot popper. She was able to get it well above the treeline and drop it in time to get away from the immediate blast radius."

"Clever girl." Kay held up her finger to Cleo, who pecked it, then turned to look out the windows again.

"Go on, love. You've earned an early rest tonight. I'll see you back home." Mara raised her hand, and Cleo flapped off into the darkness.

"You too, I should say. Leasse has Seeli down there now scouring the valley, but she hasn't seen anything. We'll send her farther down to see if we can figure out where the humans controlling those hoverballs were. They've sent out scouts to patrol the lower valley to see if they can find the skinfuckers, but they're probably holed up far away. We now think the range is up to thirty miles."

"Thirty miles?" Mara shook her head. "There's no way we'll find them."

"Doesn't mean we shouldn't try. Between Seeli and the scouts, it's worth a shot."

Mara nodded, covering her yawn. Her head throbbed from the frequent shifting, and the image of the bright pink explosion was still burned onto her brain.

"All right, I'm going home to check on Cleo and grab some shuteye. You said three nights off, guaranteed, right?"

Kay flashed a grim smile. "That's what we said."

"My circlet has been acting up. I may need to have the chip replaced. I hope I don't miss any messages."

"Not to worry. If we need you badly enough, someone will come find you."

Mara sighed. She wouldn't shirk her duty, even for Uffrin. There was too much at stake. But if they were going to call her up early, she had no time to waste in bedding him. The aerie clock read three-quarters dawn. She could go home, catch a few hours' nap, then invite Uffrin over for breakfast in bed.

She said goodbye to Kay and trudged down the thousand stairs back into the dark, silent streets of Kuppham. She enjoyed the city when no one was about, even with the frosty wind whipping around her ears. She force-marched back to her hightop and made it to the roof, where she saw Cleo had already taken to her roost. No doubt she needed rest after the night she'd had, and with two mice in her tummy, she didn't need to be fed.

Mara made it back down the stairs, opened her door, and collapsed onto her bed. She didn't even have the energy to sit up, so she untied her boots by pulling her legs up, then tossed them into a corner, where their thud probably woke the downstairs neighbors, but they would have to deal. If the hoverballs had exploded against the dam or at the lower gate, they would have awoken to sirens, so she considered them lucky. She closed her eyes and drifted off to sleep with visions of Uffrin, arms tied over his head, his eyes gazing up at hers with submission and want.

19

Uffrin checked his messages as soon as he awoke, ignoring the red one from the Assistant Head Artificer and reading the green one from Mara instead.

I got off early and had a nice little nap, but I'm all out of darkroot. Do you have a secret stash somewhere? If so, maybe you could bring some by, and we could have a cup together?

—Mara

Uffrin smacked his forehead, almost knocking the circlet off. He hadn't had darkroot since visiting his parents, as both markets he'd visited had been out. He considered dropping in on them to see if he could steal a bit, but it was a long trek there and back. He hopped on the market stream, searching for darkroot listings. He found a handful at five to ten times the normal price, which normally would have been out of the question, but he sucked it up and arranged to meet someone in a nearby hightop for the exchange. He washed up, brushed his teeth, and hurried out the door. He rushed back in to grab Mara's book and shove it into his bag, giving himself a little rise at the thought of the illustration and what it would be like to act it out with her.

Mara buzzed him up, and Uffrin had to pace himself on the stairs as he was getting all out of breath with excitement. He reached the door, clutched the bag of pastries under one arm, and rapped three times.

Mara opened, dressed in an orange robe that highlighted her curves while still leaving room for his rabid imagination to fill in the blanks. Her smile was closed-lipped but ripe with suppressed laughter, which seemed to overflow from her eyes.

"Ooh, he brought breakfast too! You've aced the test, Uffrin." She took the pastries and stretched up to his level, balancing with one hand on his chest as she plied his lips with slow, tender kisses. "You did bring some tea, didn't you?" Uffrin patted his bag, and Mara's grin widened, then softened as she leaned in to kiss him again, her hand slipping inside his coat to grip his shirt, twisting his chest hair beneath. A whiff of cinnamon and muskwood hit him, and he let his free hand rest on her hip, squeezing with gentle pressure. She pulled him through the doorway by his shirt, never letting go with her lips, and kicked the door shut behind him.

"Take off your coat," she said, pulling back from the kiss and gesturing to the hooks on the wall. She set the bag down on a tiny counter, then turned to watch as Uffrin hung up his coat and bag and pulled out the small pouch of tea he'd just paid 30 fen for. Her eyes grew wide as he held out the bag, which she took as if it were a delicate flower.

"Where did you get this?" she asked in an awed voice. "I haven't seen it at the market for weeks!"

"I had to do some digging, but I figured you'd need it after three nights on in a row."

"It's far from the only thing I need." She set the bag on the counter and moved to him slowly, closing the distance between them a step at a time. Her hands found him first, sliding around his hips and pulling him gently toward her. She left one hand there, and the other slid up and clasped around the back of his neck as she pulled him down for a kiss. Uffrin was dizzy with the wet warmth of her lips on his, the soft curves of her body, the taste of her, and he sank into her embrace. Mara kissed him hard and deep, pressing her body into his and pushing him backward until he hit the wall. She kept going, slipping her leg between his and grinding against him, her hands pulling his hips toward her even as she crushed him against the wall.

Her fingers crept to his chest, kneading and pinching, and she slowed her kiss as her thigh pressed into his hardness until he feared he would lose more than just his mind. She eased back with her leg as she unbuttoned his shirt the rest of the way and slid it off his shoulders, then raked her fingers across his chest. She pulled back from the kiss, her hot, dark eyes locked on his, freezing him in place as she undid his belt. Her fingers found his waistband and slipped inside, and Uffrin gasped as she grabbed him, holding as tight with her hand as she did with her eyes. Her eyes half-closed as she angled in for another kiss, loosening her grip on him but not letting go as if she could sense how close he was and wanted to keep him in this torturous limbo for as long as possible.

At last, she released him, and her lips closed on his once more. She ran her face down his neck and began nuzzling around his chest. He gave a little whimper as her tongue flicked across his nipple, then a groan forced its way out as she sucked and licked, her hands undoing his pants, which dropped to his ankles. Her hands fondled and caressed him with the softest touch, but it was still almost too much. He gripped her shoulder, knowing he couldn't take much more. She let go immediately, then sank to her knees, looking up at him with big, wicked eyes. Her hands ran up and down his thighs, inside and out. She looked down, running her fingers through his freshly trimmed hair, then glanced back up with a grin.

"You got yourself Maerscaped?" she said in a voice laced with tease.

Uffrin's heart leapt with panic. "I hope it's—"

His voice broke as she gripped him tight and took him in her mouth in one quick move, then pulled back again, holding him firm, lips glossy, eyes dancing. She took him in again, and he pressed his eyes shut, his hands framing her head, barely touching her hair. He never knew what to do with his hands in situations like this, but soon he forgot all about his hands as Mara worked him with her mouth, hands sliding around to grip his buttocks. She teased for a while, then took him deep, moving faster and faster, and Uffrin soon passed the point of no return.

He huffed a few hoarse breaths as he tried to hold off for a few moments longer, then pressed his hands tighter against her head to let her know he was close. She only redoubled her efforts, and his pleasure rose like a flash flood, bursting through his resolve. His whole body shuddered as he released. Mara stayed with him to the end, her fingernails digging into his behind as the pulsing diminished, and at last, she released him, wiping her mouth on the back of her hand as she stared up at him with a mischievous, self-satisfied twinkle in her eyes.

"Now let's see about that tea," she said, standing up and giving him a quick, salty kiss.

The darkroot tea was strong and bitter, but Mara had some lovely honey and milk, and they sat sipping their tea and nibbling their pastries at the too-small table. Mara had offered Uffrin the only chair, and she sat on a crate with rope handles she pulled from under the table. They chatted mindlessly, laughing and sipping and nibbling as if what had just happened and what was about to happen weren't the most important things in the entire crumbling world. He glanced around her room as they talked, taking in the books, the art, the little odds and ends of daily life. It was neater than he imagined, especially the bookshelves, which were filled with books of all sizes, including quite a few of the size and format of the one she'd given him, which was still in his bag where he'd left it when she'd mauled him as soon as he entered.

"You're quite the bookworm," he said, gesturing toward the shelves.

"Living alone, I need the distraction, and there's only so much of the Stream I can take. Especially these days."

"I hear you." Uffrin swallowed the last of his tea, brushing his fingers together and wiping them on the bottom of his pants. "I'm a bit of an addict myself, but lately, I've found myself tuning out a bit more. It was rough being on mission for an entire month without it, but it was good too, you know?"

Mara nodded absently, then her face sharpened. "Have you been assigned a new mission date yet?"

Uffrin nodded, his heart growing heavy as he pictured himself trudging away from the city and leaving Mara behind.

"Eight days, which is two weeks to the minute from when I returned."

Mara's hand moved across the table, and she slid her fingers between his. "Eight days is plenty of time, Uffrin. And it's not like you'll be gone forever."

"I know, it's just..." He put his other hand over hers and squeezed. "It doesn't seem fair. I haven't met someone like you in, well, ever, and now we have just a week before we'll be separated again."

"We'll just have to make sure we don't waste any of that time, then." She extricated her fingers, took him by the wrist, and moved his hand to her knee, where her robe had fallen open due to the way she was sitting on the crate. She moved his hand up her thigh, and the feel of her soft hair over her supple flesh sent tingles throughout his body. He leaned forward as her hand pulled his farther up, and suddenly she was kissing him, her lips soft and hot, her tongue caressing him with gentle licks. She moved his hand all the way up, and his fingers found the crease of her leg, lifting the corner of her underwear with his thumb.

Mara's kisses maintained a low, steady burn, and he let his fingertips ghost over her underwear, eliciting a soft groan from Mara, who deepened the kiss. She put her hand on his thigh and slid it up in a long, slow motion that ended in her fingers sliding over his hardness, circling and gliding, and he hummed into the kiss. They teased each other for a while, then Mara pulled back, sliding her hand back down to his knee. The heat in her stare sparkled with mirth, and she glanced over at his bag by the door.

"So, did you read my book?"

Uffrin nodded, unable to control his grin, and half-stood, embarrassed by his tented pants, which Mara stared at unabashedly. He angled away to retrieve the book and quickly returned to the table, where Mara had cleared away the remains of their breakfast.

"Not only did I read it—I studied it quite carefully." He opened to the first page, with the svelte Maer riding her partner, breasts jutting in the air. "The artist had a real flair for eyes," he said, flipping slowly through the pages. "I love this one." He pointed to the two Maer fellating each other, one standing on his feet and the other on his hands. "Though I do have some questions about the practicality of it."

"Where there's a will, there's a way," Mara said, scooting over so her body pressed against him, her hand sliding up and down his thigh. "Keep going."

He pointed out various things he liked as he turned the pages. They giggled about the positions and the facial expressions as their hands explored each other's laps with light touches, as if by some unspoken agreement to make the moment last. When he got close to his favorite illustration, which he could tell by the slight crease in the book's pages, he instead flipped to the back of the book and started working backward, pointing out this and that, stopping in mid-explanation at one point as Mara's tongue slipped into his ear.

"You've gone through most of the book, and you still haven't made your guess," she whispered, her breath and lips hot in his ear.

"I—I've been saving it," he managed as she squeezed between his legs and held on. "It's..." he turned to Mara, holding a finger in the air, helpless in her grip. She knew it, too; he could see it in her eyes.

"It's what?" she said softly.

"You said if I guessed right, we'd—" His breath caught as she squeezed him tighter still.

"And we will."

"But what if I guess wrong?" he gasped.

She released him suddenly and leaned back, a sly smile on her lips.

"Then I get to choose."

"But if you get to choose, won't it be the same one?"

She moved her hands to his face and pressed a kiss into him.

"You catch on quick." She kissed him again, her hands sliding down around his neck, holding loosely, and Uffrin's mind spun with the possibilities. She slid one hand down his chest, then touched the book with the other. "Show me."

Uffrin thumbed through until he reached it, glancing over at her eager eyes, which were fixed on the book. He opened the pages and laid it flat on the table, and they studied it in silence for a moment. Uffrin's heartbeat drummed in his ears. Her eyes raised to meet his, and she gripped him by the shoulders and flung one leg over the chair to straddle him as her mouth crushed his, kissing him with heat and fury. His hands found her hips and gripped hard, then slid around to her powerful backside, which flexed as she ground against him. His hands slid up her back, feeling her muscles move as she rocked back and forth, still smothering him with her mouth, bringing him close to the brink. He gasped for breath, and she gripped his face, staring at him with hungry eyes, then slung her leg back over him and stood up suddenly.

She shed her robe in a few quick movements and stood before him in all the glory of her mighty curves. Uffrin knocked the chair over behind him as he stood, unable to form words at the beauty he saw before him. She stepped to him, maneuvering her mouth in for a kiss but hovering just out of reach, their beards and mustaches tangling but their lips never touching. Her hands made quick work of his shirt and pants, and soon they were wrapped in each other's arms, bodies crushing together, speaking the ineffable language of the flesh. He lost himself in her embrace, hardly noticing as she maneuvered him over to the bed, holding onto his back as she lowered him down.

"Hold still," she said in a husky voice, her face hovering over his, and then she was gone, stepping across the room, her round behind jiggling with every step. When she returned, she had a pair of leather straps hanging from her teeth, which dangled in his face as she straddled him, settling down atop his chest, crushing half the breath out of him. She dropped the straps onto his neck and hunched over to kiss him, sliding her body down, her strong legs clenching around his, pinning his body to the mattress.

"Do you want me," she said in between kisses, "to tie you up now?"

"Yes, please," he managed, stretching his arms back above his head. She picked up the straps and moved her body forward, stretching so her heavy breasts dragged across his face. She slid her body up over his stomach, across his chest, not stopping until she was flush against his chin. His tongue explored her as she leaned forward, wrapping his wrists together with the soft, supple leather, securing them with a few good tugs on the knot. She held still as he luxuriated in her, drunk with her scent, her taste, her quivering movements.

Was this really happening? Were his wildest dreams actually coming true? He held on tightly to her goddess hips as she pressed into him, moving with rhythmic urgency. He did everything he could to keep up, and before long, she let out a low, hissing groan, then slid back down his body, kissing him on the forehead, the nose, and then on the lips. They lingered in the kiss, then she pushed up on both arms, gazing down at him and biting her lip.

"You don't think we're done here, do you?"

"Gods, I hope not." Uffrin throbbed against her thighs, which she squeezed together for a moment, then moved off him to stretch the cord tight, pulling his arms farther above his head and tying the straps off to her bedpost.

She stalked back over on all fours, straddling him again, hovering over him on strong arms, and stared down into his eyes, directly into his soul.

"Wings," he whispered.

"Wings?" Puzzlement mixed with curiosity in Mara's eyes.

"My word. Wings." He was supposed to have a word, he knew, and he'd prepared this one just in case.

"I like it." She lowered down to kiss him, then pushed back up, smiling down at him. "I don't imagine you'll need it for what I have in mind, but it's always good to be safe."

"What do you have in mind?" he asked breathlessly.

"I want to make you beg, and then I'm going to give you everything you ask for."

"Gods, Mara, I want that so much," he whispered.

"I want you to want it more."

20

Mara slid down Uffrin's body, kissing and licking, grinning at the way he squirmed, the little whimpers in his throat. She returned to all fours, then lowered down slowly, brushing against him, feeling his hardness throb beneath her. His lean muscles strained against the straps, his eyes wide and wet and full of need. She sat back on his thighs, toying him with her fingers, watching his desperation grow. When his breath grew short, she released, sliding her hands up across his chest, braiding her fingers through his beard and slipping her thumb into his mouth. He sucked it like a hungry pup, groaning as she lowered her body down again, pressing against him, keeping her eyes locked on his.

She wished she could keep him in this state forever, make the crumbling world around them disappear, and feel his desire mounting without limit. She had never felt so wanted before, so needed, and the fire in her core burned as hot as a forge, but she tempered her passion with patience. The end of the world could wait, and so could she.

She removed her thumb, slid her hands loosely around his neck, and kissed him, his breath still heady with her taste. She reveled in his tender lips, his timid tongue, the little gasps whenever she squeezed him tight with her thighs, his helpless throbbing as he strained upward for the pressure she never allowed to mount. They kissed for a very long time until the tension building up inside Mara was too great. She pulled back, held him firm, and sank down onto his length, one slow inch at a time. She held still, savoring the feeling of fullness, gazing down at him, watching for signs he might be too close. His eyes devoured her, his lips held in a desperate pout.

"Stay with me, Uffie. Just tell me what you want. Anything."

She leaned down and kissed him furiously, lifting halfway off him and sinking down again, then pressed upright with her hands on his chest.

"I want to be yours," he murmured, "always and forever."

A spark fired inside, and she kneaded his chest as she began moving, sliding her hands up around his neck, picturing the illustration from the book. He looked from her body up to her eyes and back, and she wondered what he saw, what was going through his mind. She applied a little pressure around his neck, still keeping her fingers loose for safety, and his eyes grew glassy, showing an infinity of longing. She moved slowly, stopping every so often to kiss him, but the heat inside her burned so hot it threatened to consume her, and her body sped up of its own accord. She stared down at him as her breath grew shaky, grinning as his face took on the exact look of want and utter submission in the illustration.

Mara cut loose, grinding and riding him with an intensity that surprised even her. A low wine rose in Uffrin's throat, and she moved her hands back to his chest for leverage, locking eyes with him as her pleasure coiled and spiraled beyond her control. Uffrin's wine rose to a groan, then to a series of hoarse shouts, which she matched with her own as she pounded him into the mattress, sliding it a little farther off the bed with each stroke, until at last, the dam broke. She gripped his chest hair in her fingers as she held her body quivering over his, and she felt him pulse within her. She squeezed him tight as another wave of ecstasy washed over her, and she crashed onto his chest, covering his mouth with breathless kisses.

Mara inhabited her nap fully, wrapped around Uffrin's tight little frame, her arm draped over his chest, fingers tucked under his ribs. He snored a little, but it was a cute snore, a sort of high-pitched trill that came at irregular intervals. She squeezed him tighter whenever he made the sound, and he snuggled into her body, his hard butt wiggling against her, stirring her need. She toyed with the idea of toying with him, rousing him from his sleep, the little gasps he would make, the longing in his eyes as he looked over his shoulder at her. She pressed tighter against him, swallowing the desire until the moment passed, and she settled into a sleep much deeper than she had planned. She woke up to the fading sunlight of late afternoon. She had slept the day away, and the bed was cold where Uffrin should have been. She pushed up to sit, and she sighed a smile as she saw Uffrin slowly stirring tea as if trying not to make a sound.

"I slept all day."

"You're beautiful when you sleep." Uffrin blinked, looking down, as Mara's heart spilled over. "I mean, you're beautiful all the time, it's just..." He set down the spoon and brought the tea over, handing her the mug with the handle facing her. "Never mind. It's stupid."

"Tell me," she murmured, smacking his knee with the back of her hand. "I don't think it's stupid to say nice things about people." She slid her hand up his thigh and gripped tightly, trying to bring his evasive eyes up to hers.

"Tell me."

He looked up into her eyes, then down at her body, lingering here and there, warming her with his gaze, which then returned to her eyes.

"When you're awake, the way you move, the little gestures, the touching, the sparkle in your eye, the things you say—I love all of it. But when you sleep?" He gestured around her face but did not touch it. "There's this tiny little hint of a smile, some secret you're so pleased about knowing, but you won't share it quite yet." His eyes were dancing, his face anguished at the effort of conjuring such words.

"I want you to know all my secrets. I want you to know me, every layer, every inch."

"I do, too. It's just..." He buried his face in his teacup. "I wish we had more time."

"Hey, hey, Uffie, we have time!" She softened her grip on his thigh. "We'll make time."

"I know." He nodded, his mouth quirking into a half-smile. "I was thinking we should do something fun today."

"So was I." Mara slid her hand farther up Uffrin's thigh, and his face froze as he opened his mouth to speak.

"I want to take you out tonight for drinks and handbowls," he said once he recovered. "I know a place, one of those cellar clubs with no sign and no address. It's all dark and lit with wax candles, and they have this old Maer who plays a goat-harp."

"That sounds amazing!" She ran her hand up his thigh, massaging the place where it thinned and connected with his tight abdominal muscles beneath a freshly trimmed coat of soft hair. "About the other thing..."

"Oh, make no mistake. I plan to worship your body before and after in whatever way pleases us both." He ran his hand over her knee and up her thigh, his fingernails tracing lightly across her hair, sending shivers through her body. "But I thought we might have a bite to eat first."

They went out in a cold drizzle for tri-fries, triangular fried pastries in the Southern style that were all the rage before the war started. Mara had never tried one, and when she finally held the steaming triangle in her hands and the smell of honey and cinnamon hit her nose, the cold and the wet and the long line disappeared. She burned the roof of her mouth when she crunched on the steaming pastry, but the explosion of sweet, eggy goodness made her regret exactly nothing.

"Gods, Uffrin, these are amazing! I never managed to get one when they were first out, and now I can't believe they're still selling them!"

"Who knows for how much longer with the flour shortage, so I went ahead and got some of the goat ones as well."

They huddled under the overhang of a closed shop. They took turns tasting the goat tri-fries, which were greasy and salty and spicy, and the sweet ones, which had little bits of nuts in the center with honey caramelized around them. Uffrin wiped her mouth with his thumb when she was done, and she grabbed his wrist and held his thumb there, wrapping her lips around it, sucking and licking it until Uffrin made his little throaty sound again. She dropped his thumb and pushed him back against the wall, pressing into him with her body, moving in slowly for a kiss that was sweet and spicy from the tri-fries. They kissed lightly for a moment, then she pulled back, rubbing his nose with hers, looking up into his eyes.

"What should we do now?" he murmured.

"You had said something about worshiping my body." She pressed against his hardness, which she could feel even through his coat.

His hands found her backside and pulled her tight to him, and she closed her eyes as their lips met again, soft and hot, heedless of the cold rain spattering all around them.

21

Back at Mara's apartment, they shed their rainskins, leaving a puddle on the floor. Uffrin drank a glass of water while Mara was in the water closet and handed her one as he took his turn. When he returned, her robes were on the floor, and she lay on the bed on her stomach, her gorgeous round behind with its fine coat of tawny hair drawing his eyes and stirring his loins. She rolled halfway over, propping her head on her arm, her eyes glittering with a knowing smile.

"You can take your clothes off now," she said, "if you like." She watched him undress, her eyes focused on his growing erection, which responded to her gaze. He walked over to the bed awkwardly and lay down beside her. He ran his hand over the generous curve of her hip, along her side, and let his fingers graze down across her breasts, stuttering over her nipples. She scooted in closer, and he returned his hand to her hip, letting it settle in the perfect crease where it met her waist. Her heat enveloped him, and her lips found his, kissing him gently, patiently, perfectly.

"Tell me how you want to worship me," she said into his mouth between kisses, her hand finding his buttock and pulling him closer, their bodies straightening, pressing against each other. Uffrin's mind spun with the possibilities, all the parts of her he'd like to touch, how he'd like to be taken by her, surrender to her power.

"There are not enough days in a year to count the ways," he said, sliding his hand along the round curve of her behind, inching between her legs, gripping her tighter to him.

She kissed him again, hot and slow, then pulled back, her dark eyes glittering in the lamplight. Uffrin licked his lips, suddenly eager to taste her again. His heart fluttered as he fell on Mara's lips, pressing into her, pulling her to him. Their hands roamed across each other's bodies as they kissed, caressing, squeezing, gripping, pinching. Everywhere Mara laid her hands on him warmed with pleasure, and as their bodies crushed together, he felt himself growing close, just from the kissing and the touching.

He rolled her onto her back and pushed her arms above her head, never letting go with his lips. Mara's body rocked against his, hips raising up to rub against him. He released the kiss and snuffled down her neck, giving her little bites as he worked his way down across her breasts, which he lavished with attention, though perhaps not as much as they deserved. He tightened his stomach muscles and pressed them against her, feeling her strain up into him. He meandered his way down between her legs, which she spread wide for him. His lips grazed over her wet folds, and he kissed her softly and slowly at first, then a little harder as a moan vibrated from deep within her, and she pressed into him.

He made love to her with his lips, tongue, nose, and fingers. With each circle, each stroke, he became more aware of what she wanted, what she needed. He threw himself into the task of giving it to her exactly as her body told him to. With every rising groan, each series of high-pitched huffs, he redoubled his effort, pouring not just his body but his entire heart into the endeavor.

There was nothing in the entire world more important than bringing Mara every drop of pleasure she was capable of, which he discovered was more than he would have thought possible. She exhausted him with the strength and persistence of her body, her fingers gripping him tight to her, ever directing him, guiding him to her next climax, until at last she released with her hands and flopped her arms sideways across the bed, closing her knees around his head. He let his forehead fall against her, his lips barely grazing her, not quite ready to leave this shared space.

"Whew," Mara hissed shakily, one arm sliding down to push his head away. He pushed up halfway, grabbing the bedside towel and wiping off his face, then scooched up beside her and snuggled in against her shoulder. She rolled over onto her side, gazing down at him with soft eyes, and he felt his heart melt and dissolve throughout his body, which tingled as if he'd touched a live wire.

"I love you, Mara," his traitorous mouth said. His heart re-formed in a tangled, writhing mass as he watched her eyebrows raise with surprise, laced with amusement, then lower as her face softened. Her mouth formed a half-open pout, which she lowered to engulf his lips with hers, kissing him with sudden abandon as her hand grasped its way down his body. Her fingers found him and gripped him tight as her tongue explored his mouth and her lips crushed against his. She pulled back from the kiss, breathing heavily, her eyes full of dark fire, and stroked him slowly. He was so close already, and her touch moved something deep within.

"I..." she stroked him once, holding him firm with a crushing grip. "Love..." and again, sending tingles throughout his loins. "You..." Mara squeezed him tighter still, and his legs went weak and started shaking. "Too." He gripped her shoulder as he spilled, gasping for air, his eyes glued to hers, which saw through him, into him, saw everything there was to see, and loved him anyway. He angled his mouth up for a kiss, tears leaking from the corners of his eyes. Mara's smile softened as she moved to close the distance and sealed her lips against his. As the moment stretched on, Uffrin tried to fix it in his mind, to imprint it like the patterns in the machines, so no matter how bad things got, he could return here and find an oasis from the worst the world could throw at him.

Uffrin held Mara's hand as he led her through the narrow passage between two hightops, following the dim red light that glowed from the dark end of the alley. She hovered close to him, her body brushing and bumping against him, her muskwood and cinnamon scent keeping the mucky smells of the city at bay. The light emanated from the cracks in a boarded-over window in a battered, half-rotted door. Uffrin knocked three times, as he'd read on the Stream. The door opened, and a Maer with dyed black hair and beard looked them up and down, then blinked and stepped aside, gesturing toward a dark doorway. Haunting string music drifted up from the stairs, which were barely visible in the feeble light of a single red hooded lamp. Mara held his hand tight and pressed against him as they made their way down the creaky stairs, holding onto a rickety handrail.

They emerged into a low-ceilinged room bathed in warm red light. The place was surprisingly extensive, lit by red glass oil lanterns on the walls, with candles on each of the several dozen tables and booths. Maer sat in twos and threes with drinks and handbowls, talking quietly. A white-haired Maer sat on a stool in the far corner of the room, plucking a goat harp with his eyes closed. The music reminded him of a camping trip with his parents at Eagle Lake long ago, where they'd sat around a fire sharing music with a group of campers from Gulham. Mara pointed to an empty booth crammed into a corner, and Uffrin eyed the bartender, who blinked and gestured them toward the booth. He squeezed in next to Mara, legs touching, and their hands found each other under the table.

"I absolutely love it," Mara said, caressing the pads of his fingers with hers, stirring his desire, which seemed without limit when it came to her. "How'd you find out about this place?"

"On the Backstream," he said, his heart buzzing as her fingers found his palm and traced patterns into it. "It's technically unlicensed, so expect the Shoza to come barging in any second and round us all up."

Mara's laugh was soft and indulgent. "I hope they have better things to do right now than clean out cellar clubs."

Uffrin nodded, thinking of Erliss, wondering what they were doing right now. Did they go out to clubs, or did they just train and meditate, waiting for the next assignment? His duty notice had not stated whether Erliss would be assigned to him again, but he hoped so.

A waiter with a large nose ring brought them two handbowls and two drinks, then laid four wooden discs on the table.

"Just flag me down when you're ready for more," they said, then hurried back to the bar.

One drink was blue or maybe purple—it was impossible to be sure in the reddish light—in a tall, clear glass with a wedge of dried citrus in it. The other came in a copper mug, with steam rising from it and several white blobs dissolving in its frothy surface.

"Ooh, I want the hot one," Mara said, slipping her fingers out of Uffrin's, leaving his hand feeling empty and hollow. He picked up the tall glass and clinked it with Mara, who blinked at him as she raised the mug to her lips with both hands. She took a sip, then let out a low hum as she wiped froth from her mustache. "Gods, Uffrin, you have got to try this. It's like...some kind of boozy tea, with cloves and...cinnamon, I think? And I have no idea what this creamy stuff is, but the bartender is a genius."

"The Backstream doesn't lie," he said with a chuckle, then took a sip of a surprisingly strong, tart drink with hints of berry and mint. "Gods, this is amazing!" He took another sip, then Mara pulled the glass from his hands with a sly smile and took a drink.

"Skundir's balls, that's good!" she said, closing her eyes and letting out another hum that vibrated throughout his chest, softly curling around his heart. He picked up the warm copper mug and drank, letting the creamy sweetness rush over his tongue and glide down his throat.

"Oh, and look—fried munnies!" Mara picked up a handful of the tiny fish, leaned her head back, and dropped them into her mouth. Uffrin lifted one to his mouth and took a tentative bite, then crunched the whole thing as he grabbed a handful of the salty, spicy morsels. The other bowl contained sweet cherries preserved in brandy, and they were the perfect counterpoint to the munnies.

They ate and drank, swapping drinks occasionally, and watched the old Maer playing the goat harp, which looked like it was made of the actual rib bones of a goat instead of wood, as most were. His eyes were closed, and his face bore the pained smile of concentration as he wove melodies that were spare and haunting yet always circled around to a happier place, tinged with melancholy though they were. Mara slipped one arm around Uffrin's waist, leaning into him with her soft body. His head grew light with the closeness, the music, and the alcohol. They watched the crowd, mostly Maer in their twenties and thirties, whose smiles and laughter brought back memories of lighter times.

They ate and drank whatever the waiter brought them, each time something different, but always exactly what they needed. When they'd finished the last handbowl and sat sipping their cocktails, Mara's hand slid down to Uffrin's lap, and her lips brushed his ear.

"Let's finish this drink and go back to bed," she whispered, pawing at him, milking his earlobe with her lips. Uffrin closed his eyes, his concentration shattering as her hands found their way inside his waistband and toyed with him. He pulled himself from his reverie long enough to signal the waiter, who flashed an indulgent smirk as they counted the wooden disks. Mara pulled her lips back from his ear while he paid, but her fingers continued their work, and once the waiter had collected the coins, she grabbed him by the beard and pulled him in for a deep, wet, boozy kiss. He had a fleeting worry at what the other customers would think, but he sank into the kiss, his hands finding ample places to caress and squeeze. They made out like teenagers in their dark corner amid the din of conversation and the soft notes of the harp.

Back at Mara's apartment, their clothes flew from their bodies, and they joined together once again, hands and lips and tongues eagerly exploring, caressing, stroking. When they were both worked up, and Uffrin felt ready to explode, Mara took the lead, pinning his arms above his head and covering his mouth with hot kisses. She slid her body back, raking her fingernails across his armpits and down to his chest, then reached between her legs to grab him and hold him firm. She did not sink down on him this time, however; she bent him backward and slid her backside against him, moving back and forth as he pressed against her soft, downy cheeks.

Her fingers moved back up his chest, gripping and pinching, twisting and flicking, until Uffrin's pleasure rose so fast he was powerless to stop it. Mara seemed to sense how close he was, and she eased forward onto his stomach. He just managed to hold himself together. She lowered her mouth to his and kissed him, softly this time, hunching her back as she scooted farther up. Her fingers found his throat, running up his chin, sliding across his cheek to rub his ears. He could feel her wet heat on his chest, smell her intoxicating scent, and he tried desperately to deepen the kiss, but she kept pulling back each time. At last, she stopped, brushing the backs of her knuckles across his cheek. She smiled down at him, then got up on all fours and turned around, lowering herself down, blocking out the light as she pressed herself onto his eager mouth.

He made love to her as she to him, lavishing kisses and licks and little nips all over, teasing and pushing each other to the limit, then back down. Uffrin's mind hovered in a delicate balance, wanting to please Mara, to hear her moans and stuttering breath as he plied her with tenderness and brute force. He lost himself in the ecstasy of her lips on him, the soft sweep of her tongue, her hums of pleasure vibrating into his core. As he felt his control crumbling, he gripped Mara's strong thighs and buried himself in her, responding to her hungry movements, chasing down the exact pressure and speed she needed and staying locked in, even as he overflowed into her gasping mouth. She bore down, quivering, flooding him as her moan rose to a desperate whine. She pulsed against him, slower and lighter each time, until, at last, she rolled over onto her side and collapsed on the bed, heaving for breath as her arm flopped onto his stomach.

They lay intertwined, covered in each other's scent, fingers tangled in each other's hair. They slept, and when Uffrin wasn't sleeping, he was staring at Mara's face in the light of the lamp neither of them had bothered to turn off. She looked so peaceful, so content, he didn't want to move his arm from beneath her, though it had fallen asleep and was tingling painfully. He extricated the arm, and she snuggled into him, resting her forehead under his chin, her breath warm on his chest. He drifted back to sleep, secure in her embrace, his heart filled with the certainty that nothing could ever keep them apart.

22

The sound reached her as a distant throb, like a headache half numbed by alcohol. As she stirred from her sleep, it sharpened into a noise like a great metal door grinding shut over and over again. Her heart sank as the piercing wail sent bolts of jagged panic through every bone in her body. It was the invasion alarm, which was sounded once a year at Midsummer as a test.

This was late autumn.

This was not a test.

"Uffrin, what's happening?" she mumbled. She knew perfectly well what was happening, but she wanted him to tell her it was just a drill. He shook his head, grim-faced, as he put his circlet on and closed his eyes. She found her circlet and put it on, and a black message filled her view:

Exploding hoverballs have damaged the dam, but it still holds. All handlers should meet at the aerie at half dawn and prepare for imminent deployment.

There was nothing behind the message, no Stream, just darkness. Tears soaked the hair on her face, and she looked at Uffrin, whose eyes were wet as well.

"I'm getting called up. I leave tomorrow morning." His face broke as he tore off his circlet, pocketed it, and wrapped Mara in his arms. She crushed herself against him, squeezing him with all her strength, as sobs wracked her body.

"It's not fair! It's not fair!" Uffrin wailed, and she clasped her hand around the back of his head as he rocked in her arms.

"Sshh…" She tried to will calm into him as she did with Cleo. "They're not here yet. The dam still holds. We're still safe."

"Safe?" Uffrin pulled back, his wet eyes glaring. "The only time I feel safe is in your arms, and now they're taking that away too!"

Mara grasped his face in her hands and pressed her forehead to his.

"Uffrin. Baby. No one can take that away from us."

"Didn't you get called up too?" His voice cracked, sundering Mara's heart in two, but she had to hold it together. She had to be strong—for Uffrin.

"I did. We'll just have to be careful, that's all. If we do our jobs, the armies can protect us, and we can be together again."

They held each other for a while longer, Mara offering little reassurances in between bouts of crying until her well of tears was spent, and she pulled back with a shuddering sigh. Uffrin's face had hardened, and the kiss she planted on his unmoving lips did nothing to soften it.

"Do you have a map?" he asked, his eyes suddenly burning.

"I…I'm sure I do…" She slipped from his arms and stepped over to her bookshelves, scanning until she found the beaten atlas her father had given her before he'd left for Gulham. Uffrin tore it from her hands and flipped through it madly, his face tense with concentration, until he stopped on a page, scanning with his index finger, which he pushed into the yellowed paper.

"Here, see this little blue dot?" He sat down on the bed, turning the book to face Mara. She saw it, the kind of little blob that indicated a small lake, of which there were thousands scattered across the Silver Hills. "This is Eagle Lake. My family went camping there when I was a kid. It's about three day's walk from Gulham at the bottom of a steep trail. Hardly anyone goes there."

"Okay, I don't see what—"

"This is where we'll meet if Kuppham falls. My mother told me to meet her there if the worst should happen." His voice trailed off, and he stared blankly out the window. "She...she knows things sometimes, things that haven't happened yet. I didn't take her seriously when she said it, but now I see it."

"Okay, Uffrin, if the city falls, we'll meet at Eagle Lake, of course." Mara repeated the words, but none of it seemed real. How was there a world outside of her and Uffrin, and why did it have to tear them apart?

"Study it, Mara!" Uffrin was almost shouting, his finger jabbing at the atlas. "Study these lines here," he said, his voice softening. "See these concentric ovals? Those show elevation, and—"

"I know how to read a fucking map, Uffrin!"

Silence filled the air after her shouted declaration. Mara's heart deflated, and Uffrin covered his face with his hands. Mara grabbed his hands away and kissed him. He acquiesced, his lips softening, and she felt his breath calming.

"I'm sorry, Mara. Of course, you do. Just...study it, okay? If you've never been there, it could be a little confusing, and with the Stream down, I'm not sure if we'll be able to message each other if things get bad."

"I will," she said softly. "And you think it will be safe there?"

Uffrin nodded slowly, then more vigorously. "I do. It's far enough away from any city. Even if the humans invade, they won't be venturing far from Valleys Road and certainly not that deep into the countryside. There are groups of Free Maer in the area, but they don't pose any threat, I don't think. With any luck, they might even help us out."

"Okay," she said in a small voice as the enormity of the situation shrouded her heart like a lead blanket. "If things go south, I'll meet you at Eagle Lake."

"I will be there, Mara. I don't care what happens, what the fucking humans do, I will find a way, and I will be there for you. Now let me tell you a little more about the lake."

The meeting at the aerie was packed with somber faces. The handler who'd been on duty the night before had thrown herself off the aerie staircase to her death, and the rocks were still stained with her blood. Her owl had been killed by one hoverball, and two more had made it through and exploded against the base of the dam, which had cracked a bit, but still held.

Sergeant Kay led the meeting, which was mercifully brief. Two handlers would be on duty that night, alternating with two others the following nights. The rest, including Mara, would be sent out on mission, each with a Shoza scout. Some would be positioned at the foot of the valley to scan the pass leading south, and the rest would be sent toward the front lines, near Mount Galantz. A contingent of the Maer army was preparing for the arrival of a horde of humans, who moved along the Plains Road and would make contact within three or four days. As Kay called out names for pass surveillance, Mara crossed her fingers, hoping to hear hers, but Kay stopped, then turned the page and announced the names for the front lines. Mara's was the second name called, and she clutched her hands together to quell the shaking that started immediately.

"You'll meet here at half-dawn on the nose with your birds in shadow cages." Kay's words were sharp, with none of the soothing demeanor she showed in the aerie. "You'll meet your scouts then, and you'll travel as a group to the pass, then split off to your deployment zones from there. You're responsible for your own bedroll, blankets, personal affairs, and any weapons you'd like to bring. Daggers and slings will be made available to all those who wish them. Food and water will be carried by the scouts, and you'll resupply in the pass as needed. Any questions?" She paused, making eye contact with each handler, and Mara's stomach clenched when Kay's eyes fell on her.

"Expect to be gone for several weeks at least, and quite possibly longer. This is a military operation—make no mistake. The security of Kuppham, and of all of Maerdom, depends on the work you and your birds do. You should prepare yourself for a long, dangerous deployment, and there's no guarantee you won't see combat action. If you have any affairs that need settling, any letters to write or goodbyes you want to say, you have the rest of today to do that. Mail to and from the field is always tricky, so you may or may not be able to communicate with your loved ones once you leave the city." She stopped, chewing on her lip, and Mara wondered who Kay would be leaving behind, what goodbyes she would need to say.

"Dismissed."

Mara drifted in a fog, dragging her leaden heart down the thousand stairs and into the city. Tears leaked from her eyes as she thought of the mission ahead: the cold wind, the hard stone, the gruesome skin-covered faces of the humans, the hatred burning in their eyes. She thought of Uffrin, alone and shivering in some distant valley, and Friend, trilling softly at Uffrin, trying to cheer him up. She clutched her hand to her chest to try to hold in the sobs, but there was no stopping them.

She pictured the figure she must cut to the passersby, crying and sobbing her way through the streets as if she were in a mourning parade. Maybe they didn't notice her, wrapped up in their own doom preparations, or perhaps they were sobbing too. She moved through the silent tunnel of her grief, heedless of the ghosts gliding along the periphery of her vision. Her tunnel led her back to her apartment, which was cold, stale, and bleak in the thin sunlight peeking through the clouds. Empty. No Uffrin.

She hit the tarpipe until her throat burned, then fell back onto the bed. Her eyes were too dry for tears, her stomach too knotted to eat, though it gnawed at her in a way that made her want to throw up. She must eat something, and maybe some tea would help. She stayed still for a while longer, struggling to move an inch from where she lay plastered to the bed. Then she thought of the tea Uffrin had brought, how he might be coming back from his meeting any minute. He would surely appreciate a cup of fortifying darkroot tea when he returned. It took her a little longer to peel herself from the mattress, but when she got upright and set the water boiling, she felt just a little bit better. She tried her circlet, but the Stream was completely down, without even any ominous black messages filling her view.

She sipped her tea at the table, not even bothering to open a book. She just stared at the wood, at her hands, at the steaming cup. The city sounded different today, less boisterous but busy, footsteps and wagon wheels moving just a bit faster than usual. When she finished her tea, she pulled out the atlas and studied the pages Uffrin had pointed out. In truth, she wasn't the best at reading maps, and it took her a while to get oriented. Once she did, she was pretty clear about the way from Gulham to the lake. She sketched the route on a piece of paper, writing directions in Ormaer, figuring no one who might try to steal her map would be able to read the languages of the Time Before.

She suddenly remembered that it was market day. Kaela would be expecting her. Kaela, whom she would be leaving behind to go on mission and who would be stuck in her group house as the humans rampaged through the city. She covered her mouth as tears formed anew in her eyes, and she turned the page in her sketchbook and started drawing another copy of the map. She wasn't sure if Kaela would be able to use it or how she would even get out of the city if the worst should happen, but it gave Mara something to do with her hands, and it distracted her for a few minutes. She didn't write the directions, though; she'd have to give those verbally and hope for the best.

She scribbled a quick note for Uffrin, saying she'd be back in a couple of hours. She had just set down her pencil when the bell rang, and she buzzed Uffrin up.

23

Mara wrapped Uffrin in a hug before he could even make it through the doorway. He held the bag of fish rolls awkwardly to the side as he pressed against her, breathing into her hair, arms clasped around her shoulders.

"Gods, Uffrin, I was just heading out to see my sister. It's—"

"Market day, I know. I was hoping to get back in time to join you. I found fish rolls in a stand near my work, and I bought them in case—well, I didn't know if all the vendors would be selling, but I just thought—"

Mara silenced him with a kiss, taking the bag from his hand, then she kissed him again and again. He had hoped to keep a sense of normalcy, but Mara's kisses were so soft, almost desperate, that he forgot everything he'd planned to say and do and lost himself in her lips.

"I love you, Uffrin," she said, and he felt wobbly on his knees, like he needed Mara's support to even stand. "I've been studying the map, and I made a copy so I can take one with me, and I—"

"You made a copy for your sister, of course. Perfect!" Uffrin paused, gripping her shoulders. He was nervous about his proposal, but Mara was family now, wasn't she? "Listen, I've been wondering... Do you think she'd like to come stay with my parents for a while? Maoti would love to have her, I'm sure of it, and Maofin too. I don't know if Paodo's going to be around much, and they could use the distraction."

"I'm sure I couldn't...I mean, that's really kind of you, but..."

"Then it's settled!" He'd formed the plan on the walk over, and he hadn't run anything by his parents yet, but how could they say no? As far as Mara had told him, her sister didn't have anyone else in the city, and he doubted the group homes would be able to stay staffed much longer. She'd probably end up in one of the unhoused camps, which were the last place you wanted a family member to be.

"You've really thought of everything," Mara said, setting the bag on the counter and peeking in. She stepped back to Uffrin and wrapped her arms around him again. She didn't kiss him this time, instead burying her face in his beard, moving her hands softly up and down his back. He held her, trying to quell the tears that threatened to burst forth. It was half-noon already, and the market might not be open all day.

"You think we should go ahead and..."

Mara nodded, stepping up to give him a peck on the lips, then placed the paper bag carefully in her shoulder bag, along with a waterskin. She breathed in deeply through her nose, then let it out, and a smile popped onto her face.

"Let's go to the market."

A Maer a few years younger than Mara stood in front of the group house, wearing a thick wool cloak with the hood up over her head. She watched them as they approached, the scowl on her face softening as she looked at Uffrin, then back to Mara, then back to Uffrin again.

"She's going to be so pissed I'm late," said Mara, leaning into Uffrin as she sped up her gait. "But she'll be excited to meet you. Kaela, my dear, so sorry I'm late! I hope you haven't been waiting out here this whole time?"

Kaela's eyes burned into Mara's, then darted toward Uffrin for a moment, her eyebrows raised in question.

"Kaela, this is Uffrin. My boyfriend." She squeezed his hand as she said it, and a little tingle of joy made its way to his heart. "Uffrin, this is Kaela. My sister."

"Nice to meet you, Kaela! I've heard so much about you!" Uffrin wasn't sure how to greet her, so he pressed his hands to his chest and gave a slight bow. Kaela's eyes sparkled with laughter as she repeated the gesture, and he could see the family resemblance. Mara had said Kaela didn't talk, but the intelligence behind her eyes was no less vivid for her silence.

"She's heard a thing or two about you, too," Mara said, kissing Uffrin on the cheek. "Come on, let's get to the market before they sell out of whatever little bit is left."

Mara filled the air with small talk as they walked, and the sun warmed the air enough for Uffrin to unbutton his coat. The market was busier than he'd ever seen it, with hundreds of Maer lining up at the relatively few stalls open. They didn't need any food since he'd brought the fish rolls, but they found a shortish line for honey-roasted nuts and hot apple cider, and Uffrin bought enough for everyone. They sat on a little stone wall by an empty fountain with a sludge of wet leaves in the bottom, which normally would have been cleaned out, one of the many ways the city showed its exhaustion.

Kaela took a bite of a fish roll and raised it in appreciation, smiling with little tufts of rice clinging to her lips. Mara raised a hand to wipe them off, but Kaela shouldered her away, wiping them off with her own hand and giving Mara a sulky shrug.

"Sorry," Mara said, touching Kaela lightly on the arm, and Kaela blinked acceptance of the touch. "So, Kaela, have you been studying your farming and fishing books?" Kaela nodded, chewing, her eyes moving from Mara to Uffrin and back. "I can't imagine what's so interesting about that, but I guess any reading is good reading."

"Oh, I love fishing," Uffrin offered, turning to Kaela, whose eyes lit up. "Paodo, that's my father, used to take me all the time, though, to be honest, he's just about the worst fisherman. I think he just likes to be away from all the talking all the time, which, I can't blame him for that." Kaela's smile showed she understood. "Do you fish often?" Kaela shook her head, and Mara burst out laughing.

"I don't think she's ever been, have you?" Kaela blinked no. "Well, maybe next spring, we can try our hand together. I expect the water's gotten too cold for much fishing by now."

Kaela studied her face with serious eyes. Mara's smile faltered a little, and she put a hand on Kaela's knee.

"So, I guess you heard the alarm last night. That was quite the rude awakening!" Kaela's gaze only grew more intense. Mara took Kaela's hand in hers and bit her lip, obviously fighting back tears. Uffrin put a hand on her back and rubbed in a slow circle. Kaela's eyes softened, taking on a pained expression, and she clutched Mara's shoulder with her free hand. Mara took a deep breath and sighed it out shakily.

"I guess it's time we talked about what's going on. I don't suppose they told you anything?" Kaela gave a little shake of her head. "The dam was hit with two explosions from what we call hoverballs. Human bombs, like little pink marbles floating through the air." Uffrin glanced around to make sure no one was listening; the information was supposed to be classified, and the official line was that the alarm was a precaution only, but no one was ever convinced by the Council's messaging. "I've been working with Cleo, along with the other handlers and their owls, to intercept these bombs before they get to the city. Until last night, we've been successful." She paused, leaning forward to press foreheads with Kaela, and Uffrin let his hand slide off her back so they could have their moment.

"Kaela, I have to go away for a while. They need me and Cleo to go down below the valley to keep the city safe." Kaela threw herself around Mara, gripping her tight. Uffrin's arms felt empty as he watched Mara rock her sister, then peel herself away and pull back, still holding onto Kaela's hands. "I don't know how long I'll be gone, and I'm not sure if the group house is the best place for you with all that's going on. What do you think about going to stay with Uffrin's parents for a little while, so you'll have someone to help you out, in case..." She paused, and Uffrin could hear the tremor creeping into her voice, see the hurt in Kaela's eyes as she glared at her, then over to Uffrin.

"Maoti and Maofin would love to have you. Paodo too," he said, wanting to hug Kaela and tell her it would be okay, even though he was pretty sure it wouldn't be. Kaela sat straight up and cocked her head, blinking at Uffrin as if she wanted him to say more. "They have a lot of books, and Paodo is a great cook. And Maoti has the loveliest garden." Kaela tapped his arm when he said 'Maoti,' and he glanced at Mara, who shrugged, then raised a finger and her eyebrows.

"You're not going to believe this, but Cloti is Uffrin's mother. Or one of them, anyway. You know who she is, right?"

Kaela's eyes lit up, and she nodded vigorously, then closed her eyes and pressed her hands together at her chest.

"You...you practice?" Mara asked incredulously. Kaela opened her eyes and showed a shy smile, putting her thumb and forefinger close together. "A little?" Kaela nodded again. "Did the group home take you to one of her sessions in the park?" Kaela blinked yes, then opened and closed her palms like a book. "You have one of Cloti's books?" Kaela closed her eyes again, forming a circle with her arms above her head, then lowered them slowly to her sides.

"Well, that settles it!" Uffrin touched Kaela lightly on the arm, and she didn't flinch. "You're coming to stay with my parents until this all blows over." She nodded, eyeing him warily, perhaps because of the last bit; she had to know this wasn't going to just blow over.

"But let's get down and check out the book stalls first, yeah?" Mara tapped Kaela on the knee. "We should get you a couple extra since I won't be around for a little while."

Kaela nodded somberly, then stood and brushed a few grains of rice from her cloak. She linked her arm with Mara's, and Uffrin linked Mara's other arm, and they made their way down to the book stalls, which were much busier than Uffrin had ever seen them. Something about the end of the world made people want to get lost in a book, he supposed. He looked for a portable map of some kind, but all he could find was a bulky atlas in worse shape than Mara's. He wasn't sure why he needed one, and his parents surely had several, but it was the only thing he could think of that might be useful. After flipping through the pages for a minute or two, he left it there. Someone else was sure to need it.

While he waited for Mara and Kaela to finish shopping, he wandered along the stalls, and a heart-shaped flash of gold caught his eye. He stopped at the stall, which was run by an older Maer who hardly looked up from her book as she sold him the trinket, a vintage heart pendant on an oxidized chain. It felt silly to give Mara such a trivial gift, but as he studied the heart, he pictured her pulling it out of her robe to run her fingers over it as she traveled and decided it was better than nothing.

"There you are, Uffie!"

Uffrin stuffed the necklace in his pocket as he turned toward Mara and Kaela, who were both carrying books. Mara had found a well-worn pocket-sized book of vintage erotica, and Kaela had picked out a book about birds, one about deer hunting, and a carpentry manual.

"Again with the random book picks," Mara said, examining them. Kaela flashed her a side-eye, and Mara put an arm around her shoulder. "No, I love your bookish omnivorousness! I just got another one of these naughty picture books. Not like I don't already have enough of them, but this one is pocket-sized." She slipped it into her pocket, and Kaela fished it out, flipping it open and turning away with an awkward glance toward Uffrin.

"You didn't find anything?" Mara asked him, wrapping an arm around his waist and pressing against him.

"Nothing I could take with me," he sighed. "Friend's case is heavy, and to be honest, I'm not that much of a reader."

"I'll find you something small for your trip. I have too many books in my apartment anyway."

Kaela turned back around, handing the book back to Mara with her eyes down.

"See anything you like? Ow!" Mara said as Kaela swatted her arm. "There's nothing wrong with liking sexy pictures, Kaela. I can get you a book if you want."

"If it's sexy books you want, you're going to love my parents' library. They have entire shelves of that stuff." Uffrin had spent many hours as a teenager drooling over those books while his parents were working or meditating or hosting their sex parties. In recent years, he'd mostly just used the Stream, but Mara's gift had piqued his interest again.

Kaela shook her head shyly and clutched her books to her chest.

"Well, I suppose we've embarrassed you enough for one day. Do you want to go back to your place and get a few things to take to Uffrin's parents' house?"

Kaela froze, tears welling in her eyes, then nodded. Mara pulled her in for a big hug, and Uffrin teared up as well. He didn't know much about Kaela, but he couldn't imagine it would be easy adjusting to a new environment, especially with all the uncertainty going on. He was sure his parents wouldn't mind, and Maofin would dote on Kaela nonstop.

"Come on then," Mara said, easing out from the hug and clutching Kaela's arm in hers. "Let's get you settled."

24

Mara stood arm in arm with Kaela at the ornate wooden door to Uffrin's parents' house, which was halfway up the North Bluffs, overlooking the river and the aerie. The brick exterior ended in the bluffs themselves, indicating a much larger dwelling within. A winding flagstone path led from the Bluff Road through a fading but well-maintained garden of flowers and shrubs. Mara had known Uffrin came from money, but this was beyond what she had imagined. Kaela stared up at the bronze knocker, which was shaped like a boar's head, and Mara gestured toward it.

"You want to do the honors?"

Kaela flashed a small smile, reached up, and rapped against the bronze plate on the door, sending a heavy thudding sound echoing through the garden. The door opened seconds later, and Uffrin smiled at them, ushering them in with a sweep of his hand. Mara stopped to give him a kiss, then followed Kaela, who had wandered into a large room with couches, chairs, bookshelves, and little tables throughout, big enough for a dozen people to lounge with drinks. Paintings adorned the walls, some abstract, some more realistic, mostly nudes, though in a very different style from the ones in her books. They were beautifully sensual without being explicit.

"Those are Maofin's, mostly, except for that one." Uffrin pointed to an abstract painting of a circle filled with dozens of smaller circles, arranged in such a way that she grew dizzy looking at it. "That's a Suji if you can believe it. A gift from some minister, I believe, when Paodo first made ambassador." Mara nodded, though she had no idea who or what Suji was. Kaela stood staring at the painting, making little tap-tap-tap motions with her finger as if she were popping all the little circles like bubbles.

"There are two hundred sixteen," said a Maer dressed in a collared suit that billowed around her as she walked through a doorway. "You must be Kaela. I'm Aefin." She stopped, pressed her hands together at her chest, and bowed, looking at no one else in the room. Kaela repeated the gesture, then looked back up at the painting. "It's a sacred number in the religions from the Time Before. It has a certain pleasing symmetry, don't you find?"

Kaela nodded, then glanced around at the other paintings, then back to Aefin.

"Yes, those are mine, most of them anyway. Except the Suji, which you saw, and those two above the couch are by a Free Maer artist named Iulreg who does these fabulous deconstructed traditional designs." She had her hand on Kaela's arm as she spoke, and Kaela had not stopped smiling since she'd entered the room.

"And you must be Mara," she said, turning toward her and bowing. "Cloti's very fond of you, and Uffrin told us all about you. It would be our pleasure to give Kaela a change of scenery for a little while until you come back from your trip."

"I...I don't know what to say, I—"

"No need to say a thing. Kaela can stay here as long as she likes, and if it doesn't work out, she can go back to her group home."

Kaela shook her head, drifting closer to Aefin, eyeing Mara hopefully.

"Thank you," Mara said. "I think it will be good for her."

"And for my parents, too," Uffrin said, putting his chin on Aefin's shoulder. "They get a little stir-crazy without any guests, and it's not exactly party season."

"You're not wrong about that," Aefin said, reaching back to pry his chin from her shoulder. "Why don't I show you to the guest room, and we'll get you settled in."

The room was sumptuous, bigger than Mara's apartment, with an armchair, a desk, a full-sized bed, paintings on the wall, a full bookshelf with several bronze sculptures on it, and a real bathroom with a hot water shower. And this was just the guest room.

"I know it's a little stuffy, but you get good afternoon light through the window. And sometimes green fly-eaters perch on that ledge."

Kaela peered out the window, then looked around the room, her eyes wide and incredulous. She turned to Mara, a questioning look in her eyes, and Mara blinked her approval. Kaela smiled and threw her arms around Aefin, who held her tight, patting her lightly on the shoulder.

"I'm glad you like it." Aefin pulled away from the hug and gestured toward the bookshelf. "I see you brought some books, and there's a bit of a variety here—mostly longstories and heartstories, a little history, some nature books, maybe a couple of art books as well. There are a lot more in the library, which I can show you later if you like."

Mara smiled as she watched Kaela's reaction to Aefin. The manager at her group home seemed nice enough, but she'd never gotten the impression Kaela particularly liked it there. She wondered about all the other Maer living at the home, those without connections. What would happen to them if things went all the way south? What would have happened to Kaela if Mara hadn't met Uffrin. Her heart wrenched at the thought, and the images of the skin-faced humans crowded her mind, tearing down doors bearing swords of cold steel, Kaela throwing up her hands, defenseless. She shut her eyes and tried to block out the images, but they kept encroaching, even when she opened her eyes again and saw Kaela's irrepressible smile.

A strange lightness crept into her heart then, a feeling of emptiness, of peace. The humans' faces dissolved into nothingness, their cries, the clash of metal dying out like whispers in the wind. Aefin kept talking, and Uffrin and Kaela kept listening, but Mara turned away, drawn by the source of the calm growing inside her. Her eyes fell on Cloti, standing at the base of the stairwell, a wistful gleam in her eye, her face full of kindness. Cloti blinked, and Mara felt the greeting in an almost physical way. She blinked back, and as Cloti's eyes shifted away from hers toward Aefin and Kaela, Mara caught her breath. The feeling faded, but she was calmer now, less full of dread.

"Welcome, Kaela." Cloti took Kaela's hands in hers and bowed low to her until her forehead touched Kaela's knuckles. "Thank you, Mara, for trusting us. I consider you and your sister family."

Mara blinked away tears, suddenly filled with the sense that it was true somehow, that this woman she barely knew was connected to her and her sister and Uffrin in ways beyond the present time. The moment passed as Cloti turned back toward Kaela, but the sensation of belonging lingered like the aftertaste of sweet mushroom wine.

They stayed for an early dinner, a simple affair of beans and rice with pickled greens, served with a delicious dry wine. Aefin drove the conversation, keeping the topics light. She asked many questions of Kaela especially, seeming to intuit her responses, and Mara was flooded with guilt at not spending more time with her sister. She typically saw her only once a week, on market day, and now she wondered how Kaela spent the rest of her days. Her work as a laundress had shut down a few weeks before, and though the home had various activities for the residents, Kaela had never seemed very interested when asked about them. Given the growing cold and the physical disabilities of some of the residents, she wondered if they were still taking walks in the park, one of the few things Kaela had shown some enthusiasm about. Surely she had friends in the home, but when asked, she'd always shrug. It had to be a lonely life, and Mara should have been there for her more. Aefin had only just met her, and already Kaela seemed happier than Mara had seen her in years. She hid her tears, smiling and laughing along with Uffrin at Cloti's stories of when he was little until dinner was finished and Aefin cleared the table and started washing up in the kitchen.

Cloti's smile faded into a sort of resigned calm as they sat, silent, around the empty table. She eyed each of them in turn, and Mara was briefly soothed as Cloti's gaze fell on her. Everything would be okay in the end, Cloti seemed to say with her eyes, despite the pain suffered along the way. She was stirred from the moment by Uffrin, who broke the silence.

"Maoti, can we talk about the lake?"

Cloti blinked slowly, and Mara fingered the copies she'd made from her atlas.

"Of course, dear. You've told Mara, I assume?" Uffrin nodded, gripping Mara's hand. She pulled the folded papers from her pocket, handing one to Uffrin and sliding the other across the table to Kaela, who pulled it closer, studying it intensely.

"I made these copies from my atlas." Mara watched Cloti, who smiled softly at the drawing, furrowing her brow as she studied the coded directions.

"You've studied the language from the Time Before."

"I'm not an expert or anything, but I like the poetry, and I figured—"

"You did well. No human would be able to figure out what this is, and very few Maer either. Kaela, this is a map to a place called Eagle Lake, though it's more of a pond, really. It's in the Free Maer territory, several days east of Gulham, which I believe is that little star?" She glanced up at Mara, who nodded. "You know the humans are coming," she said to Kaela, who nodded, glancing up at Mara, stirring a twang of regret in Mara's heart. Of course, she knew. "We still hope for an end to hostilities, and Ludo is working very hard to make that happen, which is why he's not here now. But they are coming, one way or another, one day or the next. The only question is where we will be when they get here. I will be leaving soon on a mission to the South."

"Maoti—" Uffrin's voice raised almost into a squeak, but she silenced him with a gently raised finger.

"My fate is not in question, love. I must do what I can for the Time to Come, as must we all."

"Fuck the Time to Come!" Uffrin's voice cracked, and he clutched his mother's hand, even as she maintained her placid smile. Mara glanced at Kaela through the haze of her own tears and saw her sister's eyes blazing bright into Cloti's.

"Our time is almost over, whether we want it to be or not, but it will give birth to another and another. The Time to Come begins with you. It begins here." She stabbed the paper with her finger, right on the spot where Mara had drawn the lake.

"You speak with such certainty of things you can't possibly know, Maoti." Uffrin's voice was raised in anger, but Cloti's countenance remained unchanged as she looked up at him. His face fell as he released a stuttering sigh. Cloti tented her fingers and stared down into them for a moment.

"We don't have time to talk metaphysics, unfortunately. I want to make sure everyone knows where to meet if we can no longer stay in Kuppham. Mara, if you're going to the southern front, you might not be able to get there via Kuppham. You'd have to go around here." She pointed to a blank space on the edge of the map. "It's Free Maer territory, and while I wouldn't expect any trouble, you'd want to remember that you're a visitor in their land. We've got maps, which I'll get in a moment, that can show you the way. Ludo is the expert, but I can tell you it's not going to be an easy trip. I hope your boots are in good shape."

Mara glanced down at her boots, which were scuffed and weathered but had plenty of life left in them.

"Thanks for the heads up! I'm sure I can manage. I've always been a strong hiker."

"Stronger than Uffrin, I should wager. No offense, dear," she added when Uffrin's face raised with offense. "But you're both young and out and about all the time, working, walking. You'll be fine. Kaela, we might need to build up your walking stamina. It's a long walk to Eagle Lake, a week at least. I could stand to do a bit more walking myself, as my trip will take me in the opposite direction."

"Where are you going, Maoti?" Uffrin asked in a low voice.

She shook her head. "It's something only I can know about. It's for the Time to Come. That's all I can tell you." Uffrin rolled his eyes a bit before closing them and nodding.

Mara redrew the map once Cloti brought her atlas, showing the approach from the east, which would take her past the ridges leading down from the Great Tooth. The legends said scale dragons lived on that mountain, which filled Mara with dread. Though there were no scale dragons anywhere near the Maer cities, there were said to be some in the Free Maer territories. Some Free Maer were even said to commune with dragons, control them, and even ride them. She hoped if she did run across a dragon, there would be someone to control it.

When Aefin returned from washing up, she brought a steaming pot of tea and poured it into thick glass teacups with wooden handles and elaborate floral designs etched into the glass.

"I expect you'll have to go soon to get your things ready and to make love before your trip," Cloti said, handing Mara and Uffrin teacups. Mara's ears burned, but she couldn't repress her smile as Uffrin gasped and threw his hands in the air. "I am happy for you to have such a special time together in such urgent circumstances, which often help forge the strongest bonds. You'll need them to be strong for what is to come. That is what will carry you through to the other side."

Mara's mind spun—was she really hearing this from her boyfriend's mother? She squeezed Uffrin's hand tight, and he squeezed hers back, comfort flowing through the warmth and strength of his grasp.

"I was hoping you'd agree to a short cycle together before you go. After our tea, of course." Cloti spoke in a quiet voice, which immediately smoothed the surface of Mara's mind. She looked to Uffrin, hoping he'd agree; he'd said he didn't practice, but surely he would honor his mother in this. Uffrin closed his eyes, lightening his grip on Mara's hand, then nodded.

"Of course, Maoti. It's been far too long."

Cloti's eyes shone, and she took another sip of her tea. They didn't speak much as they sipped, and Mara felt herself sliding into the meditative space long before Cloti narrowed her eyes and formed her hands into a circle at the center of her chest. Mara did the same, as did the others, and she felt an immediate connection from the strength of Cloti's energy in this intimate setting.

This was more than just meditation; it was magic, powerful and deep, beyond anything she'd ever achieved in her training. She felt a nudge, and the intrusive thoughts drifted beyond her mind's horizons, repelled by the almost magnetic tension of the five of them moving their arms slowly skyward at the same time. Mara felt the gloom lift from her heart, up through her arms, and escape through her fingertips, replaced by a pure, hopeful light rising from deep, forgotten places within her. This energy kept cycling upward, flowing out into the air and then falling like snow.

As their arms moved through the simple routine, Mara felt the wonder in Kaela's heart, Uffrin's grudging acceptance of his mother's practice, Aefin's deep love and commitment to Cloti, and her protective instincts over them all. From Cloti, she felt only her own energy reflected back, but stronger somehow, more resilient. As it settled down inside her, its roots laced tightly throughout the soil of her mind, holding it all in place against the ravages of weather and time.

When Cloti's hands released their final circle, Mara slipped back into herself as one waking from a nap, slightly confused about the world she'd re-entered, whether or not it was the real one. Kaela breathed a humming sigh and rested her chin on her hands, and Uffrin turned to Mara, squeezing her fingers, his eyes bright but calm now.

"Thank you, Cloti, for sharing with us," Mara said with a slight bow. "I will carry your practice with me in my travels."

"Then I will always be with you, in a way." She cupped Uffrin's cheek with one hand as she took Aefin's hand in the other. "With all of you."

25

U ffrin followed Mara up the stairs, past her apartment, and up onto the roof of her hightop. It was colder up there, the wind slashing in through the gaps in his coat. She pointed toward a roost attached to the side of a chimney, and Uffrin could just make out the white face of an owl peeking through the opening.

"Cleo's a little shy," Mara said, "but she's always hungry. I'm going to try to will some calm into her. Just stand there, and don't move until I say so."

She put on her circlet and reached out a hand toward the owl, which stuck its head out, and its body followed. She held up a little mesh bag, and the bird leapt from the perch and flapped over on silent wings, landing on the railing next to Mara. She held the bag up and lowered her other hand, and the owl seemed to shrink, settling its wings down its back.

"Come on," she said, gesturing to Uffrin. He took a step closer, and she handed him the little bag, which he could now see contained a dead mouse. "One step closer, nice and slow, and hold the bag out in front of her, a little higher than her beak." He did as he was told, and the owl's head swiveled toward him, its golden eyes fierce and piercing, staring through him. In a flash, the bag was snatched from his hand, and the owl dropped it and tore it open with its claws. Within seconds, it had seized the mouse in its beak, turned its head skyward, and swallowed it in two quick gulps.

"You see, Cleo? Uffrin's one of the good ones." Cleo ruffled her feathers and sank back down again. "You should go hunt now. Get a good stretch in, girl. We're going on a big trip tomorrow, and you're going to be spending a lot of time in your box."

"I bet she hates that." Uffrin thought of Friend, wondering for the first time if his machine might be awake in the box on this trip now that it had taken control of its own on-off switch.

"She doesn't like it, but at least she feels safe there. I can feel that through the circlet."

"How come mine doesn't do that?" he joked, pulling it out of his pocket and putting it on his head for a moment, just in case. The circlet was operational, but the Stream was still completely down. He briefly wondered if it would ever come up again and if he would ever know what happened to all the friends he'd made on there. They *were* friends, some of them closer than many of the Maer he knew in real life.

"I've been trying to work on keeping in touch with Cleo even with my circlet off, but it's a lot harder, and the connection's never half as strong."

"I wonder how the Free Maer do it," Uffrin mused; mages of some of their tribes were said to commune with or even control animals.

"If I meet some, I'll be sure to ask them." She bent down, lowering her face to Cleo's level, and the bird pecked at her nose softly. "You go on now, girl. Go catch yourself something warm and furry to eat." Cleo turned away, spread her wings, and flapped off in eerie silence.

Mara slipped her arm around Uffrin's waist, pressing her body into his. "And we need to get in out of this cold and see if we can't find a way to keep each other warm."

Mara's eyes were different as she slowly removed his clothes, shining with a softer hunger than before. Uffrin's body responded to her eyes, which she kept locked on his as she fondled him gently with both hands. Her lips parted and angled up toward his, and he took her face in his hands and kissed her—softly at first, then harder as her mouth seemed to pull him in, inviting him to explore and taste her. He was never one to take the lead when it came to kissing or sex, but the deft touch of her fingers and the subtle flicks of her tongue left him no choice. He fell headlong into the kiss, and Mara's little gasps and groans drew him further out of his shell. His hands moved down her body, hefting her breasts through her robe, sliding down along the curve of her hips, running up and down her thick, powerful thighs. He gripped the bottom of her robe with both hands and wrestled it up, breaking the kiss for long enough to pull it over her head and toss it into the corner, where it knocked over something on a shelf.

He kissed her more softly now, feeling her desire in the cadence of her breath and the angle of her hips toward him. He slid his hands down her back and cupped her soft behind, kneading, pulling her body tight to his, keeping her now frantic tongue at bay as he slowed the kiss even further. She fell into the new rhythm, her hands roaming gently over his body.

He slid one hand across her hip and down between her legs, and her kiss faltered as his fingers found her, tracing delicate lines up and down her wet folds. He deepened the kiss for a moment, increasing the pressure of his fingers, then pulled back suddenly, savoring the hot surprise in Mara's eyes as he dropped to his knees, gripped her hips, and buried his face in her. If this was to be their last night together, he needed all of her, and he needed it now.

He teased her with his tongue, using only light pressure as he explored her, circling around and around, heedless of her growing whines and her straining movements to direct him to where she wanted him to go. He pulled back for a moment, looking up into her eyes, whose stark desperation pulled a cord tight within him. He sank into her again, licking her hard and fast now, gripping her behind as her hands held his head tight to her. His tongue found its target and hammered her relentlessly, and she roiled against him, her moans rising to a series of high-pitched shouts. Her fingernails dug into his scalp as she pulsed against his mouth, and he clamped down and held on for dear life until her shouts descended to softer and softer moans, and she gently pulled his head away.

He stood up, took her by the shoulders, and kissed her as he walked her slowly backward toward the bed. A spark flashed in her hot, dark eyes as they reached the edge of the bed, and he pushed her down a little more roughly than he intended.

"Yes, Uffrin, yes!" she hissed, and he threw himself upon her, kissing and squeezing and pressing against her. She lifted her legs up and wrapped them around him, clamping down with soft power as he throbbed against her wetness. "I need you inside me," she said between sloppy kisses. "Fuck me into the Time to Come!"

Uffrin pushed himself up on one forearm, reached down, and guided himself halfway inside her, closing his eyes and clenching his jaw at the lush heat threatening to pull him over the edge. He paused, staring down at Mara's eyes, which shone in the darkness. His heart filled with sparkling energy, settling his body down just enough. He lowered his mouth for a kiss, keeping their bodies apart for a moment, then sank down into her as their lips clashed.

Uffrin started out slow, savoring their closeness, the gentle blooming of pleasure on every nerve. When she angled up into him, he lightened the pressure, heedless of her whines and groans. She wanted this, wanted him, *needed* him like no one ever had before. He took his time, hammering in with a few quick thrusts, then moving in softer waves, pressing down on her as her thighs threatened to crush his hips.

"Uffrin, please," she whispered, touching his face and sliding her fingers around his neck.

He stopped moving, grabbed her hands, and threw them above her head, pinning her biceps to the bed as an unforeseen heat scorched through him. Her eyes grew wide, and he lost himself in their depths as his body moved of its own accord, driving faster and faster against hers. Her gasping breaths showed she was growing close, but not quite enough. He released one of her arms and maneuvered his thumb down to wiggle against her as he bore down harder and harder.

Her whines took on a more urgent tone, triggering the final onslaught in his body. He fought through the pain and fatigue in his back and legs until his own shouts merged with Mara's. His brain flooded with ecstasy, and he braced against Mara, gasping for breath as his pleasure flowed through him like a river swollen with spring rain. Her eyes and mouth shot wide as she clenched and shuddered against him, then she slowly unwound, lightening the pressure around him. Her eyes slitted, and her mouth softened, finding his, kissing him as her hands moved over the sweat-soaked hair on his face and neck.

Uffrin half-slept, snuggled tight in Mara's warmth, comforted by her scent, the rhythm of her breathing, the shadow of her hip in the moonlight. When the middle-morn chime sounded, he unglued himself from her, shivering in the cool air of the apartment, whose heat had not yet been turned on. He dressed in the dark, making as little noise as possible. When he came out of the water closet, the lamp was on, and Mara was standing in front of the counter naked, making tea. Her smile cracked Uffrin's heart, and he moved to her slowly, wrapping his arms around her, growing aroused despite the tears threatening to burst forth.

Mara buried her face in his beard, her breath hot on his neck. Neither of them spoke. They held each other until the kettle whistled, and Mara angled up for a quick, soft kiss, then turned to pour the tea. Uffrin gazed at her curves, setting them in his memory, as this would be the last time he'd see or touch her for a very long while.

As much as despair plied him with its hooked fingers, something Maoti had said stuck with him, shining a small light from deep inside.

The Time to Come begins with you. It begins here.

She'd pointed to the map, to Eagle Lake, and the liquid certainty in her eyes was hard to shake. When he was a kid, she'd told him stories about visiting the Time to Come, but he'd never thought of them as anything more until now.

Mara handed him his cup, and she leaned back against the counter, blowing on her tea, giving Uffrin another chance to fix her in his memory: her shape, the warmth of her smile, the knowing glint in her eyes.

"I don't mean to be reductive, but Mara, you are the most beautiful Maer I've ever met. You are a goddess." His tears spilled over as he quavered the last words. Mara set down her cup and moved the two steps it took to wrap herself around him, her eyes going soft and wet before closing as she angled in for a kiss. Uffrin's teacup hand wavered as his lips met hers, and they kissed, gently, for a long moment. Mara pulled back from the kiss, touching Uffrin lightly on the chest, then let out a little giggle as she looked down and saw him tenting his pants.

"I like how you like me," she said, running her finger along his stomach and pushing his erection down for a moment. She let go and turned to pick up her tea, staring at him as she took a sip. Studying him.

"What's wrong?" Uffrin touched his beard, his hair. "Is there something—"

"You look adorable." She waved him off. "I'm just...I want to keep looking at you so I remember you better."

They stood, drinking their tea and looking at each other, until Uffrin's internal clock told him he needed to get moving. He set down his cup carefully so it didn't make a sound. He had a ways to go to get to his apartment, pick up his pack, then go retrieve Friend and meet Erliss at the gate at half dawn. He was already cutting it close.

"Mara, I have to..." She nodded, biting her lip, and set down her cup. Uffrin pulled the necklace out of his pocket and held it in his closed hand. "I...I got you something. It's stupid, but I just thought..."

Mara peeled open his fingers, putting her hand on her chest as she lifted the chain, and the brass heart dangled between them.

"It's not stupid, Uffrin. It's impossibly sweet, just like you. I'll wear it always." Her voice hitched with tears as she attached it around her neck.

"I have to—"

"I know." She studied the heart, then turned her soft eyes up to Uffrin. "Be careful out there, Uffie," she said, her face wet with fresh tears. "Keep Friend safe, you hear?"

His laugh hiccupped through his tear-choked throat. "I'll tell him if he gets us through safe, he'll get to meet a very special owl named Cleo who will teach him all her owl-y ways."

Mara stepped to him, gripped his collar, and kissed him, pressing hard and holding him in place for several moments. Their lips stuck together as they pulled apart, as if even their skin were fighting this unjust separation. Uffrin touched her cheek, shouldered his bag, and turned toward the door.

Mara pulled on his elbow, then slipped a coin into his palm. Uffrin chuckled as he saw that it was one of Cloti's meditation coins.

"For good luck."

Uffrin tossed the coin in his palm, then slid it into his pocket.

"I'll see you at Eagle Lake."

26

Mara trudged across the already-busy city, lugging Cleo's box on her back. It wasn't so much heavy as cumbersome, and she had to remind herself not to jostle it overly, though her new suspension harness did help keep the box more stable. She'd coaxed the bird into the box without using her circlet, and she could tell she'd made some kind of connection since Cleo hadn't so much as pecked at the door the entire trip. Mara tried to project calm into the bird. Even through the wooden box, it felt like some of that had made its way through.

A half-dozen handlers were scattered in the plaza beneath the aerie with their birds in boxes: owls, falcons, and even one vulture. A group of gray-clad Shoza scouts stood in a tight circle, talking quietly amongst themselves. Leasse walked over to Mara and gave a little wave.

"Leasse? They pulled you too?" Mara asked. "I didn't hear your name called."

"I got subbed in. Can't say I mind, really. Everyone's so tense here all the time. And with Ulver's cough coming in with the soldiers from the front..." Leasse shook her head, and Mara's lips pinched together in acknowledgment. Soldiers back from the front had been asked to quarantine in camps by the river because of the influx of the disease. "Might as well get out there for some fresh air, peace, and quiet." Mara smiled; she'd been so focused on getting Kaela squared away and on Uffrin that she'd forgotten how much she missed the truly open spaces.

"You got pass or southern front?" she asked.

"Front." Leasse shook her head. "Which is why I brought this." She slid her hand to her side and pulled out a sword about as long as an arm. Mara recoiled a little, and Leasse lowered it back into its sheath.

"Sorry, I just...it makes me feel safer."

"You know how to use it?"

Leasse shrugged. "I got some training. Enough to give me a chance, anyway."

"Let's hope it never comes to that. I'll be headed to the front as well, it seems. Not exactly the kind of work I'm suited for, but one does what one must for one's people." Leasse didn't seem like the scary patriotic type, but Mara had learned to speak softly on political topics.

"One does."

Sergeant Kay called out the names of the handlers and the Shoza, who walked directly to their assigned partners without having to ask who was who.

"Gielle," said a Maer with tight muscles and tighter braids, wearing two short swords on her belt and carrying a heavy pack, bow, and quiver on her broad shoulders.

"Mara, nice to meet you." Mara's hand felt soft and weak in Gielle's firm grip.

"You're the one who caught the popper and spotted the other. I feel lucky to be working with you."

Once all the pairings had been made, Sergeant Kay gave another little pep talk about how the security of all of Maerdom depended on their work, how the dangers were very real, and how they needed to prepare for extended deployment in difficult conditions. Gielle shook her head as the speech went on, and Mara stifled a giggle.

Soon they were led through the big bronze door to the lower staircase, and they descended through the shadowy stairs, lit only by the gray light filtering in through the slats facing the valley below. They walked past several groups of guards sleeping on the landings and another group at the bottom, fully armed and ready as if heading into battle. The three bronze doors were unlocked one at a time, then they emerged into the mist from the falls above and the roar of water rushing between the rocks, which they could hear to their left but not see because of the mist.

They followed a narrow path with rope guides leading along the edge of the river, which quickly calmed as the terrain leveled out. The path moved through a thin pine forest, the ground littered with coppery needles and dotted with the occasional fern or mossy log. Mara knew every inch of the terrain, having scoured it with Cleo dozens of times looking for hoverballs. A chill wind poured through the valley, softening as it widened into the denser forest area.

Mara kept an eye out in the trees for birds, smiling when she noticed a butterside wren picking at the bark of a tree. It cocked its little head at her, then flitted off into the canopy, oblivious to the coming destruction. The path here was sloppy, with half-decomposed pine needles and mud in places, testing the fitness of her boots, which fortunately showed their quality. Several of the handlers walked barefoot, following naturist traditions common among the Free Maer and among Cloti's acolytes.

She wondered if she ended up traveling the long way around to this mythical Eagle Lake Uffrin and Cloti seemed so sure about, how long her boots would last, and what she would do when they wore out. Would she be able to get another pair?

If the humans reached Kuppham, would they destroy the city or merely occupy it? Would commerce and industry continue? Would schools? Would it be a place worth going back to or a ruin? It was impossible to conceive of, this city where she'd lived most of her life, the center of all Maer civilization and culture, falling into the monstrous skin-covered hands of the humans. If that was the future the Maer had in store, the fabled Time to Come was going to be a long time coming.

They made it to the forest edge, where two scouts saluted them from their posts along the perimeter. The valley stretching below was mostly grazeland for herds of goats and stenbuffel, tufted with groves of meager trees and scrub brush. A few farms dotted the landscape, but the soil was better suited for grazing than farming, so it was only sparsely populated.

"This terrain is a nightmare for surveillance," Gielle said, speaking for the first time since they'd left Kuppham. "It's no wonder they keep getting their mages through."

Mara nodded. It would be easy for an individual or small group to move through the landscape unnoticed, darting from copse to copse, as the mages controlling the hoverballs presumably had. She wondered if they used magical means to conceal themselves as well; human mages were said to be very versatile, and their magic had a power that exceeded anything the hand channelers could produce.

"You think it'll be easier near the front?"

Gielle shook her head. "There, we'll be in rocky mountains, so there are not many places they can hide. But there's a lot of territory to cover, so many ridges and valleys, making it like five times the amount of land pushed together."

"Not to mention the fact that we'll be, you know, right by where the fighting is happening." Mara's throat grew dry, and she uncorked her waterskin and took a careful sip.

"It's not the army you have to worry about. You can hear them coming miles away—plenty of time to find a hideout. It's the scouts like me who they'll send out to hunt down Maer like you."

"Not the kind of reassurance I was looking for just this moment," Mara snapped, only half playfully.

"Sorry, but look, I'm the best there is, plain and simple." Gielle braced her hands on her hips, spreading her broad chest wide. "No skinfucker's going to get the jump on me."

"Well, even if they do, I've got this." Mara pulled out her knife, which she had only the most limited training in using. It felt light in her hand, slim but deadly sharp. She could imagine it sinking deep into flesh with a good solid jab.

"I'll make sure it doesn't come to that," Gielle said with a gentle smile.

They camped in a copse that had lean-tos and piles of rushes for sleeping, used by defense patrols as they traveled through. The handlers let their birds out one at a time, as they could be cranky when first emerging from their boxes. Mara noticed most of the handlers using their circlets, but she could feel Cleo faintly through the box, and she kept hers in her pocket. She'd need to use it for surveillance, of course, but she thought it would do her and Cleo some good to work on communicating without it. The circlet's chip wouldn't last forever, and in case things went all the way south, she wanted to have a fall-back plan. When she opened the door, the owl hopped right onto her glove and stared at her intently. Mara lost herself in the fractured gleam of those golden eyes, and their connection seemed to intensify for a moment. Cleo pecked her in the beard, moving one claw toward her pocket.

"Go ahead then," Mara said, and Cleo fished out the mouse with her claw, then took it in her beak and gulped it down with a few spasming movements. "There you go. Got some water here for you too." She held her glove toward a bowl of water sitting atop the box, and Cleo hopped off, studied her new surroundings for a few moments, and had a long drink.

"Go catch yourself something tasty. You're off duty tonight."

Half the group split off in the morning to posts in various parts of the valley, some with hawks, most with owls, and one vulture, whose cage had to be pulled in a small cart. The handler was a tall Maer with a round belly and a deep, rumbling laugh. Mara had met him once at a training and thought he had dating potential, but she hadn't run across him since. She hoped he made it through okay.

The group, now half its former size, continued south down the pass as it narrowed again, heading for the Rugged Mountains, the last before the South. They were greeted by periodic patrols along the way, and whenever Mara saw a hawk or vulture soaring above, she wondered if it was one of theirs. It took three days to reach the half-reconstructed ruins of Three Cliffs Fort, which she had always imagined being much higher up. It was perched atop a hundred-foot-tall butte with three sheer sides, rendering it nearly impregnable if not for its crumbling walls.

Since peace with the South had reigned for hundreds of years, the fort had been abandoned and fallen into disrepair. She could see why they'd decided to re-occupy it, given its position of power. The pass was narrow here, with the old road crumbling into the riverbed in spots, rendering wagon travel painstaking and dangerous. If the humans attacked from this direction, it would be slow, bloody going.

They camped among several hundred soldiers who had set up semi-permanent tents lining the valley wall. Gielle went to talk with the other Shoza after dinner, and Leasse sidled over to squat by the dwindling cooking fire. There was hardly enough wood to make tea, let alone keep them warm, but the idea of the fire, the comfort it brought to Mara's heart, was almost as important as whatever heat it provided. She toyed with her locket, holding it up so the red coals of the fire reflected on its golden surface. She popped it open and studied the random Maer whose face adorned the heart-shaped interior. Uffrin was an idiot, but he was a well-meaning idiot, and she missed him so much she struggled to draw a full breath.

"Got a special friend back in Kuppham?" Leasse said with a sly lilt in her voice.

"Very special." Mara hummed a little as she thought of Uffrin's eyes, how soft they got when she angled in to kiss him.

"They got a name?"

"Uffrin." The name sounded funny now that she thought of it, and she giggled a little.

"He's lucky to have you, that's for sure."

"Gods, he so is. Can I just tell you?" Mara shook her head, covering her smile. "How bout you?"

Leasse huffed a small laugh. "Not like that," she said. "but I have friends who mean the world to me." Leasse closed her eyes for a moment.

"Oh, sorry, I—"

"It's fine. So what's he like?"

Mara closed the locket again and tucked it inside her robe. She stared into the embers for a moment.

"He's awkward and timid but so eager, you know?"

"He sounds like a dish." Leasse shouldered her, and Mara's smile felt like it would split her face.

Uffrin visited her in her dreams, eager but so, so patient, seeking only to give her pleasure over and over, leaving her gasping for breath but ever hungry for more. She dared not touch herself, given the close quarters, so she slept fitfully, haunted by these visions, daring to hope they might one day come to pass.

They walked for three more days, into a wider valley that spread out to the east. A substantial contingent of soldiers was stationed around another crumbling, long-abandoned fort, with scattershot posts dotting the landscape like pegs on a Siege gameboard. The group was stopped well short of the army camp by a dozen fully armed soldiers, whose apparent leader wore the gray cloak of the Shoza. He stepped forward and spoke in a quiet but commanding voice.

"We're glad you've arrived. We need an accurate count of the human forces, and we've already caught a few of their spies and assassins. We've also lost a few good Maer to their blades as well. They slip in at night and wreak havoc, and they always seem to know who the leaders are, which means they've been watching us." He glanced around at the ridges on either side of the valley and ahead to where it continued between two mountains. "Wherever they are, they could be watching us right now. Which means we are all targets. Your job is to find them and warn us."

He conferred with the Shoza for a few minutes, gesturing here and there, then they returned to the group. One of them explained that they'd be split up in various places and given individual duties, as well as long, thin whistles whose sound could carry for several miles in open terrain. Mara and Gielle were stationed at the base of the north ridge, which was perhaps slightly better because it was farther from the actual front itself. On the downside, it was the area most likely to have scouts and assassins creeping through it.

"You got the north ridge?" Leasse asked, studying the terrain behind Mara.

"Yeah. Where are you?"

"South ridge, just behind the scattershot line. I'll be making sure they aren't moving any advanced units in overnight. Sounds like the humans are camped less than a day away." She clenched her jaw, staring out past the scattershots to where the pass led out onto the plains of the South, toward the human army. "Fuck, I can't believe this is actually happening. I just keep thinking it's not real—it can't be real. I mean, a week ago, I was eating tri-fries and drinking darkroot with my mom, and now this?" Her voice quavered, and she sniffed.

Mara reached out and took her hand, which lay limp for a moment, then gripped hers back.

"Look, I don't know about you, but I'm getting out of this alive, one way or another." Mara felt her resolve hardening with every word. "If the humans break through the line, I figure there won't be much need for any owls down here. Once that happens, I'm not sticking around to wait for the skinfuckers. I'm headed north to meet Uffrin."

"What about your Shoza? Won't they, you know, make you stay?"

"She can try, but I bet she'll have bigger things to worry about. And besides, who says she wants to stick around if the worst comes to pass? Will there even be a Shoza after all of this goes down?"

"Fuck, I never even thought of that."

"Come with me." Mara squeezed Leasse's hand. "If things go bad, we should stick together. Meet me..." She looked around for inspiration. "Meet me at the fort. We can beat the humans if they're coming this way and warn the fort. I don't see anyone stopping us."

"They might press us back into service." Leasse's voice dropped at the end as her Shoza returned.

"Remember what I said." Mara gave Leasse's hand one more squeeze, then rejoined Gielle, who waited just off to the side, studying a map, which she then folded up into a neat square and snapped inside a slim leather case.

"How's our spot looking?" Mara asked timidly.

"Like a fucking nightmare," Gielle said with a hard smile. "But don't worry. I've got your back."

Mara tried to feel reassured as they walked toward the shadowy ridge rising to the north.

27

Uffrin sat staring at the coin Mara had given him, running his thumb over the raised pattern of the eye, then flipping it and caressing the other side, which was perfectly smooth, like a mirror. He tilted it so he could see the fire reflected in its shining copper surface. He turned it back over, staring at the eye, trying to remember the meditation pattern that was supposed to go with it. Maoti had given him one when she'd first had them made, and he'd carried it around in his pocket for a while, but it was now sitting in a drawer back in his apartment, which he wondered if he'd ever see again.

If the humans took Kuppham, would they move into the hightops? Uffrin tried to picture a human picking through his belongings, opening his drawer, flipping the coin over a few times in their hairless fingers, then tossing it back in. He imagined them sliding open the box containing his now disassembled mechanical owl, fingering the little feathers and tools. Would they try to assemble it or perhaps give it to their children? There wasn't much in his apartment he'd miss, but his eyes grew misty as he thought of that box. He should have brought it, though it was bulky and would have been an encumbrance.

Of course, he had Friend, but he'd avoided bringing him out of his case too often, not wanting to use up his hotiron power source. He supposed it might be possible, even if Kuppham fell, to acquire hotiron from the Timon. That would require a long journey to the east, and rumors told of large groups of Timon fleeing to the south after the attacks on their mines. He couldn't blame them; the humans were said to have killed hundreds of Timon, civilians as well as soldiers, in those attacks. Despite their relative lack of sophistication compared to the Maer, the humans seemed to have a singleminded desire for destruction. The murderous resourcefulness and ingenuity they'd shown left Uffrin's heart chilled with despair.

"Is that one of your mother's tokens?" Erliss asked, lowering themself to sit cross-legged beside Uffrin.

"It is, but she didn't give it to me. Mara did."

"Does she practice?"

Uffrin nodded, eyeing Erliss, whose face showed nothing more than calm and curiosity. The way they'd phrased it—*Does she practice?*—was exactly how a practitioner would say it.

"I don't think she's been at it very long, but she seems to have taken to it. I kind of wish I'd spent more time with it myself, but with Cloti being my mother and all..."

Erliss chuckled. "I can imagine." They glanced around at the fires of the other handlers and their scouts, which were spaced out, according to what apparently were new Shoza guidelines after a hoverball attack on a camp had killed a dozen in one explosion. They looked down at the coin and held out their hand.

"Do you practice?" Uffrin asked as he let the coin drop into Erliss' hand. His stomach clenched as he spoke since Cloti's practice was frowned upon in official circles, but Erliss' nod soothed his worry.

"I can't go to any sessions or follow on the Stream, but I do, in private." They turned the coin over and seemed to study the eye. "If you'd asked me on our last trip, I wouldn't have answered truthfully, but I'm done worrying now. And I don't mind telling you that most Shoza practice in their own way. I could teach you what I know if you want."

How could that be? How could members of the very organization that persecuted Uffrin's mother and suppressed her speech follow her teachings in secret?

"I'd be game to try once we get to our post." Uffrin stared down at the coin, thinking of the peace on Mara's face as they'd done the cycle with Maoti. "We're going to need something to keep our minds off the chaos."

"Or the boredom, most likely." Erliss poked the fire with a stick. "We're probably going to be asked to hole up in one spot and not move for weeks at a time. I'm not even supposed to hunt. I'm just supposed to guard you. So, it looks like sporecakes for the duration unless I can kill something to make jerky from on the way. But with so many soldiers and handlers and scouts moving through, there's not likely to be anything left to catch."

"Gods, I don't know if my stomach is going to survive that." Uffrin paused, glancing at his case. "Unless..."

"You think your owl could catch game?"

"It has hunting patterns built in, so in theory, sure! I've never actually tried it, and I don't know if it's the best use of his power source, but maybe if he was already out on surveillance and just happened to see something on the way back..." Erliss cocked their head, and Uffrin paused.

"You said *it* at first, then *his*, and *he*."

"I did? Oh, I guess I did. It's just...you know, the longer you work with a machine, the more you tend to project a personality onto it." Erliss glanced over at the case, then fixed Uffrin with a curious stare that suggested they might not have bought his brush-off.

"Have you come up with a name for him yet?"

Uffrin laughed, thinking of Mara's reaction to the name. "I just call him Friend."

"Well, if he catches us something nice to eat, he'll have earned his name."

When the fire died to embers, Uffrin lay down on his bedroll and snuggled tight in his sleeping bag, which kept the cold at bay. He ached for the warmth of Mara's body, the soft comfort of spooning her. His heart felt empty without the pressure of her body against his, no matter how tightly he wrapped his arms around his shoulders.

As he lay there struggling to find a comfortable position to sleep, other thoughts crept into his mind, ones not easily dismissed: the hot spark in Mara's eyes when she'd looked down at him, tied to the bed and helpless against the power of her will, the wet fire of her kisses, the unstoppable strength of her thighs. He tasted her in his mouth, felt her lips on his body, her fingers caressing every inch of him, toying with him, teasing him, then sending him straight to the moon with a flurry of sudden movements. He pressed his eyes shut in a vain effort to quell the flood of desire. A trickle of tears filtered through, wetting the hair on his face, which suddenly felt the chill of the mountain air.

He wondered if she were lying by a fire in some distant valley, thinking of him, of the things they'd done together and the things they would do when they finally met again. He drifted in and out of sleep, conjuring new permeations of their lovemaking, mixing memory with fantasy. Though it wasn't the best night of sleep he'd ever had, it was far from the worst.

Erliss kept them clear of the returning soldiers, many of whom had the barking cough he'd just started to hear in Kuppham before he left. Ulver's cough was a vicious flu that could lay a Maer out for weeks at a time and even killed some, especially those not in great health to begin with. The soldiers, living in rough battlefield conditions, were especially vulnerable, and Erliss found a spot to camp well away from the main group whenever there were soldiers about. By the time they reached Giant's Pass, it was harder and harder to avoid the soldiers, but Erliss let Uffrin hang out at the valley's edge while they went into camp to get their orders, covering their face with a scarf.

Uffrin did a mental count of the automatons and was pretty sure there had been more the last time he was here. He wondered if they'd been destroyed by the hoverballs or if they'd been deployed elsewhere. When Erliss returned, their face was grim, and they closed their eyes and sighed before they spoke.

"The humans are massing in the Archive Valley, and we're being sent to the ridge just to the east of it to do surveillance."

Uffrin's stomach dropped. "You mean we'll be sent out in front of the army?"

"We could have Friend scope out our path for us to make sure we don't run into any of their scouts along the way. A couple of the other handlers are being sent into the hills to the west and the rest to Burrows Valley and beyond."

Erliss had also brought back a sack of supplies. Much to Uffrin's surprise and delight, a box of tea was included, along with too many sporecakes and too little jerky, nuts, and dried fruit. He reached in to grab a dried apricot, but Erliss swatted his hand away.

"Don't touch anything from the camp until tomorrow. Trust me, you don't want to catch Ulver's cough."

Uffrin pulled his hand back, shaking it, though it didn't hurt. Erliss had been lightning-quick but gentle. Their hand moved so fast that Uffrin hadn't registered it until it had swatted him. He had heard some Shoza had enhanced training that included bodily arts magic. If Erliss did, it made Uffrin feel a tiny bit safer around them.

They moved on quickly, as it was already afternoon, and they had only a few hours to travel before night fell. They made it just to the edge of the Maer-occupied zone, where rows of scattershot towers filled the valley, with encampments of soldiers at the base of each. A dozen or so automatons were spaced evenly behind the scattershot fields. They set up camp well clear of the scattershot and any soldiers. Erliss went in to converse with the Maer at one of the towers, and when they returned, they eyed the case.

"Looks like there's been a slight change of plans. Friend gets his first job tonight. They just lost an owl to an exploding hoverball, and their coverage is spread thin. They want Friend to scope the western valley wall, from the top of the ridge to the ground, looking for hoverballs and spies alike."

"That's a lot of ground to cover." Uffrin gazed out at the hill, dark purple in the growing dusk, veined with little ridges and crevices ideal for passing unseen.

"Would you rather hike ahead of the army to the Archive Valley, where the humans are massing their forces?"

Uffrin smiled and nodded. "Fair point. How do we want to approach this, then?"

"Start with the part closest to us to make sure there's no one lurking in there waiting to take us out, then work your way out and up from there. I promise to keep you safe while you guide Friend."

Uffrin's heart warmed a few degrees at the sincerity of Erliss' promise, though he doubted even one as skilled as they could guarantee anything in a circumstance like this.

"And I'll make sure Friend keeps us both safe and the rest of Maerdom as well." Uffrin snort-laughed, and Erliss even cracked a smile.

A low trill sounded from the case. Uffrin's gaze shifted to Erliss, who stared at the case intently, with a kind of pleasant curiosity in their eyes.

"Sorry, the new orbus is a little dodgy sometimes. Just turns on and off for no reason." Uffrin turned to open the case so Erliss wouldn't read the deception on his face. He was pretty sure he was a terrible liar.

"Seems he turned on when we started saying his name." Erliss squatted by Uffrin as he opened the case, and Friend's shining yellow eyes flitted from one of them to the other. He hopped toward Uffrin, who held out his nose, and Friend obliged him with a peck and a headbutt.

"Good to see you too, Friend." Uffrin chucked Friend under the chin, and the owl nipped his fingers gently with his beak. "You remember Erliss, right?" He wondered if Friend did remember, how aware he'd been on their last trip. He gestured toward his partner, who stuck out their hand, knuckles forward. Friend hopped over in front of Erliss' hand, then swiveled his head back to Uffrin, blinking and emitting a little purr. "Yes, they're here to protect us. You can trust them." Friend looked up into Erliss' eyes, which were wide and bright with fascination, then lowered his head and butted it against Erliss' knuckles.

"Thank you, Friend, for helping us." Erliss turned to Uffrin. "Can Friend really understand us?"

Friend trilled at Erliss, staring hard into their eyes, then settled down again, swiveling his head toward Uffrin and blinking.

"I'm sure he understands more than we think."

***

Uffrin guided Friend through the pattern Erliss had suggested, arcing out from their campsite and up the valley wall in a rainbow pattern, hopefully clearing each area and looping back fast enough to prevent any incursion between sweeps. Within a couple of passes, Friend began turning before Uffrin had signaled him to, and before long, Uffrin let go of control entirely to focus on scanning Friend's field of vision. It was tricky terrain, with all the little folds and wrinkles of the land, but through Friend's eyes, it was almost like daylight, though with an odd sepia tone. Friend's mechanicals were all operating smoothly, and he seemed to be turning just a bit more efficiently than usual. Friend had bucked the pattern or changed it somehow.

Uffrin returned his focus to the ground below, and it wasn't until Friend had flown another ten seconds farther across the ridge that he realized he'd seen something. It had taken his brain a little while to put the pieces together, but the shape of a rocky shadow stuck in his mind. A hundred yards further, the image came clear: it was the shape of a crouched figure, moving ever so slightly.

He nudged Friend to circle far enough away that it wouldn't be obvious if the spy was watching, then loop back around for another look. On the second pass, he saw movement, and the figure took off, sprinting along a jagged path down toward where Uffrin and Erliss were sitting. He broke his concentration for a moment while Friend circled back around.

"Erliss! Spy, headed our way. A couple hundred yards up, I think."

Erliss nodded, silently unsheathing their swords. They crept toward the nearest outcropping and disappeared into the shadows. Uffrin wondered if Friend would be able to find them if need be, if their skills were equal to or better than the humans.

Uffrin flew the owl down to hide in the branches of a pine tree close to the bottom of the ridge, where they grew sporadically. He'd guessed the direction the spy would be coming from based on the path they'd been following. He knew they could have headed straight downhill, off the path, but that would likely kick up some debris and ruin the chance of surprise they thought they had. He smiled as they came into view, moving low to the ground like Erliss with the same soft, deliberate footsteps. They paused, studying the terrain, and took a sharp turn straight downhill, circumventing the rock Erliss had hidden behind. The spy would still have to cover a fair amount of ground in the open, but if Erliss wasn't expecting it or was in the wrong position, it could spell disaster.

Uffrin pulled out of the owl's view for a moment and shook his head to focus his eyes. He couldn't see much in the darkness other than the vague shapes of a few nearby trees. Certainly not enough to spot a trained spy moving with stealth down the hill. He shifted back into the owl's vision, wincing at the sudden brightness of the view until his vision settled in. Friend must have flown to another tree, one with a direct line of sight to the spy, who was moving quickly toward the bottom of the ridge no more than a hundred yards from their camp. There wasn't much to make out except for a gray cloak and sword, as well as what looked like a crossbow strapped to their back. It could just as easily have been a Shoza, except for the skin on their hands.

Uffrin hoped the angle of the tent would make it hard for them to shoot at him with the crossbow and that Erliss would realize what had happened in time to do something about it. He fingered the hilt of his dagger, stomach roiling. He wondered if he'd have the nerve to use it if the human burst into the tent.

As the figure reached the bottom, they sprinted from tree to tree, stopping for a moment behind each one to peek out ahead, then continuing their jagged progress toward the camp. Friend flapped out of a tree and powered up into the air, surprising Uffrin, who slipped back into control mode for a moment, giving Friend a light touch, a reminder. He could not tell if Friend had understood his gesture, but he no longer felt like he had the right to command Friend to do anything. If Friend was flying up high, it must be to dive, though he couldn't see why Friend would think it was a good idea to—

Uffrin's mind froze as Friend powered down into a dive, knifing through the air toward the spy as they burst past the last tree before the camp and bolted across the open space. The owl swooped low, extending his talons, and Uffrin could sense every movement as it was happening, but he did not try to exert control. The spy whirled, drawing their sword just as Friend's talons were about to make contact. Uffrin seized with his mind, trying to pull Friend out of the dive at the last second. As they struggled for control, a blur of shadow and metal surged forth and plowed right into the spy, who crumpled with a wheezing cry.

Friend crashed to the ground hard, bouncing several times before coming to rest against the edge of the tent, the view showing only the canvas. Uffrin was thrust violently from the owl's view. He sat up, gasping for breath, and tore the circlet from his head. He was dizzy, disoriented, and sweating, but he suddenly remembered there was something—yes, the spy! He pulled his dagger and stood on wobbly legs to peek around the edge of the tent.

There wasn't much light from the moonless sky above, but it was enough to see Erliss crouched over a lifeless body, wiping their blades on the spy's clothes. Uffrin sheathed his dagger and stumbled out, turning to see Friend sprawled against the edge of the tent, one wing sticking out at an unnatural angle. A trail of white silk feathers showed where he had crashed, bounced, and rolled to a stop.

"Oh, Friend, my gods—" Uffrin stopped as a coo sounded, and Friend struggled to right himself. "Let me help you." Uffrin lifted him gently by the torso, supporting the damaged wing with one hand as he stood Friend up. Friend blinked at him and gave a quiet trill that sounded surprisingly cheery.

"Is he okay?" Erliss crouched next to him, staring at Friend with real concern in their eyes.

"He's going to be just fine as soon as I get enough light to re-set his shoulder." He moved it a little and could feel where the ball joint had popped through, probably tearing the bracket in the process. He had the tools and replacement parts to fix it, though he would miss having a proper table to work on. He supposed he could just use the case as a table.

"Well, on the bright side, there's one less human spy to worry about. If you can't fix him tonight, you might as well catch up on some sleep, as I imagine things will only get more interesting from here."

Uffrin cradled Friend in his hands, leaning his nose in to rub against Friend's beak. The peck he got in response broke his face into a smile and jerked a tear or two out of his eyes.

"You rest now, Friend. We'll get you all patched up in the morning, and then you can go play hero again tomorrow night. How's that sound?"

Friend's trill vibrated straight through to Uffrin's heart.

28

Mara held her meditation coin flat in her palm. She circled the edges of the eye with her vision in five slow cycles, then did the same with the iris, letting her mind tickle over the fine ridges there as if she could feel them on her fingers. When she reached the center, she narrowed her focus, and the edges of her vision grew dark. The sound of clanging weapons in the distance set her heart racing, distracting her for a moment. She could tell from the cadence it was just the sparring they did every day, filling the valley with tinny, discordant music. She re-focused by circling the outer and inner rim, then sank again into the void of the center, which took on an emptiness that pulled her slowly in.

She closed her eyes, and her mind held onto that emptiness, which carried her aloft like a dandelion seed in the breeze. She floated, weightless, buoyed by a soft swell from beneath her, and the void began to take on texture like unseen clouds. She passed through the clouds to a velvety darkness interspersed with coppery threads twisting and coiling all around her, extending into the infinite void, connecting her, though with what, she could not have said. She soon got lost in their twists and curls, and the connection snapped like a thin thread. Sensations came rushing back in: drops of icy rain pattering on her face, the breeze lifting the edge of her hood.

When she opened her eyes, she saw Gielle watching her from a distance, sharpening her sword. Gielle quickly turned away when Mara looked at her, but not before Mara saw a spark of fascination on her face. Though Cloti's practice was not illegal, her treatises on human and Maer commonality were regularly censored from the Stream. Mara was sure the Shoza were forbidden from practicing. She wondered if that stopped them or if there were some who did so in private.

"You still have time to catch a nap." Gielle glared at the sky, which spat intermittent icy raindrops and snow but didn't seem inclined to make up its mind one way or another. "It's going to be a long night, I'm sure."

"Long nights are nothing new to me, but a nap does sound like a good idea. I'll give it a try." She returned to the tent, which Gielle had covered with brush to make it harder to spot from a distance, and slipped into her sleeping bag. Cleo emitted a little trill from her box. Mara considered letting her out but decided the owl needed the rest too. Cleo trilled a couple more times, then went silent. Mara dozed lightly between visions of Uffrin's face, his soft eyes, and his kissable little mouth, which mostly kept thoughts of the horrid, skin-covered human hordes at bay.

Gielle walked the lower reaches of the ridge before dark and returned with a grim expression.

"There's no one here now, but I saw footprints that were too long and thin to be Maer. There are spies about, and I bet they'll try to come down over the ridge once night falls."

Mara bit her lip, trying to quell the shaking that crept into her fingers.

"Hey, don't worry; I've got your back." Gielle lay a gentle hand on her shoulder, and Mara could feel the restrained strength of her grip, which was a small comfort. "No one's getting anywhere close to you. But you want to circle back to this area often, just to be safe. There are a thousand little places to hide."

Mara nodded, putting her hand on top of Gielle's. "I'm scared," she said. "I know you're here, and Cleo is as sharp as they come, but..." She gestured vaguely at the lines of scattershot towers in the distance and at the mountains all around. "I just can't believe it's come to this."

Gielle blinked, squeezing her shoulder for a moment, then stood, scanning the ridge top in the growing dusk.

"We can't control anything but what happens on this ridge right here. We have to do our part and trust the others to do theirs. Inhabit what is before you and let go of what is beyond your reach."

Mara gave a start at the words, which she remembered from one of Cloti's texts. The Shoza were the very ones who enforced the ban on Cloti's practice, so why did Gielle know her words?

"Right," she said, pulling her bracer tight before opening the box. Cleo hopped right up onto her arm and began clawing at her pocket before Mara had stood all the way up.

"Don't be so grabby." Mara pulled her arm away a little, and Cleo straightened up, looking her in the eye and blinking. Mara blinked back, softening her eyes, and she might have been imagining it, but it seemed like the owl's gaze cooled slightly. Mara moved her arm closer again and let Cleo pull the mouse from her pocket and gulp-gulp it down. She put on her circlet and locked eyes with Cleo, creating the shared space and moving into it more quickly and fluidly than usual. She turned and pointed toward the ridge, running her finger in zigzags through the air as she pushed forth the image of flying across the terrain. She'd spent time earlier practicing so she could better present it to Cleo. She chucked Cleo under the beak and got the commensurate peck in response, and Cleo ruffled her wings a little, as she did when she was getting ready to take off. Mara held her arm wide and gave it a little shake.

"Go find us some bad guys."

Cleo seemed to have understood Mara's desires. She flew slow arcs across the lower part of the ridge, requiring little direction, then began working her way up, methodically swooping over each outcropping and crevice. At one point, she started to dive on a tree rat, but she pulled herself out of it before Mara even had time to correct her. When she reached the top of the ridge, Cleo did a wide circle to scan the other side. When she wheeled back around, she saw them: hundreds of tiny pink lights streaming into the pass toward the scattershot field. She called Cleo back, then slipped out of owl view and fumbled for her message pad. She figured they'd already heard from the owls on the other side of the valley but quickly wrote a note to the central command post:

100s of poppers incoming.

Gielle hovered, reading the note over her shoulder.

"It's begun."

Mara shook her head, struggling to calm her trembling fingers to roll up the note for transference. She had just gotten it rolled tight when Cleo fluttered down to land on her bracer. She slipped it into the band and put her nose out toward Cleo, who was breathing heavily, her eyes bright and alive with the action.

"Fly like a tornado is chasing you."

She guided Cleo to the command post, which was situated just behind the scattershot field. The transfer went smoothly, and soon Cleo was flapping across the valley floor. Mara slipped out of view and nodded to Gielle.

"She got them the message."

Gielle squinted into the distance, where Mara could now see a faint glow from beyond the scattershot field.

"I doubt it's going to make much difference if it's hundreds like you said."

A bright pink flash lit up the valley, and the boom of the explosion hit a half-second later. Another flash, another boom, and Mara could see debris flying from a scattershot tower in that instant of intense light. Another, and another, and another, their booms echoing and overlapping as the sky lit up like a thunderstorm. Soon the entire valley was a giant fireworks show, with flames raging from the struck towers, which slumped to the ground as debris rained down all around. The sound was deafening, and Mara gave a start when Gielle grabbed her shoulder and twisted her around.

"We have to start moving north fast," she shouted over the cacophony of the explosions. "That's the only way to keep you safe. And we need to send word to the fort."

Mara nodded, her heart seizing with panic. Cleo fluttered down onto her bracer and gave Mara a slow blink. Mara blinked right back, leaning in for a peck on the nose, which settled her a little. She whipped out her pad and held her pencil above it, eyeing Gielle.

"Just tell them the attack has begun and the scattershots have been destroyed." She looked back at the field, where the pace of the explosions had slowed, replaced by the din of shouts and screams. Mara scribbled the note, clenching her jaw to keep her hand from shaking, and tucked it into Cleo's band. The fort should be within the range of her circlet, though it might be a little dicey toward the end. She pulled out the last mouse, holding it just out of reach of the attentive bird.

"You ready to fly?"

Cleo spread her wings wide, then tucked them halfway, eyeing the mouse. Mara moved it in front of her mouth, and Cleo snatched it up and gulped it down.

"Make sure there's no one waiting for us along the way, yeah?"

Cleo clacked her beak, then sprang from her arm and powered off into the darkness.

Mara maintained a low-level connection with Cleo while trying to keep up with Gielle, who moved ahead and to her right, scanning the ridge as she went. Mara could barely see well enough not to trip over the rocks littering the valley floor. She couldn't imagine how Gielle would be able to spot a spy, but the scout's vigilance was a little reassuring. She wondered about Leasse, who'd been stationed on the other side of the valley, closer to the fighting. She might well have sent her owl back to the fort as well, assuming she hadn't been caught up in whatever was happening. They'd moved around the bend in the valley, and she heard only indistinct sounds, which could have been a battle or just general commotion following the explosions. She hoped Leasse's scout saw things the same way Gielle did; it was easy to imagine her being kept there to keep tabs on the movement of troops and the fighting, assuming that's what was happening.

And Uffrin. Poor Uffrin, alone with his scout gods knew where along the northern front. As much as he'd played off his fear during his last trip, he was bound to be terrified. She imagined him watching a series of explosions like the ones she'd seen, the liquid terror in his eyes, the shriveling of his resolve. She wished she could hold him and keep him safe somehow, wrap her cloak around him, and hide away from the skinfucker hordes, tucked into some cave or crevice, clinging to each other amid the chaos of war breaking all around them. She forced a deep breath in and let it out slowly, then another, until she had completed a cycle of five, and her breathing steadied. Cloti's words rang out in her mind, spoken in Gielle's voice:

Inhabit what is before you and let go of what is beyond your reach.

She brought her mind back to owl view, following Cleo as she flew like an arrow toward the fort. Cleo remembered the terrain, and the connection was still strong, so Mara focused on her breathing and her walking and soon fell back into the rhythm of Gielle's steps.

Cleo reached the fort in about an hour. Mara guided her to the makeshift aerie, which she'd been shown when they'd camped below. The connection remained steady, and Mara watched as the handler fed Cleo and removed the note. They passed it to another figure, who shouted something, and further voices echoed the shout. Another note was affixed to Cleo as she drank from a bowl of water the watcher provided, then Mara nudged the bird off the perch and back toward her.

She released the view since Cleo knew her way back without her and signaled to Gielle.

"Cleo's delivered the message, and she'll be back with their response in an hour or so. Then we'll need to rest."

Gielle nodded, pursing her lips, then turned to study the terrain to their right, which consisted of a series of small hills.

"If we hurry, we can make it to the cliffs ahead." Gielle pointed, but Mara saw only darkness. "It'll give us better cover than these hills, where any number of humans could be lurking, though I haven't seen or heard anything."

"Maybe they're all back in the valley," Mara said hopefully, though when she pictured Leasse and the other handlers in the midst of such chaos, her heart sank.

"Not all of them, if they're anything like us." Gielle chewed her lip thoughtfully. "But we're a lot safer here than back there. Let's get to those cliffs and hunker down before Cleo gets back."

Mara trudged on through the darkness, trying not to focus on the indistinct shadows of the hills to their right or the unseen skin-covered faces of the human spies watching and biding their time.

29

Uffrin decided not to use the field lab, given the spread of Ulver's cough, but he sorely missed the bright lights and big tables. His travel tool set was decent enough, but there was no replacement for a cleanly arranged wall full of cogs, tools, and spare parts. He spread his tools and the parts he thought he would need on a flat rock covered with a black workcloth and strapped on his examiner's cap with a headlamp and flip-down lenses. Friend's eyes popped open as Uffrin set him on the cloth. The bird stared at Uffrin for a moment, then looked down at the array of bronze parts laid out before him.

"We're going to fix you right up. You did so good last night, they want us to go off to where the real action is at. How does that sound?"

Friend's trill was high and strong, a brave little sound, Uffrin thought.

"I'm going to open your rear cage to see what's going on with your shoulder. I'll have to turn you off unless you'd rather do it."

Friend put one bronze talon on Uffrin's hand, blinking slowly. Uffrin shook his head, wiping an unexpected tear from his eye.

"Right then. Just turn around, yes, that's it, and now..." He triple-tapped his gauntlet, and Friend powered down with a soft mechanical whine. He unscrewed the shoulder access panel, then donned his goggles, vest, and gloves. There shouldn't be any leaks, as the power source and orbus were heavily shielded, but hotiron was not to be messed with. He lifted off the panel, which got stuck for a second because the cage had been bent during the crash, and everything in that area was just a little skewed. He studied it for a moment, angling his light to see the damage from different angles. He could straighten the cage all right; they were designed to be flexible and able to be re-shaped without too much fuss. Just as he'd thought, the shoulder ball and socket had ripped free of the bracket, which wasn't built to withstand the kind of blow it had sustained.

He had the spare bracket he needed and all the right tools. He picked up a pair of pliers and set to work on the cage. He had to reposition a couple of braces that had bent, but he was able to get everything back into position. It should be sturdy enough to take the force of flight and landing, but there was no way to reinforce it against another potential crash.

"Might want to keep an eye on the clock." Erliss eyed a bank of purple-rimmed white clouds rolling in on both sides of the Great Tooth. "That's a whole mess of snow heading our way."

Uffrin took a deep breath, then switched tools and started unscrewing the bracket. He worked methodically and as quickly as he could, given the gloves. He had to pause at one point to retrieve a tiny screw that had fallen down inside the mechanism, but he was able to tweeze it off of the lifter casing it had landed on. The new bracket went in without a hitch, and he fitted and adjusted the ball joint, spritzed it with a little lube, and carefully wiped off the excess. The first snowflakes drifted into the cage, and he quickly bolted the shoulder cover back on and triple-tapped his gauntlet.

Friend gave a soft hoot, then spread his wings slowly. He extended them fully and tucked them in again, where they snuggled neatly down his back. He blinked and trilled at Uffrin, who stuck out his fist for a headbutt.

"Just like I told you. I wish we had time to touch up your feathers since you lost some in your fall, but..." He held out his hand, and a fat snowflake hit his glove, lingering for a moment before melting. "You think you can manage another flight or two with what feathers you have?" Friend narrowed his eyes at Uffrin, then whipped his wings wide again, his eyes now blazing and fierce.

Snow had begun to fall in earnest as they left the camp, skirting around the groups of soldiers clustered here and there between the dozen or so automatons remaining. Uffrin kept his scarf over his mouth and held his breath each time one of the soldiers coughed. It wasn't until they were clear of the camp and past the frightening rows of scattershot towers that he felt like he could breathe again.

The snow was troubling, as it was wet and heavy. Friend could fly in powdery snow or even rain, but wet snow and freezing rain each posed challenges, as they tended to adhere to the feathers a bit and could weigh the bird down considerably. They couldn't afford another crash, so Uffrin kept Friend in his case as they walked. Besides, it wasn't like he'd be able to see much in this snow. It wasn't technically winter yet, but this storm looked ready to pack a serious punch.

Erliss found them an overhang behind a big rock that protected them from the worst of the storm, which thankfully didn't come with a lot of wind. The temperature had dropped, and the air was heavy with the wet chill of the snow. They couldn't have built a fire in the wet even if they didn't need to stay hidden. Uffrin set up his sleeping bag against his pack so he could recline and possibly nap but still watch the opening. At the rate the snow was falling, anyone who knew where they were could get to within ten feet before he'd have any idea they were there. Maybe Erliss, with their training, could detect someone a little earlier, but there was nothing to do but hope the weather would deter their would-be assassins. If the rumors were true, the humans dealt with cold and snow worse than the Maer, which helped ease his mind just a bit.

He must have dozed. When he awoke, the snow outside was twice as high as it had been when he'd first sat down. It would now be up past his ankles if he were walking in it. It was getting harder and harder to imagine a group of humans moving through this mess. He closed his eyes again, pulling his feet in closer to his chest, as the chill of the stone had crept in and left his toes clammy and cold. Erliss glanced over, looking tired and haggard in the dim light reflected from the snow. They crouched with a blanket over their shoulders, but their feet had to be cold, and they must have been exhausted. Uffrin had calculated that Erliss was getting no more than four hours of sleep a day. They were usually on watch at night while Uffrin was flying with Friend and when Uffrin slept as well. Uffrin did short watches on and off while Erliss napped, but they hadn't had a solid block of sleep since Kuppham.

"I don't imagine the humans would come after us in this," Uffrin said.

"I think we're safe for a little while."

"Do you want to..." Uffrin lifted the corner of his sleeping bag. "It'll be warmer if we share blankets."

Erliss glanced over at Uffrin, then out at the driving snow. They turned back to Uffrin, blinked their agreement, then scooted over and nestled in next to him, wrapping and tucking their blanket to create a space of common warmth. Uffrin leaned into Erliss, glad of another body, and he felt himself growing drowsy, his head drooping down onto Erliss'.

"It's okay if you need to nod off, too," Uffrin mumbled. "I think we're safe for now, and if the humans come to gut us in our sleep, at least we'll be warm."

Erliss gave a single chuckle, then their frame relaxed a bit into Uffrin, whose toes were already beginning to thaw. His head grew heavy with the warmth, and he fell asleep to the muffled patter of falling snow.

Uffrin awoke to a bright sun reflecting off the snow, which lay a foot or deeper in the pass. Erliss stood at the edge of the overhang, staring into the distance through their field scope. They lowered it and turned to Uffrin, blinking hard.

"I can't see much with the glare of the snow, but you'd best send Friend out to see what's what."

"Okay," Uffrin mumbled, stretching against his pack to unkink his back, which had been stuck in the same position for however long he'd slept. "Maybe this snow buys us a little more time."

Erliss' expression showed they did not share his assessment, but they said nothing, turning again and raising the scope to their eye.

Once he'd relieved himself and had a bite of sporecake, Uffrin opened the case and saw Friend's bright yellow eyes staring back at him.

"Fancy a little spin in the sunlight?"

Friend trilled as Uffrin undid his straps. The owl hopped onto his arm, swiveling his head to look out at the glaring white of the pass. The owl's sensors should automatically adjust for the daylight, but Uffrin couldn't help wondering if Friend preferred the night, a side effect of the owl behaviors Uffrin had laid over his base patterns.

"See the Great Tooth there?" Friend turned toward the mountain, shining white in the sun, then swiveled his head back around and blinked at Uffrin. "The valley between that ridge there and the one beyond is where the human army was last seen. Let's go make sure they're all snowed in like they should be." He put on his circlet and linked to the owl, closing his eyes as he switched to Friend's view.

He didn't even need to touch the control pad as Friend rose up, steadying himself against the uneven crosswind, and powered away toward the ridge. The pure, unbroken expanse of the snow was serene, a wonderland he could never have hoped to see in any other circumstance. Though the reasons that had brought him out to this gods-forsaken corner of Maerdom were tragic, he clung to the beauty of the landscape, which buoyed his spirits as Friend soared on the updrafts. The white of the snow was broken by a large mass halfway to the ridge, and Friend dove lower to get a better look. Uffrin's heart lurched when he saw the columns of soldiers, their swords and armor shining in the sun, led by a large group on horses. There were thousands of them, several times as many as the Maer had massed at Giant's Pass, and they had covered ten miles overnight in the snow. If they kept up this pace, they would reach the pass by nightfall.

A bright light flared among the group, and three pinkish glowing objects snaked through the air toward Friend, moving many times faster than the hoverballs he'd seen near the ground. He didn't need to urge Friend back, as the owl had already wheeled and begun flying back at top speed, but the pink balls were gaining on him rapidly. Uffrin panicked, unsure what to do, but Friend rose higher and higher, the pink balls hot on his tail, then dove in a wicked curve past them, using the momentum of his dive to carry him back toward the human forces. *What are you doing?* Uffrin pushed out, but if Friend received the message, he did not respond. Instead, his speed increased as he dove, and the pink balls glowed more brightly as they sped up to catch him.

"No, Friend, no!" Uffrin said aloud as Friend swooped in low, buzzing the horsemen, most of whom ducked out of the way, but several took wild swings at him with their swords. A flash of pink filled the view, and Friend was pushed forward by the strength of the blast, his talons grazing the snow before he managed to angle his wings and soar straight up into the sky. He wheeled around and saw a dozen or so horses and their riders scattered on the ground. A hail of arrows fired up in his direction, but they fell well short. Soon Friend was soaring back toward Uffrin, swiveling his head around periodically to make sure there weren't any more of the pink balls following him. After a few minutes, he winged into the crevice, his beak and talons shining in the sunlight. He alighted on his case, trilling high and loudly at Uffrin.

"Gods, you did amazing!" Uffrin chucked Friend under the beak, and Friend trilled at him again, softer this time.

"What happened?" Erliss pocketed his field scope and crouched beside Uffrin.

"The humans are only ten miles away. They must have started moving when the snow began. They tried to shoot Friend out of the sky with their magic, but he showed them, didn't you, Friend?"

Erliss closed their eyes and shouted, "Fuck!" Their hoarse cry echoed out across the snow.

"There's nothing we could have done, Erliss."

"I knew it. I fucking knew it! The second I saw that snowstorm coming, I should have warned them."

"Well, Friend can warn them now. Right, Friend?"

Friend spread his wings, his eyes bright and fierce.

"How many were there?"

"I have no idea...Five thousand? Ten thousand? I'm not trained at that, but it looked like a hell of a lot more than the soldiers we have at Giant's Pass." Uffrin's heart sank as he realized what that meant. "But we have the automatons and the scattershot field, right?"

Erliss shook their head. "Their mages will turn our equipment into a wreckage and half our army with it. If they really have thousands, there's no way our forces hold."

Uffrin nodded, fingering the coin in his pocket. "And there's not much between Giant's Pass and Kuppham to stop them, is there?"

Erliss pursed their lips. "There's a garrison at Gulham, a few thousand strong, but they might elect to try to defend the city rather than being drawn out into the open. The humans could head straight to Kuppham, and with that number, they would take it."

"And that would be the end." Uffrin pulled out the coin and stared into the eye, wondering if there really was an infinity locked within the image, if he could take refuge there as the world burned. He flipped it over, studying his haggard face on the smooth side. What would Mara think if she saw him like this? And what was happening to her down on the southern front?

If things were as bad there as here, how could she possibly be safe? How could anyone be safe? If anyone knew the answer, it would be Erliss. Uffrin looked up at them, studying the glint in their eye, despite the hard lines of their face.

"Not the end." Erliss touched him on the shoulder. "A new world? Yes. But will the humans really try to occupy all the Maer lands? They have enough to conquer but not to hold. Not forever." They shook their head, gazing off into the mountains behind them.

"So, what, then? We go live among the Free Maer?"

Erliss spread their hands wide. "What else are you going to do? Go back to Kuppham, see what the humans do to it when they arrive? You really think you're going to go back to your hightop and your tarpipe and your workshop?" Erliss' voice was more animated than Uffrin had ever heard it as if they'd ripped off a mask and were breathing free for the first time.

Uffrin put both hands on Erliss' shoulders and looked them dead in the eyes.

"I know a place, a mountain lake, far enough from the cities it might be safe. If things go all the way south—"

"I will join you. But first, you must write that note and send Friend off to deliver it."

The human army passed in mid-afternoon, seemingly endless lines of armored men marching through the snow that the rows of horses trampled down. Friend had delivered the message and returned with an order to stay put, which was an easy one to follow. Erliss had rigged up some concealment, and the humans seemed to take no notice of them as they passed, row after row after skin-faced row. Erliss watched through their field scope, reporting what they saw: the number of mounted soldiers, the number on foot, and the groups of mages scattered throughout.

"With the kind of power those mages have, they need no siege equipment." They spoke with an almost reverent tone, full of grudging respect. "There is no force in Maerdom that can stop them." They turned to Uffrin, a smile growing on their face. "And there is no one among them who can track me through the mountains. As soon as they're well and truly gone, we leave this whole mess behind."

"Just like that?" Uffrin's chest buzzed with nervous excitement. Who was this new Erliss, and where had they been hiding?

"Just like that."

30

Mara huddled in the cave, which they'd had to climb a bit to get to. It wasn't an easy climb, but that was the point; this high up, the humans would be less likely to investigate it. There was barely room for both of them to lie down, and the floor was uneven and jagged, but it gave her some small sense of security, not being visible to the humans. She'd fed and watered Cleo and left her in the box to rest; she was calmed by it, perhaps in the same way that the cozy confines of the small cave comforted Mara.

Gielle crouched in the opening as the last of the light leaking over the mountains dimmed. Soon there was nothing to see but snow and stars.

"Do you hear anything?" Mara asked.

Gielle shook her head. "We're far enough away the sound of battle might not carry with the snow to muffle it. But from what we saw, it's hard to imagine the fighting hasn't ended." Her voice fell, and silence crept in as the realization hit Mara. If the humans won the battle, it was only a matter of time before they continued up the pass toward the fort. And if that fell, there was absolutely nothing between them and Kuppham.

"So, what do we do?" Mara asked in a small voice.

Gielle turned away from the cave mouth and stepped around the jutting rock to sit on her bedroll and remove her boots.

"First, we get a good night's sleep." She slipped into her blankets, half-turning toward Mara. "You don't mind sharing body heat, I hope?"

Her calm, matter-of-fact tone was just what Mara needed. The cold from the cave floor had managed to seep in through her bedroll, and she was not entirely warm.

"No, of course not!" Mara lifted up the edge of her blanket and scooched closer. Gielle turned her back to Mara and wiggled up against her, then tucked the blankets tight around her.

"Wow, you're like a furnace."

Mara giggled. "I do have my uses."

Gielle's frame shook with silent laughter.

"Anyway, once we've all had a bit of rest, you should send Cleo back to scope out the situation. If the Maer held their ground, we check in and see what they want from us. And even if the humans won the battle, they won't be able to move right away. They'll need to tend to their wounded, deal with the prisoners, resupply, that kind of thing. It'll take them a day or two, at least. Which gives us time to get to the fort and regroup."

"Do you think the fort can stop them?"

Gielle snorted. "For like an hour, maybe. But they'll blow that thing off the three cliffs with their hoverballs. You saw what they did back there."

"And after that?"

"It's every Maer for themselves."

When Mara awoke around midnight, she sent Cleo back out, and it was as they feared. The scattershot field was completely destroyed, along with the command and surveillance posts. Bodies littered the field, most of them Maer, many of them charred. Groups of Maer stood with hands tied behind their backs, watched by stern human soldiers with swords at the ready. Mara's heart sank into an abyss of despair, and she tore the circlet from her head and collapsed against the cave wall, tears flooding her face. Strong arms closed around her, and Gielle held her as she sobbed, her mind spinning with visions of charred bodies and the defeated faces of the bound soldiers. She had nearly cried herself dry when she felt a peck on her knee. Cleo stood next to her, gazing up at her with wide, excited eyes.

"What on earth?" Mara asked, slipping the circlet back on. Cleo turned and flew out of the cave mouth, soaring low over a lone figure who trudged through the snow toward her. It was Leasse, and her owl circled around Cleo, who led them slowly to the cave.

Gielle lowered a rope to help Leasse up since the snow and ice had made the climb tricky. The hair on Leasse's face and beard was matted with frost, and she held her left arm gingerly.

"Gods, what happened to you?" Mara gestured toward her arm, and Leasse winced as she pulled back her torn sleeve to reveal a blood-soaked bandage.

"One of the human spies snuck up on us just before the attack. My scout saved me, but unfortunately, she couldn't save herself."

"You were with Piban?" Gielle asked in a quiet voice. Leasse nodded, and Gielle closed her eyes, inhaling slowly as she clenched her jaws and bit her lip in the way one does when they're trying not to cry. It was Mara's turn to comfort Gielle, who stiffened for a moment before falling into the hug, moaning softly into Mara's shoulder. Gielle mastered herself before long and moved with Leasse to the back of the cave, turning on her headlamp and getting out her first aid kit to tend to her wounds. Mara coaxed Seeli into her box, with help from her circlet, which allowed her to form a thin bond with the owl, though Mara had not worked with her before.

They made plans to leave before dawn. The human army seemed to be in much better shape than anticipated and would not tarry. They would be slowed by the snow and the prisoners, assuming they kept them alive, but there was no time to waste. Gielle took the lead, showing them the distance on the map and discussing timelines and the speed of armies and a lot of other things too depressing for Mara to consider. They would head to the fort to see what use they could be and decide what to do from there.

The first light of dawn turned the snowy landscape into a glittering wonderland, broken only by the occasional tracks of deer or rabbits. On Gielle's suggestion, they had sent their owls out early to hunt, and they had each returned with a rabbit, which still had most of their fall coloring and must have been easy to spot. They sent the owls out for a second hunt while they marched, and they returned again with rabbits, which Mara and Leasse let them devour while they stopped to rest and choke down a sporecake. Gielle ran off to fill their waterskins from a trickle flowing down from one of the cliffs, and they were soon on their way again, the bright sun warming their upper bodies while the melting snow froze their feet in their boots.

They arrived at the fort near dusk and found space around a small fire, along with a dozen soldiers who were coughing and sickly. Gielle whispered into Mara's ear that they should find a place to camp away from the group, and she begrudgingly gave up her spot before her toes could fully thaw. They made rough camp against a large rock; Gielle's tarp was hardly big enough for two, but the three of them squeezed in and made a heap of their combined blankets that kept them warm if they snuggled tight against each other.

The next day was a chaotic mess as the soldiers from the fort hurried to set up rock barricades between the half-dozen scattershot towers spread too thin across the pass. They traded one of their rabbits for barely enough wood to build a small fire, which Gielle tended with great care, keeping would-be guests away with a stern glare. It was hardly enough for the three of them, and parts of the rabbit were undercooked, but they gobbled down every bite and sucked on the bones. They took stock of their food stores: enough sporecakes to last a week if they were frugal. The rest of the camp seemed to be in even worse shape.

Mara sent Cleo off to scope out the humans, and she found them organized and active, looking as if they were preparing to move very soon. They had maybe a hundred horse-mounted knights in addition to thousands of footsoldiers, despite whatever casualties they had taken. The fort wouldn't stand a chance against this number. She'd reported the intelligence to the aerie watcher, who came down in the morning to check in with the handlers. The news did not surprise him. He looked around as if to make sure there was no one in earshot and leaned in close.

"When the battle commences, you should run. To Kuppham or to somewhere else if you have anywhere to go. With the height of the fort, we can see the battlefield without your assistance. Best we keep our feathered friends out of harm's way." He winked, clapped her on the arm, and wandered off to find another handler to chat up.

His cheery demeanor buoyed her spirit a little, but the way he coughed as he walked away left her holding her breath. It sounded a lot like what she'd begun to hear from the soldiers coming in from the northern front. Ulver's cough. There hadn't been a major outbreak in her lifetime, but older Maer grew silent and long-faced when the topic was raised.

She hurried back to their little tent, where Leasse was sleeping, with Gielle crouched in the opening, watching warily.

"You shouldn't be talking that close to anyone here if you can help it." Gielle gave her a hard, concerned look, raising her scarf over her mouth.

"You're right, but he's the aerie watcher. I report to him. I had no choice."

Gielle nodded, closing her eyes. "You're fine. I'm sorry, it's just—"

"I get it." Mara touched her on the arm, and Gielle flashed a soft smile for a moment before hardening her visage again.

"So, what's the plan?" Leasse said, yawning and pushing halfway up.

"The plan is you get some rest so your arm can heal. But first, you get this piece of jerky." Gielle held it out toward Leasse, then pulled it back. "Make sure you get every bit of that juice out of there."

"Yes, sir." Leasse did an awkward military salute, and Gielle's smile burst forth, breaking her mask again.

"The aerie watcher said once the battle starts, we should leave, either back to Kuppham or..." Mara wanted to ask them to join her, but how would Uffrin feel about that? Would she be crashing his family's apocalypse getaway with two total strangers?

"Kuppham won't be safe for long," Gielle said. "And I wouldn't be surprised if the same thing isn't happening on the northern front. Kuppham could get squeezed from both sides."

"We could always go live with the Free Maer." Leasse laughed, but the tone of her voice suggested she wasn't entirely kidding.

"If they'd have us." Gielle stroked her trim beard, eyes distant. "I know a little of their language, but the dialects can vary widely, so it could get interesting. There are bound to be a lot of refugees, though, and their welcome might wear out pretty quickly."

Mara looked from Gielle to Leasse, then at Cleo's box. She imagined herself trekking for weeks across unknown mountainous terrain with these two, and a spark lit in her heart. She could hardly ask for better traveling companions, nor more competent. She was sure Uffrin would see that the skills they brought would make them all stronger together. If they could help her find Eagle Lake and get her there safe and sound, they deserved a place in her life, and Uffrin would embrace that.

"I...I have a place in mind." Mara stepped into the tent and sat down on the bedroll, pulling her map from her bag. "I'm not going back to Kuppham. I'm going...here." She laid the map out between them and pointed to the blue dot.

Gielle crouched down to study the map, running her fingers here and there, turning it one way, then the other, until finally, she touched a spot on the edge of the map.

"We're here."

"Yes, I...I think so, because this..."

"Is the fort, and this is Kuppham. So, it says we head north here, past the turnoff toward Kuppham, and skirt around the Millipede." She ran her finger along a line of rounded curves symbolizing mountains. "Then we pop out here on the path that leads toward Gulham, but it's several days' travel, and there are no real cities here. And this writing? It's ancient Maer, right?"

"Yes, in case it were to fall into human hands. No way would they be able to read the description of how to get there."

"Well, read it!" Leasse sat up all the way now, looking more animated than she had since she'd first joined them in the cave.

Mara looked them both in the eyes and knew in that moment that she could trust them with her life.

"Okay. I'll tell you now in case we ever get separated. There's a spring near the cleft of two small mountains, hidden in a tangle of brush, that's supposed to be visible to the north of the path. Directly above, where the lower ridges of the mountains meet, there's a pine forest with a trail leading through it. You follow it for half a day, then look out for a narrow, rocky path on the left, marked with a stone. It leads down several miles to a little lake, or more of a pond, called Eagle Lake. Uffrin's family used to go camping there."

Gielle snickered, and Mara glared her down.

"What?"

"Camping. It's just…I mean, the idea that someone would have to go out of their way to, I don't know, *be* out in nature…" She waved her hands, then let them drop. "Never you mind. It sounds amazing."

Mara felt her face grow hot for a moment, but she stilled her annoyance.

"He says there are wooden lean-tos, proper ones, and with any luck, they won't all be taken by the time we get there."

"We, as in you and her and…" Leasse pointed each of them in turn, then touched her chest.

"Gielle just said Kuppham is a no-go." Mara leaned a bit closer to Leasse. "You can go wherever you want, but I'm saying, if you want to come with me, I would be thrilled to have you." She looked up at Gielle, whose face was twisted in thought. "*Both* of you."

"I'm in!" Leasse leaned over awkwardly and hugged Mara with her good arm.

Gielle moved her hand from her mouth, which broke into a soft, wide smile.

"I don't know about staying in a campground with a bunch of tourists, but if you're going to travel along that path, you need a guide who knows the area. Especially…" She circled with her finger near the line of mountains she'd called the Millipede. "Right around here."

Mara's mouth hung open at the ominous tone of Gielle's voice.

"And why is that?" Leasse asked in a small voice.

Gielle's smile widened, and her eyes glinted with unexpected merriment.

"Dragons."

31

Uffrin watched the battle through Friend's eyes, tears streaming down his cheeks as the hoverballs obliterated the automatons and the scattershot towers and sent the troops sprinting in every direction, trying to flee the explosions. Their escape was short-lived, as the mounted knights swept through the burning debris with spears and swords, routing the scrambling Maer forces and killing anything that moved. Human mages sent jagged bolts of blue lightning streaking through the chaos, picking off the Maer archers and mages who tried to stem the tide. Uffrin pulled Friend back before the human infantry moved in. He had seen enough. The battle was over before it had begun.

The end of the great Maer civilization was at hand.

He reported the news to Erliss, whose tears flowed more stoically than Uffrin's, but they flowed just the same. They clung to each other, rocking side to side gently until Erliss pushed back and wiped their eyes with a dirty handkerchief. Uffrin did the same, and soon Friend fluttered down and landed on his case, eyeing Uffrin with eyes that shone a little less brightly than usual.

"Thank you, Friend." Uffrin squatted by the owl, who gave him a profusion of head-bumps all across his face, trilling softly. "I know it's hard to believe, but that life is over now." Tears flowed anew as he thought of Maoti, Maofin, and Paodo. And Kaela, who'd been staying with them. Would any of them make it to Eagle Lake?

"Are you ready to start on the new one?" Erliss stood with their pack on, a slight smile on their face. "We'd best get moving as soon as it's all the way dark. We'll be a little exposed until we get around the end of this ridge, but I think we should make it in a couple of hours, and once we're away from the valley, we can find a place to hole up and make time in the morning."

Uffrin stared off to the south, toward the battle. Toward Kuppham. What would become of the family he'd left behind? Maoti had spoken of a mission to the South, and something told him she knew what she was doing, though she was the only one who did. Uffrin could see Paodo sticking it out until the end, hoping to salvage something of the work he had done as an interpreter and ambassador. Would Maofin be able to find a way to help Kaela get to the lake? Maofin would surely stay behind with Paodo, waiting for Maoti's return from her mysterious mission. They had enough money to hire someone to guide Kaela, and he hoped they had already sent her. It wouldn't be long before the humans were at the gates of Kuppham. Once that happened, there would be no escape.

"Uffrin?"

"Yes, sorry, it's just..." Uffrin closed his eyes, chasing away images of Kuppham burning by picturing Mara, the gentle spark in her eyes, how she truly saw him in a way no one else ever had. He imagined her expression when they met again, exhausted and ragged after long travels but afire with joy. Kuppham could burn, the walls of every Maer city could crumble, but if he could find her again, in some forgotten corner of the mountains, maybe it would be as Erliss had said. A new world, more difficult perhaps, but also freer. No circlets, no Stream, no brightstone chips or hotiron. Just Maer and mountains, as it was in the Time Before.

"Yes," Uffrin said, sniffing and rolling up his bedroll. "Yes, I'm ready. What about you, Friend? Are you ready for a new adventure?"

Friend spread his wings, trilling quietly, then hopped down from the case and pulled the door open with his talon.

"It's going to be a long trip, but when we get to where we're headed, I'm going to introduce you to a very special owl named Cleo."

The humans did not find them that night, nor the one after. By the third night, they risked a fire to cook a baby marmot Friend had snagged for them. He'd proven quite adept at hunting, and with no humans in sight, his eyes quickly focused on finding prey. He seemed to delight in bringing them back something, and each night he brought a bird or mammal he'd caught as he returned from his surveillance flights. When he'd delivered their meal and gotten his praise, he'd put himself in his box, waiting for Uffrin to strap him in before turning himself off.

They ran across several groups of Free Maer, who eyed them with suspicion, no doubt aware of the goings-on between the Maer and the humans. Erliss obviously didn't speak their dialect perfectly, but they knew enough to convince the Free Maer they posed no threat, and they passed through unmolested. One group traveled with a frasti on a stout leather cord. The beast glared at them and bared its yellowed fangs but stayed under its master's command. The others had crows shadowing them in the trees above, and one of them looked to be communicating with the birds through hand gestures.

"A bit like Mara," Uffrin said, almost to himself.

"She'll fit right in." Erliss stared up at the birds before thanking the Free Maer. After much pointing and gesturing, all parties seemed satisfied, and they went their separate ways.

"Have you had a lot of interaction with the Free Maer?" Uffrin asked as they continued in a light mist of icy rain.

"Here and there. I've never had any trouble. Not even with the Skin Maer."

Uffrin shuddered. They were said to be reviled even by the Free Maer, only venturing out of their caves at night to kidnap solo wanderers for their dark rituals.

"Is it true what they say? That they have no hair at all on their bodies, not even on their heads?"

Erliss chuckled. "I never got very close, but they definitely had hair on their heads and beards, though the rest of their faces were as bare as humans. They stay out of the way, for obvious reasons, and the Free Maer leave them their space."

"I can't say I blame them. I've heard the Free Maer can be kind of...territorial?"

Erliss shook their head, grinning out of one side of their mouth.

"Kind of like how Kuppham has high walls and heavy gates and armored guards and surveillance birds? That kind of territorial?"

"Point taken," Uffrin said, a grin burning through his embarrassment.

"But you're right. They can be if you don't respect their boundaries. Same as any Maer."

"I guess it helps if you speak their language, too."

Erliss shook their head, sucking their teeth. "Different dialect. I only caught about two-thirds of what they said."

"You seemed to do all right. Where'd you learn that, in Shoza school?"

Erliss' eyes gave a fluttering half-blink, and they smiled. "I'm no Shoza. Not anymore." They gestured behind them. "That life is over now. I'm just me." They spread their arms wide. "Whoever that is."

"Okay, well, you may not be Shoza in the traditional sense, but if we're starting a new society out here, we're going to need Maer with your skill set to protect us."

"Oh, we're starting a new society now?" Erliss laughed, a genuine, joyful sound untarnished by the events of recent days. "And what will your role be in this mountain utopia?"

"Everyone who comes will probably have some piece of tech, a circlet at least, maybe one or two other little things. I might be able to cobble something together out of whatever folks bring with them. We might need an artificer yet. And if not, well, we're going to need engineers. We may not have forges and metal tools right away, but we'll be building things, designing them. I'm sure I'll be of use."

"Very good, and Mara can work with birds, and I can hunt, so we have a few good bases covered. Though it would be nice if we had a farmer."

Uffrin threw up his hands. "I'm completely useless in that regard, I'm afraid. When my mothers arrive, maybe." His heart swelled with sorrow as he realized he might never see them or anyone else he knew again. They might make it out all right, though—they *should* make it out all right. Maoti had seen it, hadn't she? But he had to accept the possibility that they wouldn't. It was too much to bear, so he chose to believe they would find their way here, just as Maoti said.

As long as he found Mara again, he could withstand any heartbreak the world threw at him.

He recognized the cleft between the two little mountains above a field grazed by a handful of goats in the greenish-brown patches between the melting snow. A Maer no more than ten years old tended the herd, watching them warily. No doubt the sight of two Old Maer, as the Free Maer referred to them, was suspicious, but the goatherd soon returned to their animals, prodding a couple of kids who were tumbling in the grasses to rejoin the herd. A vulture soared overhead, which Uffrin hoped wasn't an ill omen. Erliss watched it for a time, then continued up the hill, scouting a bit ahead of Uffrin.

A sparse pine forest filled the space between the hills, and the scent brought back memories of his childhood trips here. They walked along the well-traveled path through the orange-brown carpet of pine needles. Erliss stopped here and there to examine tracks, which they always concluded were small groups of Free Maer.

"No animal tracks with them, so either they don't have animal companions, or their companions fly or are too small to make tracks."

"I'm pretty much okay with not running across any more frasti to be honest, unless it's in a stew."

"Even this far out in the Silver Hills, you won't find many frasti except those kept by the Free Maer. They're too dangerous and too tasty for Maer to just let them be."

Uffrin chewed on the thought in silence as they walked. He'd always imagined the Free Maer lands to be wild and untouched; they'd certainly seemed that way when he was a kid as if they were still living in the Time Before. But maybe the Time Before wasn't as wild as he'd thought. Maybe it was in Maer's nature to kill, fell, and build, to shape the world to suit their needs. The goatherd out in the field was living today just as they might have lived a thousand years ago, in a land that was no wilder then than now.

Uffrin's reverie was interrupted by the approach of a pair of Free Maer carrying wooden instruments on their backs, laughing and singing little bits of a tune as if they were composing as they walked. Erliss stopped, pressed their hands to their chest, and bowed, and the Free Maer did the same, surprise and perhaps a little amusement in their glances.

"It's a little late for camping season, isn't it?" The taller of the Free Maer spoke in the standard dialect, with just the hint of an accent. Both Maer eyed them and their equipment, especially Erliss' swords and Uffrin's case, with curious eyes.

"I take it you haven't heard?" Erliss' voice was serious, and the smiles washed from the Free Maer's faces. They shook their heads.

"The humans have routed the army at Giant's Pass. They'll be on their way to Gulham by now and then Kuppham."

The taller Maer's mouth dropped open, then he covered it with his hand.

"We knew there was a war going on, but we had no idea it had gone this far." He gazed off the path where Uffrin and Erliss had come from.

"No one's followed us," Erliss said with calm confidence. "Nor do I expect anyone to come looking for us here."

"Except Mara and her sister. And possibly my parents," Uffrin blurted out.

The taller Maer shook his head. "Well, Bogadan will be glad of the business, I suppose."

The shorter one stepped forward, a soft smile on her face. "Can you tell us what happened? We can sing it around, spread the word, so everyone knows."

Uffrin looked to Erliss, who closed their eyes and nodded. Uffrin took a deep breath and recounted what he'd seen, including Friend's daring deeds. They took great interest in the story and in the hoverballs and the massacre, which left them somber and silent.

"We are truly sorry for your loss," the taller one said. "With your permission, we will compose a lament and an ode to your brave Friend." He eyed the case, then raised his eyebrows at Uffrin. "I don't suppose you'd mind showing us?"

Uffrin chewed the inside of his cheek, tempted to look to Erliss for guidance, but he resisted. Erliss wasn't Shoza anymore, and Uffrin didn't answer to anyone. Friend was his, and if these Free Maer wanted to make up a song to commemorate him, who was he to argue? He set down his case, reassured by the soft blink of Erliss' eyes, and opened it. Friend's eyes popped open, and his head swiveled to the Free Maer, who had approached but stood at a cautious distance. They drew in sharp breaths as Friend trilled at them, then took a step back when Uffrin released Friend's straps, and he fluttered over to land in front of them.

"He's beautiful," the tall Maer said.

"Yes, you are," the shorter one said, squatting and holding out a hand toward Friend. The owl swiveled his head back toward Uffrin, who shrugged. Friend hopped forward and gave her a quick peck on the fingers, and she laughed, shaking her fingers and examining them.

"He's just saying hi. He'd never hurt anyone. Would you, Friend?"

Friend trilled at Uffrin, then tucked his wings back and lowered his body in a kind of bow toward the Free Maer. They bowed back, and Friend turned and fluttered over to the box, backed in, and shut himself off. Uffrin wondered if Friend had made such a brief appearance out of a desire to conserve his power source.

"Did you make him?" the tall Maer asked.

Uffrin shook his head. "I tweaked the skeleton, reconfigured the wings a bit, and put in most of the patterns, but the important parts are made by someone way above my pay grade."

"Maer are going to go nuts for this," the taller one murmured.

"We'll change the location in the song," the shorter one assured them. "So no one comes looking for you."

"That's...that's good, I guess. Thank you."

"Thank *you* for sharing your story with us and for letting us meet Friend. We will make sure his valiant deeds are not lost in the fog of war stories that are sure to follow." She glanced at the horizon and said a few words in their dialect to her partner. "Weather's coming. Looks like maybe snow."

"Or sleet," the other commented.

"Either way, we have another couple of hours walk ahead of us, as do you. Might do well to hurry, as you don't want to be heading down the lake trail if it gets icy."

"Thank you." Erliss bowed again. Uffrin joined them this time, and the Free Maer repeated the gesture.

"The keeper's name is Bogadan. He's not much of a talker, but you can trust him."

Uffrin thanked them, and they all made awkward goodbye gestures and continued on their way. Close to dusk, with fat flakes of wet snow filtering down through the trees, they found the path on the left that led down into the valley with Eagle Lake at the bottom. They couldn't see the lake through the trees, but Uffrin recognized the pointed stone marker indicating the trail.

"How far down did you say it was?" Erliss asked.

"An hour or two, if memory serves."

Erliss studied the ground near the trail, moving the pine needles with their fingers.

"No recent footprints. We should set up camp here and head down in the morning."

Uffrin shivered as a snowflake melted on his neck. "You think it's okay to light a fire?"

"If we get started quickly. Try and find some dry tinder, and I'll work on splitting a few branches. You think Friend could catch us some dinner? I've seen a few tree rats here and there."

Uffrin salivated at the thought of fresh meat. Friend trilled even before Uffrin had opened the case as if he'd been listening in on their conversation. Uffrin barely had time to put on his circlet and gauntlet and find the hunting pattern, which was already lit up.

"Do a sweep to make sure we're not being watched first."

Friend blinked and ducked his head, almost as if he were nodding, then spread his wings and fluttered up into the canopy. Erliss sharpened their hatchet, watching Uffrin as he removed his gauntlet.

"Don't you need to keep that on, just in case?"

"I've hardly used it since after the battle. I can still pop in and check on him using the circlet, but Friend doesn't need direction anymore."

32

Mara sent Cleo out at dusk, as instructed, to make sure the humans had actually stopped. She saw tents and fires, as well as more human soldiers than she could count. The Maer prisoners huddled in a guarded enclosure with no blankets, no tents, and no fire. There were more than a hundred horses, and the foot soldiers surely numbered in the thousands. She'd also identified several dozen unarmored figures she thought must be mages, each guarded by a heavily armored human with swords drawn at all times. This wasn't going to be a battle. It was going to be a slaughter.

Once she'd delivered her report, she'd boxed Cleo and woken Leasse, who was snoring softly. Gielle was awake and already packed, watching the rest of the camp. Almost everyone was asleep, and they'd picked a spot on the northern edge of the impromptu camp where a few hundred Maer soldiers awaited certain death. They packed quietly, then stayed still for a long time on Gielle's insistence. Near middle-morn, Gielle rose from her crouch, blinked at them in the dim starlight, and started walking. They followed her in silence, and Mara did not dare to look back until they had walked for several minutes. The camp was still and silent, and no one followed them. They were on their way.

They ran across a small contingent of soldiers in the morning coming from the direction of Kuppham. Gielle exchanged a few words with them while Mara and Leasse waited to the side.

"I told them we were headed back to Kuppham and said they should hurry to the fort. They have no idea what they're headed into." Gielle shook her head, looking down, and Mara felt her grief. Shoza were part military, so this whole disaster had to be hitting her differently, but her face remained strong. She adjusted her pack and gestured forward, toward where the Niekupp valley spilled out onto a hilly space between the mountains. "Once we're past the valley, we're into Free Maer territory. We keep our heads down, be polite, and we'll be just fine."

"Do you think the humans will follow us eventually?" Mara asked. "Once Kuppham falls, I mean. Won't they set out after the Free Maer?"

"I doubt it." Gielle motioned with her shoulder and started walking, and Mara had to hurry to keep up. "Their war is with us, not the Free Maer. And occupying Kuppham, Gulham, and the other cities will be more than they can handle, especially with winter coming. If we can make it to this lake before the real snows come, we should be safe for a good long while."

They traveled through rain, mist, and snow, with the occasional sunny day interspersed. The owls kept them in small game, though Gielle warned Mara and Leasse not to hunt in certain areas, which were marked by a system of wooden poles with symbols carved in them, designating different Free Maer territories. They ran across a handful of Free Maer: hunters and goatherds mostly. Gielle spoke their language, though it was clear that she had a harder time communicating with some of them.

Mara could only make out a little bit of what they said, but all the interactions seemed cordial enough. The hunters were accompanied by a species of dog with pointy ears and curly tails, ever attentive to their masters' calls. They also met a Free Maer couple who sold them what they claimed was frasti jerky. Mara gave up a few of the coins she'd brought after Gielle had bargained with them. It felt odd to be using the currency of a civilization that would soon be obsolete.

The weather turned frigid as they passed alongside the mountain range known as the Millipede. They clung to each other at night, sharing their blankets against the cold air and colder ground. As she spooned Gielle's muscular body with Leasse's softer form pressing into her back, Mara thought of Uffrin, wondering if he had someone to share a blanket with to keep the mountain chill at bay. She longed to lay with him again, hear his contented little hums as he snuggled into her, his desperate whines as she toyed him gently with her fingers.

She tried to push the thoughts away, as it was awkward to feel like this while pressed against two other bodies. It had been so long, and she'd never missed anyone so much. She slept fitfully, tormented by images of Uffrin's lean body pressed beneath her, his eyes soft and pleading, his timid hands gently cupping her backside. When she finally got to Eagle Lake, she was going to throw him down on whatever passed for a bed and show him, in great detail, just exactly how much she'd missed him.

As they traveled the next day, Gielle stopped suddenly, motioning them back with one hand while pointing at a set of openings in one of the small mountains of the Millipede with steam billowing out. Leasse gasped, and Mara studied the openings until she saw it too, and every hair on her body stood up. A dark shape lurked amid the steam from one of the caves, then emerged, long and sinuous, and started moving at an alarming rate down the mountain. It was hard to tell from this distance, but it had to be at least forty feet long, including its thick tail.

"Was that—" Leasse whispered.

Gielle nodded. "Scale dragon, probably a *waadrech* or a *berdrech*. We're in dragon Maer territory for sure." She started walking again, and Mara scurried to keep close.

"Is it safe to pass through here?" she asked breathlessly, partly due to fear.

"Safer than walking a hundred miles or more out of our way. The dragons won't attack us unless we piss off the Free Maer. If we're really lucky, we'll get to see one up close."

Mara shared a glance with Leasse. She wasn't sure it would be lucky to see a dragon up close, but Mara felt a spark of childish excitement mixed in with her abject terror. She'd grown up on stories of dragons, but they were mostly the made-up kind that flew, breathed fire, talked, and hoarded treasure. She knew, in theory, that real ones existed and that they weren't much more than oversized lizards, but the thought of seeing one with her very own eyes filled her with jitters she couldn't shake.

It turned out they didn't have long to wait. They rounded a bend in the trail and stood facing a pair of Free Maer fifty feet ahead, with a hulking dark brown shape behind them. Mara's heart raced as it poked its head between the two Maer and bared huge yellow teeth. One of the Maer put a hand on its snout, which was as big as his entire body, and the creature's teeth disappeared. It snorted, a muffled sound that carried even at this distance, then turned its wide, unblinking eyes toward them.

Gielle called out some kind of greeting and bowed, and the Maer bowed back. One stayed with the dragon, petting its snout and bending low as if whispering to it. It lowered its body flat on the ground, curling its clawed feet underneath its chest and slitting its eyes.

"I think I'm going to piss myself," Leasse whispered.

"If Gielle says it's safe, I trust her," Mara reassured her, trying to convince herself at the same time.

Gielle spoke with the Maer, using a lot of hand gestures, pointing back toward them, then forward. The Maer listened intently, then nodded as Gielle slipped something into their hand. They signaled to the dragon handler, who tapped the creature on the snout. It raised up on all fours, flashing its teeth once more, and veered off the path. It climbed atop a boulder just above where it had been sitting and watched them with its cold, golden eyes.

"Come on then." Gielle gestured them forward, and both Free Maer stepped to the side, standing beneath the boulder. The dragon crouched ominously, its eyes following them as they passed. It was as thick as an ox, with eyes like cake plates, rows of horrible jagged teeth, and a forked tongue that slid in and out of its mouth as they approached. Mara flashed a smile and a brief bow to the Free Maer, who did the same, though their smiles were restrained and their bows perfunctory. The smell of rotten meat lingered in the air where the dragon had been, and Mara walked on shaky legs until they were around the next bend.

"See? Nothing to worry about, just like I said." Gielle's grin was a little self-satisfied for Mara's taste, but she had gotten them through the encounter unscathed, so she got a pass.

"Gods, I have to pee so bad!" Leasse said, hurrying behind a rock to relieve herself. When she returned, she walked with lighter steps, and her smile had almost returned.

"Just a few more days, and we'll be past the Millipede, and a couple of days more will take us to this lake if your map is accurate."

"It is," Mara said firmly. She'd copied it with the utmost care, knowing one false pencil mark could be the difference between meeting Uffrin and never seeing him again.

"We should be out of their territory by midday tomorrow. Best we don't hunt until then. I've still got a couple of spore cakes left, plus a bit of that jerky, which I'm pretty sure is marmot, not frasti, but I've had worse."

They made camp near dusk in a little pocket between boulders to the side of the path, eschewing a fire on Gielle's recommendation. They ate a meager half-meal, rationing their food as best they could, but they'd need to rely on the owls to catch them something tomorrow. Mara went to bed with a growling stomach and cold feet, but she found comfort and warmth in Gielle and Leasse's arms and slept better than she had any right to, given the circumstances.

They traveled through a cold rain the next day, which turned to sleet, then back to rain, then to wet snow. If Gielle hadn't found a sheltered crevice they could squeeze into, the night would have been unbearable. They sent out their owls in the early morning once the snow had been replaced by biting cold and were rewarded with a pair of cliff rats and a skinny rabbit. They let the owls have the rats, and they roasted the rabbit for breakfast, seasoned with a bit of spice mix Leasse had brought. It wasn't nearly enough, and Mara was beginning to wonder how they'd make it through the winter, eating rodents and gods knew what else.

Gielle managed to scrounge up some edible roots that grew beneath unassuming brown grasses, which they roasted for dinner. They were bland and stringy, but with their sporecakes and jerky almost gone, they had little choice. It gave Mara terrible gas, which coincided with the tail end of her period, so she slept miserably. She awoke knowing they only had two or three more days of travel, assuming her map was indeed accurate, which she had begun to doubt more and more with each passing day.

The last few days of their journey passed in a haze. Mara's heel developed a blister, which became raw and infected. Gielle put some kind of salve on it, which she said would keep the infection from spreading, but it still burned with every step she took. The owls did their best to keep them fed, and Gielle scrounged up a few more roots, along with some nuts that required a great deal of work to get at very little bitter meat, but it kept them moving. Mara could already feel her cloak hanging a little looser from her frame from the long distance and the paltry rations. She didn't mind losing a little weight; her body would right itself once she got a steady diet again, whenever that might be. And she was sure Uffrin wouldn't care one way or another.

Her body began to hum when they reached the pine ridge shown on the map, the last stretch before they reached the turn-off to the lake. Uffrin was nearby. She could smell it in the air and feel it in her bones. He had to be here. And every step she took brought her closer to his heart.

They were still a little too far to send Cleo out to check on Eagle Lake, especially with Free Maer who might be able to control birds around. They slept one night in the forest, whose pine needle carpet was infinitely softer than the rocky beds of the previous weeks, and the needles provided a little insulation underneath. She snuggled between her two companions, her heart throbbing as she thought of Uffrin, how easy it was to get him hard with a kiss, how completely he surrendered the moment she put her hands on his tight little body.

Gielle wiggled against her, and her narrow, muscular bottom gave Mara a spark of desire. Her frame was wiry like Uffrin's beneath Mara's arms, her muscles a bit more pronounced but lean like his. Mara pressed her eyes tight and concentrated, centering herself slowly until the physical urge drifted to the outskirts of her consciousness, replaced by Uffrin's smile, the way he looked down when she caught his eye, then squinted when he turned his eyes back up. Her body relaxed into Gielle's, and Leasse hugged her tight from behind. She drifted off into a deep and beautiful sleep.

The path was right where the map said it would be, and Gielle nearly jumped when she spotted the trail marker. Her smile was as bright and joyous as any Mara had seen in a very long time.

"I think I can tell you now that I doubted the accuracy of your map, but you have proven a most able cartographer." She gave a little bow, and Mara giggled.

Leasse took a half-step forward. "And I want to say for the record, before we go down to the lake, that if I ever have to flee the end of civilization as we know it again, I want to flee it with you two." Mara sank into her embrace, and Gielle surprised her by wrapping them both in a vigorous hug, nearly lifting them off the ground.

"Do you want to send the owls first?" Gielle eyed the crates. Mara looked to Leasse, then turned back, shaking her head, feeling suddenly nervous and vulnerable.

"No. When I see Uffrin again, I want it to be with my very own eyes."

33

Uffrin trudged back up to the lean-to, his feet and hands numb from plucking horsetail roots from the muddy cove the Free Maer had granted them harvest rights to. Friend was allowed to hunt only in the pine forest above, which Uffrin didn't like, as it would wear out his power source too quickly. He dumped the roots on the edge of the wooden platform and added a few pine needles and twigs to the coals to warm his extremities. When he could feel his fingers again, he set to work shucking the roots, dropping the meaty pulp in the pot to cook later. One of the Free Maer fisherfolk had brought him a pouch of tiny fish, which were abundant in the pond, and which they caught in wide nets spread between poles. He had given their chief councilor most of the coin he'd brought from Kuppham as a gift on Erliss' suggestion. The councilor had accepted the money with great reverence. Uffrin didn't know if the coins would have any value once the Maer had finished losing the war. Perhaps they would take on greater value here, where they were comparatively rare.

One of the curly-tailed dogs the Free Maer used for hunting bounded up to the edge of the platform. It cocked its head at him and let out a small bark, then turned and scampered back in the direction it had come. Uffrin's chest buzzed when he realized it was headed toward the path leading up out of the valley, the very path Mara would take to get down here. His heart raced in panic, and he hurriedly rinsed the slimy residue from his hands and splashed some water on his face. He looked down at his muddy pants and root-stained jacket; there was nothing to be done for it. He was a mess, and his other pants were still damp from the morning's wash. He took a deep breath, ran his fingers through his beard and hair a few times, then hopped off the platform and marched toward the path.

He stopped in his tracks when he saw her familiar shape picking her way down the last rocks of the trail. When she reached the flagstone path, she looked up, and their eyes met across the brown landscape. They both froze for a moment, then Uffrin took off running, his bare feet slapping on the stone.

Mara unshouldered her case, handing it distractedly to one of two other Maer with her, and bounded toward Uffrin. Both of them slowed as they approached, stopping several feet from each other. Uffrin's breath came in shallow gasps. Tears flooded his eyes, and his heart leapt up into his throat. Mara's face broke as she threw herself at him, almost knocking him over with the force of her embrace. He pulled Mara tight to him, his body responding to her softness and warmth, his hands moving up and down her strong back. She pulled her head away, gripping his collar in her fists. Her eyes slitted as her plump lips inched closer, her breath hot on his face.

And then they were kissing. First a dozen small, frenetic kisses as they relearned the landscape of each other's lips. Then a long, slow kiss with little movement, just softness and building heat. Mara slid one hand up his neck and behind his head, fisting his hair and crushing her lips against his. Her tongue coaxed and teased, going deeper each time he responded with his. Her other hand found his backside and gripped it so hard it hurt. She ground her body against his, ratcheting up the pressure of her kiss, then stopped suddenly, pulling back with heavy breath and eyes ripe with dark heat.

"Mara, I..."

She stopped him with a simple kiss, her eyes growing soft, her hand releasing his hair and grazing his cheek.

A pair of hands clapping broke the spell, and another pair joined it, and several more. Uffrin and Mara giggled at the same time as they looked around. Mara's two companions, a scout and another bird handler, stood clapping and smiling at them. Uffrin turned to see Erliss and the boy whose dog had come to deliver the news clapping with hands held high.

Uffrin turned back to Mara and kissed her softly, letting his fingers trace up her arms and over her shoulders to hang gently around her neck.

"Welcome to Eagle Lake."

Uffrin watched as Mara devoured the gloppy horsetail stew, twisting her mouth sideways as she chewed on one of the little fish. She looked as if she was going to spit it out, but she swallowed it and kept going. He had poured himself a small bowl, giving more to Mara and her companions, who fell upon it like it was a Solstice feast. Gielle was a Shoza, or had been anyway, and Leasse was an owl handler, who he realized he'd briefly met when he'd visited the aerie. Once they'd finished, Uffrin primed the rickety pump, rinsed their bowls, and left them in the weak afternoon sun to dry.

Mara watched him, her face falling, her eyes suddenly sad.

"What, love?" Uffrin knelt by her, putting a hand on her shoulder.

"Kaela?"

Uffrin closed his eyes and shook his head.

"Not yet. But if Maoti said she would come, she'll get here safe and sound." He found himself believing it as he spoke. Maoti knew things, and he felt in his heart it was true.

"Promise?"

Uffrin let his forehead fall against hers, squeezing her shoulder. He noticed Bogadan standing at a distance, eyeing the newcomers with caution. Uffrin gestured him over, and he walked with slow steps toward the platform, bowing slightly toward Mara and the others.

"Bogadan here is the camp keeper. He's the one who kept these lean-tos standing all these years, and he's been showing me how to add the last wall." Uffrin gestured toward the makeshift frame covering most of the open side of the lean-to, only a small part of which had been plastered with mud and moss.

"Pleasure," Bogadan muttered. Uffrin still hadn't figured out how much Old Maer Bogadan spoke; he always seemed to understand what was said to him, but he seldom uttered more than a short sentence at a time.

"Bogadan, this is Mara, the love of my life." He touched her on the shoulder, and her warm hand slid up over his. "And these are her friends, Gielle and Leasse." Mara's companions bowed, and Bogadan acknowledged them with a subtle blink. "We were hoping it would be okay if they settled into the next lean-to over until they can figure out something for themselves."

"Fine." Bogadan gestured toward the lean-to with his head. "No one's here in winter." He studied the two as if assessing their hardiness and seemed to approve. "I'll show you how to make the wall."

"Nice frame," Gielle said, touching one of the joints where the branches were lashed together. "What's this binding?"

"Horsetail leaves. Soft when wet, tough when dry."

"And the moss?"

"Shallow end of the lake. Better in summer, but it will hold the clay in place."

"Thank you so much." Leasse stood up, bowing again. "Tell us what we can do in return."

Bogadan looked each of them up and down, then eyed the owl boxes. "What birds?"

"Cliff owls."

Bogadan's face twisted as if he'd eaten something disagreeable. "They hunt?"

"They kept us alive all the way from the Rugged Mountains," Mara said with pride in her voice. Bogadan nodded, skepticism in his eyes.

"I'll ask the councilor. She'll be by later." He bowed his head awkwardly, then turned and left without another word.

"I like him," Gielle said.

"Oh, Bogadan's great. Anything you need, just ask. He won't say much, but he can do everything."

"Speaking of everything, I'd like to check out our lean-to and get started on that frame. It looks like a solid week's work at least, and it's not going to get any warmer." Gielle hoisted her pack onto her back and helped Leasse shoulder her owl box.

"Your pump should work if you prime it hard enough," Uffrin said, gesturing toward the one next to his lean-to. "Not sure what we'll do for water once it freezes, but I'm sure they'll help us out."

Gielle looked at the pump, then back at the lean-to, studying the frame for a moment.

"Right, well, we'll leave you two to catch up." Her eyes twinkled as she spoke, and Uffrin's heart warmed as he felt Mara's hand slide around his waist.

Mara closed her eyes and hummed in her throat as Uffrin sponged her body down with water warmed on the fire pit and a cake of the rough soap Bogadan had given him. He lathered her face and hair as best he could, then wiped away the soap when Mara winced as if a bit had gotten in her eye.

"Oh, gods, sorry!"

Mara opened one eye and smiled, running a hand along Uffrin's thigh, stirring his desire and tenting his pants.

"Keep going," she murmured, closing her eyes again. She raised her arms above her head, and he washed her armpits, drying them immediately as he noticed her shivering. He washed her back, feeling the strong muscles beneath her fur, which was stiff with sweat and grime.

"Sit behind me to keep me warm while you wash my front."

Uffrin pulled his stool behind hers, pressing his chest into her back. He lathered her breasts, his erection poking her round backside, and she raised her arms again, teasing her fingers through his hair as he washed and dried her. She twisted her head around for a kiss, and he caught the side of her mouth, her hum buzzing through his lips and straight into his heart.

"Keep going," she whispered, lowering her head again and running her fingers up and down his calves.

Uffrin washed and dried her stomach, then her legs and feet, which she brought up one at a time in a feat of flexibility that was as impressive as it was arousing. Once he had finished, he rinsed the cloth and hung it on the bucket, letting the fingers of his other hand trail along her inner thighs, where the hair on her body was the softest.

"Don't be shy," she cooed, pulling the hand up her thigh and between her legs. Uffrin grew dizzy with want as he felt the shape of her, heard her breath catch as he rinsed and massaged her, perhaps more than was strictly necessary. He lathered his hand again and pressed close to reach farther down, cleaning her from front to back as her fingernails dug into his calves. When he was done, he found the towel and dried her gently. Mara braced against Uffrin's knees to stand, turning to him in all her curvy glory. She eyed his muddy clothes and shivered.

"Uffrin, I'm so cold," she murmured, her eyes dark and inviting. She unbuttoned his coat, backing him toward the opening in the fresh lattice on the lean-to. She raised her mouth for a kiss, sucking his lower lip into her mouth and teasing it with her tongue as she slid his coat off. Uffrin slipped his sleeves out of his shirt, breaking the kiss for a moment as he pulled it over his head and tossed it in the corner. Uffrin's heart swelled to see her bright eyes and crooked smile taking him in. She bit her lip and licked it.

It was exactly as he'd dreamed.

But even in his dreams, Mara hadn't looked this beautiful.

Mara's fingernails raked through the hair on his chest, hungry eyes running slowly down his body. She dropped his pants, teasing him until Uffrin feared he would lose it. She pressed in to kiss him again, devouring him with her mouth as her fingers tightened around him. Uffrin's hands moved up and down her back, massaging her supple backside as she gripped him tight, keeping him on the ragged edge. He let out a moan as she released him, then pressed her soft body into his.

"I dreamed of you every night," she murmured between kisses. Her hands clutched his behind, pulling him to her with such force he gasped for breath.

He pulled his head back, studying her face, which her absence had somehow rendered more gorgeous. "I missed you so much, Mara."

"Show me," she said, closing her eyes and angling in for a soft, wet kiss.

34

As they kissed, Mara lightened her grip on his backside and slid her hands around to his chest, creating a little distance between their bodies. Her fingers moved of their own accord, and Uffrin whimpered as they traced over his chest, moving in slow circles. He gasped, and his lips stopped moving as she gently pinched and rolled his nipples between her fingers. His hardness throbbed against her belly, and she leaned into it, suddenly hungry to feel him inside her, but she slowed her kiss and slid her arms around his shoulders, clasping her fingers behind his neck. This had been a long time coming, and she wanted to make it last.

Uffrin's hands touched her with gentleness bordering on reverence. As the kiss deepened, he gripped her with more force, kneading her backside, stirring her need. When his kisses became fast and sloppy, she slowed hers, running her thumbs up and down the muscles in his neck, eliciting a groan that spiked her desire.

This was no time to make it last.

She needed him in her now, needed to ride him and see that look of pure abandon in his eyes. She kissed him harder, pushing him back toward the bedroll. He stopped suddenly, his breath hot and heavy, his eyes shining with lust.

He pushed her to arm's length, his eyes trailing hungrily down her body, lingering on her breasts, her hips, and between her legs. His eyes found hers again, staring into them with a frank desire that melted her to the core. His hands moved up her shoulders, his fingers ghosting across her neck and down to her breasts, his gaze hardening as he hefted and fondled them. His eyes, normally so soft, pierced straight through to her heart.

His hands slid down, and he hunched toward her, licking and mouthing her nipples as his fingers slid between her legs. She was so wet, and his fingers felt so good. She moaned, cupping his head as he sucked her nipples almost too hard. She pushed his head down, and he dropped to his knees, staring between her legs with a barely restrained hunger. His hot, dark eyes stayed locked on hers as he nosed in, and her heart felt ready to burst through her chest.

His hands gripped her thighs, pushing them apart, and she moved her legs wider as his lips brushed against her, his hot breath melting her like butter in a sunny window. Her breath hitched as he buried himself in her, only his eyes still visible, still staring at her, into her. She let out a deep moan and ran her fingers through his hair. He kissed her with gentle languor, giving equal attention to every part of her except the one she really wanted.

She leaned toward him, trying to force him into position, but he gripped her backside and held her still as he continued his maddening ministrations. Her grip on his hair tightened, and she pulled him toward her. He paused, pulling back just a moment, breathing into her, his eyes bolts of dark fire in the shadows of the lean-to. After a long moment, he finally released her gaze and went in for the kill.

Mara closed her eyes and rode the waves of pleasure as Uffrin made love to her with his mouth. He pushed and pushed and pushed, ringing the same bell time and again, then slowed down just before the stroke of midnight, only to start the wind-up again. Each time she rose higher and higher on a cloud of ecstasy, and each time he left her gasping, fisting his hair as she bucked into him, straining for that one final swipe of the tongue, that last bit of suction, to push her over the edge.

The pressure of his hands on her backside ratcheted up as his lips clamped down on her and his tongue fluttered relentlessly. Her release boiled up suddenly like milk left on the stove one second too long. She sucked in a loud, gasping breath as she pulsed against him, letting it out in a series of hissing whines until at last, she relaxed her grip on his hair and unclenched her muscles, now burning with the exertion.

Uffrin sat back on his heels, wiping his beard with a ratty towel, and stared up at her with a tender, hopeful look in his eyes. He fell back onto the bedroll, stretching his arms above his head, pulling every lean muscle taut and leaving no question of his arousal or of his intent. Mara lay down beside him, not quite ready yet, but she felt a stir at the sight of his eager body. She let her hands roam over him, fingering him softly, every part of him rising to meet her touch. She reached between his legs and cradled him, rolling partway over so her thigh lay on top of his, her face inches from his. He turned his head toward her, and she kissed him, his mouth salty and ripe with her taste, his lips and tongue moving with hers, inviting her in. She closed her hand tighter around him, and his breath hitched, his hand resting at the curve of her waist. He kneaded her, gently at first, but with more urgency the longer she held him tight until he broke from the kiss, his breath coming in short huffs, his eyes wild and wide.

"Mara...please..." he moaned softly.

She released him and got on all fours, lowering her body down to brush against his, and kissed him for a while longer as he hummed in his throat and his hands roamed over her. She lowered down further, pressing into his hardness, savoring the way his grip on her hips tightened, how his hands slid down onto her backside, squeezing her tight against him. Her resolve crumbled in that instant.

She rose quickly, gripped him firmly with one hand, and sank down onto him. She held still for a moment, gazing down at his eyes as she slowly slid forward, then backward, pressing down with all her strength, bracing her hands against his chest. His eyes sparked, and he thrust up into her. She bore down harder, increasing her speed but not giving in to his desperate bucking. She steadied her breathing, finding her rhythm, homing in on the exact movement and pressure her body demanded, and hitting the sweet spot over and over. The edges of her vision clouded as she grew close, and everything disappeared except Uffrin's soft eyes, his mouth half-open as if in disbelief. Her hands slid up to grip his shoulders for leverage as she rode him with fire and fury.

Her pleasure rose and distended like she was rushing through a million stars zipping by in jagged streaks that exploded as she crested. Her arms trembled, and she let out a long, shaky sigh. Uffrin thrust up into her one more time, his fingernails digging into her, every muscle in his body hard and tense. He released a plaintive moan, and his body relaxed, though his throbbing inside her continued for a time, slowing along with the beat of her heart. She peeled her fingers from his shoulders and let herself sink down onto him, pressing her lips to his in a soft, gentle kiss.

"I want to be yours forever," Uffrin murmured.

"From now until the Time to Come," she whispered in his ear, kissing him once more before releasing him and slumping down to lay half-draped over his body.

The cold air once again began nipping at her toes and ears. The sounds of birds returned, then a dog barking in the distance, then another sound, one it took her a moment to place: a muffled trill coming from the lacquered case in the corner of the lean-to.

The councilor visited them near dusk, bringing a basket of dried foods: fish, jerky, mushrooms, berries, roots, and a sack of herbal tea. She asked to see Mara and Leasse's birds, who stared around wide-eyed as they were brought out of their boxes. The councilor offered them each a small fish from a pocket of her robe, which they gulped down with gusto as she watched with smiling eyes.

"You'll have to meet our crow handlers tomorrow and introduce your birds in a controlled setting," she said in barely accented Old Maer. She held out a finger to Cleo, who looked up to Mara for approval, then gave the finger a gentle peck. "Once you do that, your birds are free to hunt in the pine forest above, so long as they leave the crows alone."

"Can we release them after dark just to stretch their wings?" Mara asked.

The councilor paused for a moment, then nodded. "I'll let our handlers know. The crows roost at night, so it shouldn't be a problem." Her eyes narrowed as she glanced over at Gielle and Erliss, who were putting together the lattice on the neighboring lean-to. "Are the two Shoza going to be staying here as well?"

"Erliss is," Uffrin said. "But they're no longer Shoza. They're going to try to send their badge back, though I'm not sure how that would be possible."

"Gielle will probably take it. She said she's going to return to see if there's anything she can do to help." Mara's heart grew heavy as she thought of the fate that awaited Gielle, and the fate of her sister, wherever she was. Though she had known it for weeks, she still got a sharp pang of sadness whenever she thought of those who had been left behind.

The councilor closed her eyes and put her hand over her heart. "We were saddened to hear of what happened. I hope things go better than you fear."

"Your lips to the gods' ears," Uffrin murmured, and they all touched two fingers to their lips.

Mara chewed her lip, thinking of Kaela, wondering how she would fit in here, if she would be welcome. The councilor's eyebrows raised as if she sensed Mara's unspoken question.

"My sister may be coming, *is* coming, from Kuppham, probably with an escort. I hope…"

The councilor nodded, stroking her beard and gazing up the hill.

"That could explain."

"Explain what?" Mara's heart pounded in her ears, and she gripped Uffrin's hand.

"The crows spotted two figures, Old Maer, one a Shoza, the other younger and female, nearing the cleft just this morning. Could that be her?"

Mara nodded, tears welling in her eyes as the dread she had been harboring for the past few weeks was suddenly streaked with hope.

"You will have your answer soon. Anyone willing to put in work is welcome to stay here as long as space remains." She glanced off at the other lean-tos, which numbered around a dozen from what Mara had seen. "Come by tomorrow to meet the handlers, and we'll get you added to the duty roster once you've got your lean-tos winterized."

Mara nodded, still too choked up to speak, and rested her hand on Uffrin's shoulder. His arm slid around her hip, and he kissed her cheek. The councilor flashed an approving smile, bowed at them, then turned and made her way down the trail, leaning on her walking stick.

Once night fell, Mara put on her circlet and sent Cleo out to look for Kaela, hoping they would not be out of range. She spotted her camped just inside the pine ridge, curled up next to another figure who slept leaning against a stone. Mara squeezed tightly with her mind, pushing Cleo down to land a few feet away from Kaela. The sitting figure leapt to their feet, drawing their sword and moving between the bird and Kaela.

They quickly relaxed as Cleo crouched, spreading her wings low, as she had been trained to do. The Shoza woke Kaela, who blinked groggily. Her eyes shot wide as she saw Cleo, and she moved on all fours toward the bird. Mara pushed warmth into Cleo, who tucked her wings and stood up straight, allowing Kaela to touch her chest feathers gently. Kaela waved, her eyes filled with tears, and Cleo trilled, then flapped up into the trees, heading back through the forest and down to the lake.

Kaela arrived near dusk the next day, accompanied by a terse, serious Shoza. Mara showered her with hugs and kisses, even as Kaela tried to squirm out of her grasp.

"Gods, you've gotten so skinny!" Mara squeezed her sister's shoulders, which were even bonier than usual.

"We had to leave in a hurry," the Shoza said, glancing over at Gielle and Erliss, who blinked in understanding. "The trip was...difficult."

"Thank you so much for bringing Kaela here safe and sound." She pulled Kaela tight to her once again, heedless of her sister's feeble efforts to break her embrace. Mara finally released her, and Kaela shrugged off her pack, which hit the ground with a thunk.

"Gods, what's in there?"

Kaela smiled shyly, opening the bag to reveal a hoard of books: farming, fishing, carpentry, hunting, all the random books she'd been collecting. Except they didn't seem so random now. They would need this knowledge if they were going to start from scratch.

"You were collecting those for a reason, weren't you? You knew!"

Kaela shrugged, her smile widening a bit.

"Kaela, you're a genius!" Mara went to hug her again but settled for a kiss on the cheek when she saw Kaela wince.

Uffrin cleared his throat, eyeing the Shoza who had brought Kaela. "Aefin sent you?"

The Shoza nodded.

"And she's..."

They lifted their eyebrows slightly. "The humans had not yet reached Kuppham when we left, but they surely have by now. We had to take a difficult side route to avoid them." They paused, putting a hand on Uffrin's arm.

Uffrin nodded, biting his lip, and Mara took him in her arms, holding the back of his head as he buried his face in her shoulder.

They shared a meager stew made with bits of the dried foods the councilor had given them mixed with fresh horsetail roots. Gielle, Erliss, and Loachi, the Shoza who'd brought Kaela, walked off to speak in private after dinner. When they returned, Gielle announced she'd be leaving with Loachi in two days, once they'd had a chance to rest up a bit. Kaela stayed with Mara and Uffrin the first night, but the next day, Leasse took her under her wing. Kaela helped her and Erliss finish packing clay and moss onto the new wall of their lean-to. By the time Gielle and Loachi left, both lean-tos had mostly intact walls, though the doors still remained to be built, and the cold night wind forced them deep under the covers at night.

Mara and Uffrin found solace in each other's arms, forgetting for a few heated moments the tragedy they had left behind and the challenges of the new life they had fallen into.

Friend joined Cleo and Seeli in their nightly flights for a while, but Uffrin began keeping Friend back, worried about his power source. He left the door to the case open, and when Cleo flapped back from her hunt each middle morn, his eyes would pop open, and he would trill in amazement at whatever small creature Cleo dropped at his feet. Cleo would trill back at him, then hop forward, lowering her head to let Friend bump foreheads with her, though it wasn't a gesture common to owls. She would give him a little peck on the beak, then hop over to her box next to his and settle down inside. Once Mara and Uffrin had closed the doors, the two owls would coo softly for a few minutes before going quiet, while Mara and Uffrin snuggled tight under their blankets to doze in their shared warmth until the sun rose.

True winter had yet to arrive, and though each day was a struggle against hunger and exhaustion, Mara smiled each night as she lay down with Uffrin in the shelter of their little lean-to, thinking of Maoti's words:

Our time is almost over, whether we want it to be or not, but it will give birth to another and another. The Time to Come begins with you. It begins here.

She went to sleep each night believing it in her heart, for in the arms of her one true love, how could it not be so?

ALSO BY DANI FINN

The Maer Cycle trilogy: classic adventure fantasy with extra heart, introducing the Maer. The monsters of legend are real, but the legends got it wrong.

The Weirdwater Confluence duology: Sword-free fantasy with meditation magic, nature vibes, and romance.

Unpainted, a standalone arranged marriage fantasy romance in the Weirdwater romance.

The Time Before trio (ongoing): The fight to keep love alive as the great Maer empire of old was falling to the human invaders. *The Delve* is out now, and *Cloti's Song,* a steamy poly fantasy starring Uffrin's parents, is coming in early 2024.

Jagged Shard, a dungeon crawl romance set in the Time Before, is coming soon as well!

Acknowledgements

Wings so Soft is my first full-length fantasy romance, and it wouldn't have been possible without the inspiration provided by the gorgeous books written by the brilliant romance writers of the world, with a special shout-out to my indie fantasy romance colleagues, who inspired me to follow in their footsteps.

This book was brought into the world with the help of a team of absolute badasses, including, but by no means limited to:

My wife Sarah, who's twice the reader I am and helps keep me anchored in the real and bookish worlds;

My lifetime critique partner Beth Blaufuss, who helped see this book and the ones leading up to it from infancy to adulthood;

My fabulous beta reader Em Strange, who helped nudge me where I needed it and cheered me on when I was on a roll;

My editor and sensitivity reader Charlie Knight, whom I trust with my dearest fictional children and the sometimes rambling sentences they live in, and who has never steered me wrong. Wherever I may have erred either in prosecraft or in representation of identities outside my own, it is through my own fault, not theirs;

Lorraine Bondi and Peter Hutchinson, who helped me learn about owl behavior; any inaccuracies on that count can surely be attributed to my making shit up despite their best efforts to educate me.

My cover designer Virginia McClain, whose design makes me want to fly away with joy;

Kriti Khare, who made the delightful black and white owl art that graces the book's interior;

My Siblings in Smut, including but by no means limited to Krystle Matar, Fiona West, Connor Caplan, Angela Boord, Maxime Jazz, Em Strange, Erika McCorkle, and so many others;

And as always, the brilliant, glittering hordes of the online bookish community: The book bloggers who were kind and generous enough to give this odd little book a shot, and who make the bookish world run; the fantastic author community, especially my fantasy and romance peeps; and all the wonderful people I've met along the way who share my love of a good story.